Flight of the Piasa

Raymond Scott Edge

Raymond Edge

Redoubt Books

Flight of the Piasa
All Rights Reserved
V3.0

Cover art and Author Portrait by Micah Edge

Redoubt Books

ISBN-13: 978-0-9794737-0-8

Printed in the United States of America

Dedication

This book is dedicated to the thousands of students over the years that have listened to my stories and believed them to be true. Thanks for the faith. Any book written by me would be remiss if not dedicated to my wife Marilyn. "More than yesterday, less than tomorrow." Thanks for the faith.

Chapter 1

A Question of Scholarship

Daniel French stood behind the podium looking over the empty classroom: thirty minutes to go he thought, thirty minutes. He turned the overhead projector on and off, adjusting the light focus; the equipment had to be right, even the smallest screw up would not do. *Where am I going to find a spare bulb if the damn thing goes blank,* he wondered. He could feel his heart beating in his chest and felt increasing tension, like a fighter prior to the opening bell, or perhaps a Christian before his performance in the Coliseum. He laughed at his thoughts: *get a grip, gotta get a grip. I've done this before, I can do this now.* Lifting his shoulders and circling his arms about, he tried to release the tension. He walked over to the side table to once again straighten the piles of handouts he had set out and readjusted the positioning of the artifacts collected for the students to review.

This has to be right, he thought. In thirty minutes Eldredge's undergraduate archeology class would come in and expect a show. He'd helped his department chair Dr. Frederick Eldredge, with the class many times, but today he was flying solo. Well, not exactly, for today, Eldredge, the old man himself, would be in the back of the class taking notes. Today's class was a major part of his graduate seminar, and his grade would depend on it; hell, not only his seminar grade, his future with the department—as well as a potential career in archeology. He could feel his heart begin to pound again. "Get a grip," he mumbled to himself, "they can only kill you, they can't eat you." He looked down at his clothing: jeans, tee shirt, and sneakers. *Will this be all right? Will Eldredge expect me to look more professional? Christ, I'm driving myself crazy, every graduate student dresses like this.* "Get a grip," he repeated to himself. He sucked in a deep breath, loosened his shoulders again, and ran his fingers through his rather unruly hair. "Like me or not, here I am."

The minutes crept by with Daniel checking and rechecking the overhead, straightening the piles, adjusting the artifacts. Finally as Eldredge's undergraduate students drifted into the room, he took his place behind the podium. Daniel was taking roll when Dr. Eldredge came in, took a seat in the back row and opened his notebook. Daniel heard himself say, "Class, if you will," and immediately felt dumb since that was a phrase Eldredge commonly used to begin his classes. He saw Eldredge's lips curl in a half smile. *When in doubt, follow the master*, he thought. *Hope he doesn't think that was intended as a suck up.*

"Ah, my name is ah, Daniel French. Dr. Eldredge has asked me to review Illinois Indian artifacts from the Middle Woodland Period, that's about 500 BCE to CE 400, and discuss the Illinois petroglyph known as the Piasa Bird. The name Middle Woodland Period is used in a very general sense; it simply means that this is a cultural pattern found all over the Eastern Woodlands, the forested third of the nation. During this period, we see the beginnings of agriculture, permanent villages, and the first appearances of both pottery and the bow and arrow." He pointed to the side table.

"On the table are some examples from the Period. I created worksheets for your use. Grab a paper, find a partner, and identify the following items: a copper ear spool, a wolf effigy stone pipe, mica ornament, shell dipper, bone fishhook, clay pipe, obsidian ceremonial knife, and a spearhead. The spearhead will resemble the arrowheads on the table, except it will be over 2 ¼ inches long. The smaller true arrowheads tend to be of a more recent age. Once identified, make a drawing of each of these on your paper. Finally, do a sketch of one of the pottery pieces. The decoration is very characteristic of the period and is known as Hopewell Zoned Incised."

Daniel turned and wrote the term Hopewell Zoned Incised on the board. "These early people manufactured a great number of pottery pieces. Both jar and bowl shapes were common, the bases of the vessels varied from round to flat, and occasionally had four feet. The techniques of incising, punctating, and stamping along the rim and shoulder give the style its name. Let's take about 15 minutes for this exercise." He watched as the students milled about the side table identifying and drawing the pieces. Moving among them, he answered questions and gave prompts when they mislabeled a piece. After about 20 minutes, he signaled them to take their seats.

Once the students were seated, he returned to the podium. "OK, what can you tell me about the people responsible for these artifacts?" When several hands went up, Daniel referred to the seating chart to identify the students. "Miss Turner?"

Casey Turner, a smallish brunette, looked down at her paper as if to organize her thoughts. "Well, I think we can say they were trading people."

Daniel nodded, "You're right, they were, but what makes you identify them as a trading people?"

Casey smiled, feeling more confident in her answer, "Well, it's the types of materials. The shells would not be native to the area, nor would copper, mica, or obsidian."

"Right again," Daniel confirmed. "The materials would probably have come from areas as far distant as the Great Lakes, the Gulf Coast, and the Rocky Mountains. Notice also the quality of the items— probably used for ceremony and ritual—which also strongly suggests that these are trade goods. The hammered copper ornaments, the mica adornments, and ingenious spool-shaped ornaments all have the feeling of trade items. What else can we know about these people from the artifacts?"

Fewer hands went up for the second question. Daniel looked over the group and referred to the seating chart before selecting a tall boyish-looking young man whose arm was moving back and forth, seemingly eager to answer. "Mr. Chartrand?"

Tony Chartrand leaned forward, "I think we can say they were a sedentary village people."

Daniel thought for a second. "Sedentary, how so?"

Tony Chartrand stammered as if trying to get the answer out too quickly. "Well, well, I mean…how could they have created the quality and quantity of ornaments and pottery if they were a hunting/gathering nomadic people on the move? The very quality and diversity of the items tells us that they were sedentary."

"OK. I'll buy that," Daniel responded. He turned,

picked up an erasable marker and started a list on the board:

1. **gardening**, to which he commented: "Required the settlement in one place for long periods of time."
2. **construction of large ceremonial earthworks**, "Such as burial and ceremonial mounds. These earthworks foreshadow what we see a thousand years later in Cahokia."
3. **widespread trading**, "Materials derived from the Rockies, Gulf Coast, and Great Lakes."
4. **manufacture of a great variety of excellently made art works**

"All of these items distinguish the Middle Woodland period people from their predecessors. It is believed that these were the first Indians in the Midwestern region to maintain settlements in one place for long periods and to devote some of their time to growing corn. We also call this the Hopewellian Interaction Sphere because of their extensive trading network. Scientists have identified associated trading and cultural centers scattered across Illinois, Missouri, Oklahoma, Arkansas, Louisiana, and Mississippi. The Woodland Periods gave way to, and overlapped to some extent, the Mississippian Culture, which had as its nucleus the Cahokia mound site near East St. Louis."

Daniel glanced up at the clock. "We need to close up this topic." He hastily continued scribbling. "Look over your notes and be sure you have:

Middle Woodland Period, "what, where and when?"
Hopewell Zoned Incised, "distinguishing features."
Hopewellian Interaction Sphere, "meaning and justification of the term."

Daniel then pulled the projection screen down, placed a transparency on the overhead, and clicked on the machine's light. "Let's shift topics. Who can identify the picture?"

Again, Tony Chartrand's hand went up. Daniel looked over the group waiting for another hand to rise. He finally settled on a student in the back row. "How about you, Miss Nevins?"

Kate Nevins looked out through thick glasses. "It's the Piasa Bird."

"You're right, it's the Piasa, a cliff painting found in Alton, Illinois, once described as 'America's most fascinating free roadside attraction,' and 'the finest example of Native American rock art.' Who's seen it or heard about it?" Most of the hands in the class were raised. "OK, so most of you are at least aware of it. What do we know about it?" He began to list known facts on the overhead:

1. **Pre-dates western culture in area**
2. **First described by Marquette and Joliet in 1673**, and he commented "as they made their way down the Mississippi"
3. **Associated with local Miami/Illini tribal lore**
4. **A topic of cryptozoology**, "like Bigfoot and the Thunderbird," he added.

"What don't we know about it?" Daniel began a second list:

1. **Who first etched it into the stone and painted it**
2. **Why it was originally created**
3. **Location of the original**

Tony Chartrand's hand went up in the back. "You mean

the one at Alton isn't the original?"

Daniel shook his head. "Nope, our forefathers, in their infinite wisdom, saw fit to dynamite the cliffs in the area sometime in the 1870s, and somehow didn't bother to note the exact location of the destroyed petroglyph. Actually, we don't even know for sure if this is a faithful representation of the original, but we think it's at least close. We do know that the current picture is very like a logo used by a local beer company at the turn of the century. So, was the beer logo a true representation of the original, or are we now speculating about a picture found on a beer bottle, that has little to do with the original?"

"Where's the CAS when we need them?" a voice spoke up from the class. "That's what they're all about, keeping modern development from stealing our past."

Daniel looked at the seating chart to see who was speaking. It was Josh Green, a slim dark haired, dark eyed student with a scraggly beard, sitting in the back row.

"Are you planning to be an archeology major, Josh," Daniel asked, "because, if you are, you might want to cool it on the CAS stuff. The Creative Archeology Society has done more harm to our profession in the last ten years than all of the developers in the last century."

"Yeah, the developers are so benign, that's why we archeology majors are sitting here learning about a cliff painting that's probably more like a beer label than the real Piasa," Josh retorted, half standing up, "As for me, I'm with the CAS. Screw the progress-at-any-price-bastards, and the Hummers they rode in on!"

Daniel looked at Josh who was now standing, with arms out and eyes wild. He was not exactly sure how they had gotten into this political argument over the CAS, nor quite sure where to take the conversation. "Sit down Josh; this is not the time or place for a CAS commercial!" He waited as

7

the student slowly sank back into his seat. "The CAS's tactics of planting phony artifacts at construction sites may seem clever, but they're efforts are counterproductive, and they're stalling antics have caused some developers to cement over real finds rather than to deal with the cost over-runs associated with delay and legal hassles. Not to mention that several of our fields' leading scholars have published articles putting their reputations on the line, only to find that they'd been defending a hoax. It's kinda like PETA. Who could be against a group calling for the Ethical Treatment of Animals? Everyone's for that, but the proponents often engage in foolish behavior. You want people to treat animals ethically, but you don't want someone sneaking into a university lab and freeing all the research animals, or throwing red paint on someone wearing a leather vest. Some individuals in these groups go too far." Daniel paused, "Josh if you really want to continue at another time and place, fine, but for now, let's get on with the class."

Daniel looked down at the seating chart, "So, we don't know when the original Piasa was completed; we're not sure whether the current picture is like the original; we don't know who did the original and can only speculate as to the why. So, let's speculate. Who has a guess?" He selected students from the last row of the class. Over the next several minutes he listed a variety of the student's ideas on the board. Completing the list, Daniel turned back to the class. "Well, your guesses are as good as any. Some say it was the real McCoy, an ancient creature who somehow managed to survive into modern times; there have even been some recent sightings, although most, shortly after the two-o'clock bar closings." This drew several laughs from the class, and Daniel relaxed, glad they were beyond the CAS discussion. "Some have even

suggested that the original was created by the Phoenicians."
Daniel frowned. "Actually, the Phoenician idea is probably
racism speaking, just another attempt to deny credit to the
Native Americans for producing anything sophisticated.
For a time period, Europeans gave the Phoenicians credit
for the Zimbabwe structures in southern Africa, for much
the same reasons. Although the Phoenicians were great
sailors and navigators, there is neither proof nor concrete
evidence that any of their expeditions ever reached the New
World or went to southern Africa for that matter."

He laughed in self-deprecation, "I must admit I once
did a paper listing the similarities between the Piasa Bird
and the ancient Chin Shi Huang Di Chinese Imperial
Dragon Banner." He reached over and put another
overhead on the projector.

Similarities Found

➤ Red, fiery eyes	➤ A tiger's beard
➤ Scales	➤ Red, Green, & Black
➤ Deer-like horns	➤ Long wrap around tail
➤ Anthropomorphic face	➤ End of tail fishlike

"So, who knows, maybe the Piasa was drawn by
someone from ancient China, or, and this is more likely,
maybe it was used by the Indians the way a farmer uses a
scarecrow: to either scare people away, or to warn travelers
that this was a particularly dangerous section of the river."
Daniel noted that Dr. Eldredge had stood and was leaving
the room. He tried to read his face for any evaluation, but
Eldredge was a hard one, he rarely looked happy.

Daniel looked up at the wall clock, "Well that brings us
to the end of our time, but I should tell you that the last
sighting of the Piasa was April 1948. Guy named Coleman,

while riding on horseback about four miles from Alton, claimed to have sighted a bird 'bigger than an airplane." He noted that Eldredge paused to listen before leaving the class. The students were now standing, packing their bags, adjusting their coats, readying themselves to leave. "Oh, by the way, be careful out there," Daniel laughed, "and remember to look up now and then, you never know."

After the students left, Daniel repacked the artifacts for their return to the department and thought about his scheduled meeting with Eldredge. As he gathered up the class materials, he tried to critique his performance. *Not so bad, coulda been better, but not so bad.* Remembering Eldredge's expression as he had left the room, he tried not to worry. *Hell he always looks stern; he probably thought it was at least OK.*

Daniel finished replacing the Middle Woodland specimens in their appropriate department drawers and then knocked on Eldredge's office door. Hearing the professor's invitation, he entered to find Eldredge sitting behind his desk surrounded by a lifetime of academic scholarship. Awards, plaques, pictures, and certificates hung on every available inch of wall space behind his desk. His bookshelves were crammed with books and stacks of files and papers. Eldredge didn't look up but grunted an acknowledgement and waved him to a chair.

To Daniel, Eldredge looked somewhat like the poet Carl Sandburg, tall, slightly bent, with a clean shaven, lean lined face and shocks of white hair that defied any attempt to bring it into order. He liked and admired the older man, although as his department head and doctoral chairman, he was cautious and reserved around him.

Without any preliminary conversation as to how Daniel thought the class had gone, Eldredge opened his notebook and began. "Not so bad, the classroom was in order, the class began on time, but you needed a better anticipatory set to get the students attention at the beginning. Generally, student interaction was acceptable, some management problems during the CAS discussion, but that was OK, and the closure at the end needed some help in regard to review of content. All in all, it was not a bad class."

Daniel, who had been holding his breath, slowly breathed out. While not an "atta-boy, or great job," it was not a disaster either. He could handle and live with an "All in all, it was not a bad class." That should at least translate out as a B, maybe even an A, one never knew with Eldredge.

Eldredge spoke again, but this time in a gravelly tone that froze Daniel in place as he immediately recognized it as the one the professor used with those in whom he was displeased. "Now let's talk about the Piasa nonsense. What was that Chin China, Dragon Banner, stuff all about, and your final comments about looking up as if the thing could still be out there?"

Oh Shit! Daniel's mind went into frantic mode as he tried to think how he should approach the answer. "Well as you know, I'm a native to the area, and have been around the Piasa literally all my life. While I don't really know what the original looked like, it has never really looked Native American, and the current rendition has always looked like a banner or flag to me, so recently I tried to think about what banner it looked like. It's very close, lots of similarities to the Chin Dragon Banner."

"That's your reasoning?" Eldredge interrupted. "You stood before a class and put up a list on the overhead based on the deep research of 'it sort of reminded you.'" He mimicked Daniel's tone of voice. "Daniel, a hint suffices the wise, but a thousand lectures profit not the heedless." He took a deep breath, expelling it loudly, as if clearing his lungs of the disappointment and outrage he felt. "You are a fine graduate student, you may even have a future in archeology, perhaps even in this department, but—and let me say this so you truly understand it—NEVER do that again. We don't teach soft science, we don't teach hunches as fact, we don't teach fiction in this department, and we don't do 'oooooh' be careful out there jokes in our lectures. This is not entertainment, nor the history channel, and you're not an actor, you're an educator."

Daniel thought that he might say something in his defense but the look on Eldredge's face told him the meeting was over, so he stood to take his leave. As he reached the door, he heard Eldredge say, "Daniel, the class was ok, and you were right about those CAS idiots, they've cost our profession a great deal with their antics."

Chapter 2

The Skeleton

Daniel French stood in the morning sun looking up at the bluff, enjoying the play of shadows across the craggy rock surface. Having grown up along the River Road in Alton, Illinois, he had often come here as a child. Here, with the great river below and the wooded bluff above, had been his special place, a place to chase pirates, hide from Indians, and to explore. This morning, the air was cool and crisp and the sky that special blue which tells that winter is near. Daniel thought that autumn was the best of seasons, especially since the fall colors were good this year due to abundant spring rain. He looked down at the river winding its way south, languid and slow, as if loath to leave the heartland on its way to the Gulf. Daniel's mind went back over the meeting with his department chair and he shook his head, trying to clear his mind of the stinging rebuke he'd received from Eldredge. *What a disaster, he thought. Hell, maybe I'm not cut out to be an academic, much less an archeologist?*

Daniel turned his gaze to the huge painting on the cliff face. Staring back at him was a great and fearsome thing, a creature with the wings of a hawk, horns of a deer, and face of a demon. No one remembers who first painted the bird; it was there before the first white man canoed the river. Not even the oral traditions of the local Indians explain the why of its creation. Father Jacques Marquette first recorded its presence in 1673, noting it in his diary as he journeyed down the Mississippi. Marquette had given the creature its name, *"Piasa,"* meaning *"Destroyer."*

Thinking back over the lecture with the students, he wondered whether the painting above was like the real petroglyph or just a copy of the pre-prohibition beer logo. *Wouldn't that be a hoot*, he thought, *what if both the picture and location were wrong*. The location of the earlier painted carving had been somewhere out along the rock surface of the bluff, facing the river. Daniel's grandfather said that his father had actually seen it, and that the original had been upriver, somewhere near the Blue Pool, a water-filled quarry site where Daniel and friends swam during high school. That area was now fenced off, following the murder of a young woman and, later, the death of a student who had jumped from the cliff into the water, striking a submerged rock. Daniel's grandfather said that his father told him the original Piasa was badly scarred from literally thousands of arrow marks because generations of Indians had used it as a target when passing along the river below. Its placement in a recess on the outer cliff had made it a difficult target. The number of hits spoke both of its ancient origin and also of the natives' determination to erase it. One early legend had the Indians actually killing the monster, but none explained the origin of the painting itself. *One thing's for sure*, Daniel said to himself, *if it looked anything like the one painted above me, it must have scared the bejeezus out of them.*

For Daniel, the painting above him had a flatness to it, which gave it an almost banner-like quality as if someone had drawn a flag. It certainly didn't resemble any other Native American artifacts he had seen. *As many times as I've looked at it*, he thought, *it still doesn't seem to belong here.*

When he was home from college, Daniel often came to this spot to stare at the petroglyph painted on the rock surface. He loved the wildness of the creature. According to one legend, attributed to the Illini Indian tribe, the beast was a real animal, one that had survived from the time of the mastodon. The legend spoke of it raiding local villages, carrying off sheep in its great talons. The natives were said to have believed that the creature preferred human flesh, especially young children. According to the historical marker which now stands below the painting, the natives tried for years to destroy the beast, watching in helpless horror as it consumed whole villages. Finally a great warrior named Ouatoga, having received a vision about where the predator would land, hid in waiting and killed it. *Yeah, right*, thought Daniel.

He stretched in the crisp morning air, trying to clear his mind of the Eldredge matter, once again glad to be alive. Looking upriver, he tried to spot one of the migratory eagles that came to the area each year. The air was crisp, the sky blue, and today was even nicer than most because Donna was with him. He looked down the path toward the parking lot and could make out her blonde head bobbing its way toward him along the trail. "Be careful," he called, "the footing can be tricky." She was one of the cutest girls on campus, a Fine Art major who had come along to do a drawing of the Piasa Bird. He smiled to himself; today was shaping up just fine.

Daniel spread the blanket and opened his daypack to take out the breakfast he brought. The aroma of the hot coffee filled the air and he breathed it in deeply. His stomach turned in anticipation. *Life is good*, he thought, *a mug of coffee, a McDonald's Big Breakfast, and Thou*. Donna joined him on the blanket, plopping herself down, breathing heavily. She was short, blue eyed, with curly hair that framed her face, and a well scrubbed, sun freckled look that shouted Midwest small town. Looking up, she shivered.

"It looks scary as hell," she said. "It doesn't make any sense. It's clearly a bird, but has other animal parts put in for good measure. And to top it all off, the thing has a demonic human face with fangs. Why would someone paint such a horror? It's so unreal!"

Daniel shrugged; "You're right, it kinda reminds me of the multiple motifs used by some ancient cultures. Maybe the Egyptians discovered America," he laughed, "Not likely, but maybe."

"You're right! Not likely," Donna said, forcefully rejecting the idea. "Look at the thing, the beast seems more created than creature. Something cobbled together from the parts of unrelated animals is not a usual evolutionary path. Even an art major would know that this thing never flew."

Daniel shrugged, "Maybe it's—you know—like a scarecrow, meant to frighten people away, although who and why, I can't imagine."

Donna took out a sketchpad and drew the outlines of the Piasa. Daniel watched over her shoulder as she worked quickly with her pencil. "Not bad, looks like the real thing. You know, now that I can see it up close, it looks a bit like the qi-lin."

16

Donna paused, mouthing the unfamiliar word quizzically *"qi-lin?"*

Daniel straightened, "Qi-lin, the mystical creature after which the Chinese dragon is patterned." Donna didn't reply but shrugged again, looked down, and continued her drawing in silence. Daniel sensed her irritation, *God*, he thought, *Qi-lin, what graduate lecture did that come from? Better cool it or she'll think I'm a pedantic nerd. Hell she probably thinks that now.*

In between her quick strokes on the paper, they ate the breakfast in silence, looking out across the river toward Missouri. Daniel pointed up river along the bluff. "In the 1800's, the whole bluff for miles along the river was quarried to build the road, exposing these limestone cliffs. They say the original petroglyph was somewhere near Blue Pool, but was destroyed in the process of quarrying the rock. Can you imagine how valuable an archeological site it would be if the original was still there?"

Donna looked up river where Daniel indicated, "You mean this isn't the original? How do we know what it really looked like?"

"We don't really," he admitted, "but it's said to look like the original sketch Marquette made in his 1673 journal. In fact, the whole bluff area is probably returning to a more naturally rounded form due to weathering." Daniel pointed at the bushes and small trees that grew in the breaks between layers of limestone, supported by accumulated soil that washed from above during rains. "These large caves below the painting," he pointed to the fenced off openings, "were certainly not there in the beginning. In the years prior to prohibition, they were dug out and used by the local Bluff City Brewery to cool and store beer." The caves Daniel was describing were massive openings into the cliff which extended several miles up and down river under the bluff. The whole area was a honeycomb of passageways; some of the older local homes on top of the bluff even had private doorways from their basements down into the old cavern system.

Looking at the cave openings, Daniel remembered how these were a favorite meeting place for kids from his high school. Even now, he could still see names scratched and painted onto the soft limestone at the cave's entrance, proclaiming undying love—or at least lust. Embarrassed, he smiled to himself, hoping that at least one set of scratches had eroded away. It would not do for Donna to stumble onto the *Daniel loves Polly* scratched on the cave wall. He was suddenly very glad that the Alton City Council had seen fit to fence the area so the cave entrances below the Piasa were now blocked.

Daniel stood and shouldered his daypack. "We can't make our way to the top here but at the other end of the quarry we can climb above the rock face for a better view."

He pulled her up and together they made their way down and back across the parking lot to the other side of the old quarry. Here, hidden behind years of overgrowth, were other cave entrances that the city fathers had not seen fit to fence off. Like those below the Piasa, the openings along this wall were massive, with twenty-five foot domed entrances and passageways that stretched back into the darkness. Along the far quarry wall, Daniel found a path upward that they could climb. Half-way up, he found a ledge that extended diagonally across the bluff surface; they made their way out along a narrow shelf using the bushes and small trees as handholds. The bluff surface was pock-marked with shallow caves that offered places to sit and watch the boat traffic on the river below and, for the lucky, catch a glimpse of an eagle fishing the river. As a boy, he had loved to crawl into the small caves and explore them, although most only went in a few feet. He always knew he had to be careful though because some of the openings connected to the old caverns that the brewery had used for storage.

After about an hour of steady climbing, they came to a small cave that appeared to go a considerable way into the mountain. Peering in, they could only see darkness. Knowing better, but unable to resist, Daniel suggested that they explore.

"If I die in there, I'm taking you with me," protested Donna. Daniel took flashlights from his daypack, handed her one, and bending down, squeezed through the small opening. Once inside, the cave opened and he could stand. "Donna, you gotta see this, come on, it's big."

"Daniel, this is crazy, I don't want to get dirty," Donna protested as she squeezed through the hole to stand at his side. The air was much cooler inside; Donna shivered and leaned against Daniel. For the first fifty feet the cave was level, and then began a gentle upward incline. They had now moved beyond the light provided by the small cave entrance; ahead were several passages moving off to both sides. As Daniel ventured further, Donna grabbed his arm, "Daniel, let's not get lost in here."

"It's OK, we'll always take the passage to the right going in," Daniel said, "and left coming back." As they walked, the walls and floor were dry and dusty, but the air held the pungent moist smell of a bat colony somewhere in the gloom. Daniel felt a bit anxious as they continued deeper in and further from the light, but still felt sure they would be safe. *Right in, left out,* he reminded himself.

"Let's stop and go back," Donna said forcefully. "This is getting freaky." Daniel turned to look at her; he could see that climbing around in the cave was going well beyond her comfort zone. "Daniel! What if bats start flying around? This is crazy"

Daniel reached back and squeezed her hand in reassurance. "Just one more turn and we'll quit," he promised. "Besides, don't worry about the bats; they're more afraid of you than you are of them and their echolocation keeps them from flying into objects. Given that we've been going upward, we should be near ground level. I wonder if this cave has a second surface entrance."

They continued until they reached the next branch in the path. Their lights displayed a large flat rock that had fallen from the ceiling. They sat down on it to rest and Daniel explored the area with his light. He saw a smaller side passageway that went slightly to the right. The light illuminated the path for only a short way. Off to the left was a mass of rocks where the side wall and ceiling were caved in. "Wouldn't have wanted to be here when that happened," he said to Donna, moving his light across the jumble of boulders.

Donna shivered, uncomfortable in the cold air. It was clear to Daniel that the dirtiness and darkness had very little appeal to her. For Daniel, however, caving was high adventure and he was having a great time. "You know, I've always loved exploring caves. As a kid we used to go to Meramec Caverns, you know, the one with all the billboards advertising itself as a place where Jesse James hid the loot."

Donna nodded in acknowledgement; it was true about the billboards, you really couldn't drive in the greater St. Louis area and miss their endless promotion of the underground wonders of Meramec Caverns just a few miles down the road. "You have too much Mark Twain in your blood," Donna said. "Let's go back soon. I'm getting cold. Really Daniel, this is not fun."

Daniel reluctantly agreed. "Ah, sure, we can go back. Just let me look around here a bit more." He swung the light again toward the mass of boulders along the left wall. Something bright winked near the edge of the illumination. "Stay here," he said, and moved toward the shining object. "Oh my God!" shouted Daniel. "Donna come here, you're not going to believe this!"

As she approached, she saw that he was looking into a small dry alcove that had been exposed by the collapse of the cave wall. She came closer as he shined the light directly on what had excited him. Lying flat on a raised area of the small pocket was a skeleton. Something near the hand of the body caused the reflection that had originally attracted his attention.

"Wow," said Daniel, "Who do you suppose this was, and when?"

"Don't know, don't care," replied Donna, her shivering increasing from the cold, the darkness, and now the unnerving presence of the skeleton. As an art major, she

21

had little of the fascination for old dead things that Daniel seemed to have. "But I do know it's time to get out of here. It may have been someone like us who got lost and couldn't get out. Maybe he was trapped by the wall caving in." She shined her light across the ceiling as if trying to spot the next loose rock about to crash down from above.

Daniel swung his light back toward the skeleton. "I don't think so," he said, "The cave-in looks like it exposed the alcove rather than closing it off." He crouched down, trying to see what caused the reflected light. In the dust, beside the skeleton's hands, he saw something coin-like that sparked in the light. Daniel picked up the coin carefully, marking in his mind its original position near the skeleton, and placed it in the side pocket of his daypack. He left the skeleton where it lay without disturbing any of the bones. *Professor Eldredge will want to see this*, he thought. Turning to Donna he said, "Let's get out of here so I can look at the coin in the light, maybe it's dated?"

They moved down the passage toward the cliff face, always selecting the left path, and soon saw the light of the cave entrance. Once outside, they made their way back along the bluff face to the parking lot below the Piasa Bird. Daniel then took the flat metal piece from his pack for closer examination. The shiny object was indeed a flat metal coin-like piece, with a small hole near the top where one might have threaded it for use as a necklace. On the face of the coin was a half torso of a man in what looked like a feathered cloak. On the back of the coin was writing that looked somewhat like Chinese calligraphy.

"Wow," Daniel said, showing the coin to Donna, "the writing looks Chinese. Do you suppose our friend in the cave was one of the Chinese who built the railroad through here? If so, that would place the skeleton somewhere in the mid to late eighteen hundreds. Amazing!"

Donna shrugged, "That seems like a reach to me." Her tone suggested to Daniel that she didn't care one way or another, but then she added, "It's more likely a bum or something, or someone dumb like us who crawled into the cave, got lost, and died." Donna again looked up at the cliff painting of the Piasa Bird, and shivered. "Christ, that thing looks malevolent," she said.

Daniel looked at Donna; the morning with her was not going as well as he had hoped. She had once said that he reminded her of Scruffy from the Scooby Do show, tall, skinny, brown eyed, with hair hanging down into his face. At the time she appeared to think of archeology as an exciting major, and dating a graduate student as being cool, but now looking at her he could see that the morning had been a bust. What for him had seemed an adventure, was for her time spent in dirty places, with weird petroglyphs, and creepy skeletons. Whatever magic that had transformed him in her eyes from tall and lanky into a cute Scooby Do character seemed to have worn off. *Maybe, she's just tired* he thought, but he did hope that his nerdishness hadn't screwed up his chances for another date. *Oh well, fifty-fifty chance*, he flipped the coin in the air, caught it, and returned it to the side pocket of the backpack. "Maybe my roommate Michael Wang can make something of this. He's from the People's Republic. He'll at least know if it's Chinese." He turned to Donna, "Please don't tell anyone about this for a while, OK? We don't want this area crawling with college kids until we know something about the who and when. I think the bones are too old for this to be of interest to the police."

Donna nodded assent, but looked at him angrily. "Daniel, why would I want to talk to anyone about this ugly beer logo painting, the dirty cave, or the skeleton? In fact, right now, I can't even think of why I agreed to come here in the first place."

On the ride back to the SIU campus, neither spoke, as each was wrapped in their own thoughts. He was excited about the find, and assumed she was thinking beyond this moment, happy to be back in the real world, a place of clean clothes, clean people, malls, and normality. As the car moved down the river road toward Alton, Donna pushed a button on the dash, and the radio delivered a familiar country western tune about moving on, which he could see lifted her spirits.

Chapter 3

The Manuscript

When Daniel reached his dorm room that afternoon, he found it empty. *Michael must be at the library*, he thought. He decided to get a bite to eat and placed the coin on the desk with a note, asking Michael to look at the calligraphy and tell him if it was Chinese writing etched on the back. He wanted to keep this part of the search at the graduate student level, because once he showed it to a full professor, he might either be laughed at for his naiveté or have the project taken from him. Either way, he didn't want to show the object to or tell anyone anything about the cave and his findings just yet. He thought again about Donna. She hadn't said much when he let her out of the car. Probably just tired, it had been quite a day, *she'll come around.* Daniel smiled as he thought of the old adage, 'When all else fails, hope springs eternal.' He did hope that he might see her again.

He arrived back in the dorm room after seven and found a note from Michael.

Hi—it looks Chinese, but if it is, it was done some time ago. The People's Republic of China reformed the writing after 1949 to simplify the characters, as a way to help with a literacy problem. I'm not a scholar on ancient writing, but the character etched on the back sort of looks like the modern character we use for something big, maybe 10,000, could be ten thousand years, miles, lifetimes, who knows, without the context, it's impossible to know. By the way, this is strange, this is the second ancient Chinese thing I've been shown this evening. A guy, I think a graduate student, dropped by looking for you earlier with a manuscript. I'll tell you about it when I see you. Anyway, back to the coin. Whatever it is, I can't really be sure about the character. I have a friend at Northwestern who might help; he's into the older forms of Chinese characters and coins.

Daniel smiled. How Chinese of Michael to suggest a friend. Being Chinese was like belonging to the world's largest club. Every Chinese person he knew drew upon a large network of other Chinese across the country. This network helped newcomers to the United States get jobs in local restaurants, fill out applications, and provide references for schools. Michael often told him that, to understand the Chinese, you must first come to understand the obligations of relationships. In almost all situations, Michael knew someone who knew someone, who knew someone, to get just about anything done.

The next morning they had breakfast together. Breakfast was the only meal that Michael would eat at the campus cafeteria, complaining that American food killed his stomach. This always amused Daniel, given the gelatinous wiggly things Michael was willing to order and eat when they were out at Chinese restaurants. Michael took the rest of his meals off campus or cooked in the apartment microwave. It was dazzling, what he could concoct with a rice steamer and a microwave. Daniel often felt sorry for other university students who had the generic American dorm-mate. Rooming with Michael was a great lesson in gastronomic cultural relations—and the meat dumplings weren't bad either. He had come to like this tall, thin, Chinese student, with rather wild unruly black hair, dark eyes, and narrow Mongolian features.

"I think a buddy of mine in the department of Asian studies at Northwestern will help," Michael said, forking a slice of melon from his plate. "His mother worked with my father at a hospital in Beijing."

Daniel looked up at Michael. "Good, but can he keep this secret? I don't want word of this find to get out until I know what I'm looking at."

"Sure," Michael said, understanding the need for confidentiality, "I'm sure he'll keep it a secret if I ask. Oh, I almost forgot, this is the manuscript the guy brought by last night." He reached down and pulled a packet of papers from his backpack. "He claimed to be a doctoral student and sat in on your archeology class, hoping to make some contacts to see if there was a possibility for a joint Archeology/Chinese Language position at SIU." Michael shoved a thick file with an attached note across the table. "The guy said that this is a translation of some scrolls he'd found in the archives of his university back in China. According to him, the original was really old and pretty damaged."

Daniel looked at the note attached to the packet

Dear Sir,

This manuscript is a copy of a translation of an ancient text I found in my university library. From internal evidence I believe the original was created during the Ming Dynasty, but is itself a translation from an earlier document. I worked on it for several years, but it has not been well received by my colleagues, either here or in China. Your lecture regarding the Piasa Bird led me to think it may be of some interest to you.

Sincerely
Wang, Sheng

Daniel turned to look at the backside of the note. "Did he say how we could get back in touch with him? Do you know this Wang guy; is he a relative or something?"

"No", Michael replied, "never saw him before. Having the name Wang is like being named Smith or Garcia, there are a million of us; he just apologized for the quality of the manuscript. Said he had worked on it for several years in China and then when he got a chance to study here in the states, he'd brought it, hoping that he could use it to open some doors and perhaps get a position with a department after graduation. However, whenever he discussed the manuscript during interviews, he caught a lot of grief, people suspecting it to be a fiction or a hoax. Apparently, simply discussing the matter hurt his employment chances. He said it made him about as popular as someone who farts in an elevator. So he gave up on it. However, something about your lecture the other day made him think you might be interested."

Daniel picked up the packet, "Well I certainly understand how quickly you can get into shit trying to push an unpopular idea in academics. Wonder what it's about? Not that I have much time for additional reading. After the reaming I got from Eldredge, I need to be all work and no play." He put the packet into his knapsack. "Strange he didn't say how I could contact him."

"Actually Daniel, I got the feeling the guy was really bummed out about the whole thing. He even talked about going home to China, something about sick parents. You know how we Chinese are about family. Our boy Confucius coulda taught the Catholics a few lessons about guilt, at least when it comes to parents."

Daniel stood up to leave. "Speaking of parents, I think I'll go home for the weekend. Should I tell Mom that you'll be with us for the holidays? You know she loves having you about. Claims you as her Chinese son."

"No, can't, I've already promised friends in Chicago that I'd spend the holidays with them. Maybe if you decide what you want to do with the coin by then, I can take it to the guy I spoke about. But do give my regrets and love to Mom."

Daniel didn't push his VW Beetle as it made its way toward Alton, he needed time to think. The last two weeks had been hard ones for him. The trouble with Eldredge had been a real trauma. How could he have been so wrong? What if he didn't have a future in archeology? Certainly, Donna hadn't been impressed with the find, not even the finding of the coin. She'd blown the finding of the skeleton off as being a horror rather than interesting. Maybe archeology was something best kept as a hobby, something not practical enough for the real world. Maybe he needed a real major.

He pulled the bug into the front driveway of his parent's home. Grabbing his bags, he pushed the front door open and dropped them in the foyer, then made his way toward the kitchen where he heard the voices of his mother and sister. The place smelled of fresh cut pine, and he could see the Christmas tree in the dining room where no one ever dined. The family always gathered and ate in the kitchen. The formal dining room was obviously built for some other family who lived somewhere else. *Perhaps we should rename the room the Christmas tree room, as that seems to be the only time when it gets the family's attention.*

Entering the kitchen, he found his mother and sister sitting together at the table.

"How was school dear?" his mom asked. "Coffee? Will Michael be coming for Christmas?" His mother always had a soft spot for the international students with whom he had made friends, especially Michael.

"Michael is spending the holiday in Chicago with friends from the university there, so he can't be with us, but he sends his love, and as for school, this has been a bit of a rough patch." he replied, "and thanks, but no on the coffee." Daniel shook his head in frustration. "Actually this has been hell week. Got chewed out by my department head, my girlfriend isn't speaking to me, and I'm wondering if archeology is my forte. Maybe I should do something more practical, like accounting or mortuary science."

"Are you and Donna having problems?" his mother asked with eyes twinkling. "Did I ever tell you I know her mother? We served on a committee together." She laughed as if remembering a funny story. "Do you remember the old saw about always checking out the mother before you select a mate? Well dear, if you had, you probably would not be so unhappy that Donna's gone. And as for whether you're in the right major, a person can do a lot worse than to work at something they love. Perhaps, you should suspend judgment for a bit. I think that perhaps a change to mortuary science is a bit drastic, and as Scarlett said,

'Tomorrow is another day."

"You're probably right Mom, but it's been a tough week. I wasn't actually thinking of changing majors or marrying her, but you gotta admit she's cute. Can I do some laundry?" He pulled his arm up to smell the sweatshirt he was wearing. "Things are getting a bit ripe; it's time for a clean." Daniel pulled a small amber fishing buoy, the kind once used for crab pots off the eastern seaboard, from his pack and held it to the light. "Say, look what I found in a small antique shop near campus." His mother loved amber and had a collection of several hundred pieces on shelves in the kitchen.

"Oh my, how lovely," she said, placing the piece on a nearby shelf and standing back to admire it in the light. Fending off an offer to eat something, Daniel begged tiredness from the long drive, gathered his bags, and went upstairs to his room. He lay down, hoping for a long nights sleep, but again the questions churned in his mind. *Is archeology for me? Who was the skeleton? How do I get back into the good graces of Eldredge?* Finally after an hour or so of staring at the ceiling, he got up, put on his robe, and sorted his dirty clothes for the wash. *Might as well be doing something useful,* he thought. He put his clothes in the washer, and went back to the kitchen to make a snack.

It was nearly three in the morning when he finally made his way back to bed. After just a few hours of sleep, he was up early and went to the garage where he gathered some wood and materials to paint a sign. When he finished, he grabbed his daypack and drove to the Piasa Bird parking lot. Making his way to the far side of the old quarry, he found the path upward and began his climb across the bluff face toward the cave opening. Once there, he sat at the cave entrance ledge facing the river, pulled a thermos of coffee from the pack, and surveyed the river below him. Finishing the coffee, he took the sign from the pack, and hammered it into the ground. **Danger, Do Not Enter—Loose Ceiling Rocks**. He wanted to discourage any other climbers who might find the cave opening.

Once he had the sign in place, he squeezed around it and made his way into the darkness. *Oh Great!* He thought about the fact that he had just placed the sign which warned people away. *If anything happens now, I'll end up looking like the other guy before someone climbs in here.* It didn't take him long to reach the alcove that held the skeleton. It lay where he had left it. This time, however, when he shined his light around the alcove, he noticed another tunnel connected to the chamber, one with a slight upward grade. He decided to follow the channel to see if it made a connection with the ground level above. It was a bit tight and now he had to crawl. After about five minutes, he came to a jumble of rocks that blocked the way forward. If the cave ever had an outside ground entrance, it was now completely blocked. A bit frustrated, he found a place where he could turn around and began the climb back down.

He reached the chamber again and sat looking at the bones. "Who are you?" he asked, almost as if he were willing the bones to tell him. The room around him repeated the question, "Who are you?" but it didn't have the answer either. He sat on the rock with his light shining on the bones and tried to think about the circumstances that would put the skeleton and coin artifact in this place.

His flashlight dimmed, and then brightened again, reminding him that it wouldn't be wise to be sitting here without light. Grudgingly he stood, shook off the stiffness from sitting too long, and made his way toward the entrance. When he again saw the light, he slowed and moved his flashlight over the walls for a last look. Just as he was about to leave the cave, he thought he saw an outline of something on the wall. He stood looking at it, unsure that it was in fact real. Slowly, he began to see the outline of a creature, not as large as the Piasa but of the same general design. The years had faded the drawing until it was barely visible, but with a bit of imagination, he thought he could connect the lines and see it. He sat down in the path to study the painting, still unsure if he was seeing something real or just seeing a natural discoloration, and allowing his mind to build the picture. He took a camera from his pack and took several pictures of the discoloration or what ever it was. Finishing, he made his way back along the bluff to his car.

That afternoon he made a call to the *Alton Democrat* to ask if he could spend some research time in the archives. Sam Dalton, the editor and owner, was an old friend of the family.

"Sure, Danny, but what are you researching? Anything I can help with?"

Daniel thought for a moment, not wanting to lie to his friend. "Well, actually, I'm doing a piece on the Chinese who participated in the railroad building around the mid-nineteenth century. I need to see if they spent any time around Alton."

Sam told him that he didn't know anything about the Chinese in Alton, as most of their work occurred in the far west. He thought that the Alton workers were Irish, not Chinese. Nevertheless, he invited Daniel to come down and look.

"Well, I'll drop by in the morning. Thanks Sam."

Later that night, Daniel quickly finished the evening meal, begged off from the family card game, and went to bed early. He lay down and almost immediately the same set of questions whirled about in is mind. *This won't do*, he thought, *maybe I'll read for a bit*. He reached into his backpack and found the packet of papers that Michael had given him. *Why not*, he thought and started to read:

Chapter 4

The End that Begins

Bad fortune is what good fortune leans on.
Good fortune is what bad fortune hides in.
Who knows the ultimate end of this process?
Lao Tzu

My name is Sun Kai, I am of the Chin'in people. In my life I have been many things: a dutiful son, a Huashan Mountain warrior monk, a powerful governor, a loving husband, a mighty general, a betrayer of he whom I served, and finally, a wanderer lost in a distant land. Today, of these things, I am none. My quest is over; I am but a tired man, hurt and lost in a far place. My world has now shrunk to this dark hole in which I hide. When death comes, I doubt that even my ancestors will find me here.

As I write this, I do not know if any of my company

still lives, the last day having been one of running and hiding. The attack came so suddenly, so fiercely, that only a few of us fought our way beyond the fire into the darkness. At first, several of us were together, stumbling outward from the carnage, hearing the cries of our enemies as they pursued us, and of our friends as they fell to savage blows. As time slipped by, one by one our numbers grew fewer, some lost to death, others lost in darkness, and now there is only silence. I am alone and have not seen or heard anyone for the period of one light and dark time.

The barbarians who hunted me have gone with the exception of the one who found my hiding place and died for his success. He no longer hunts in this life. If the Hindi are correct and our souls are reborn, perhaps in another life he and I will meet again and it will be I who will lie dead in the cave entrance. It is of little matter now, for in the fight, he hit my leg with a blow which ends my running. Now, I scuttle about like a crab and I will not soon leave this hole in which I sought shelter.

To my left, water seeps through the walls, forming a small pool. A pale fungus that grows from the roots of the fallen tree that has formed my burrow dulls my hunger. My former mate, Snow Pine, ever loving and cautious, would have chided me about eating an unknown mushroom. "One could die from eating such things!" she would say. How I long to hear her scolding me, but that will never be.

As the new sun warms me, I reach for my journal pouch which has been my constant companion. It is time to complete the tale, for the end is now clear. With these final words I shall end a story begun long ago in our homeland. Even as I write, I wonder at my judgment, for I am sure this will not be read by anyone, anywhere, anytime. It is only the foolishness of one already dead, who chooses to continue to live in his memories, and I write only for myself.

Our story has been one of great adventure, as vast as our land, a tale filled with sacrifice, passion, love, and loss. It is a tale of great men, larger than life itself, from whose deeds an empire grew. Yet my story is also one of small human frailty, where the faithful and faithless played out our parts, where madness and confusion reigned, and where, finally, a vain grasp for immortality ended us all. It is a strange tale, and the fact that I know it to be true barely enhances its believability.

My body is chilled but its discomfort does not dim the vivid memory of the day we arrived in this land of no name, this land beyond any map. It was a warm day and the land looked beautiful in the distance. The beach was as if the gods themselves had prepared it, with sparkling white sand made even brighter by a frame of clear blue waters and tall green trees. We were as giddy children, laughing and shouting as the waves pushed us to shore. How beautiful and perfect was that moment. How beautiful was my Snow Pine, dancing in the water.

It had been almost a year since we left our homeland. In our party were those most dear to me: my beloved wife Snow Pine; my younger Brother, Fan Shaofei, with his wife and child; my faithful lieutenant, Wang Yueming and his family, along with a small contingent of soldiers. Our mission was from the great Chin himself, the Eagle Who Sees Far, First Emperor, and God Ruler. It was a mad quest, born in obsession for the secret of longevity. Having been told of a race of immortals that lived on islands in the South Seas, Chin sent us forward. It was madness, but one did not disobey. Even in the beginning, our venture was half quest and half escape, but that is a story for another time. As I write this, lost in a far land, and as badly as our story has turned out, if given the same choices, I would make them again.

Our voyage was hard. We made land three times. We first came ashore in the land of the people to the west. Theirs is a wet steamy land, with rain that comes in sheets off the ocean. Like our people from the southern provinces, they are growers of rice, which they spice with peppers and a hot yellow powder that was strange but good to the taste. We have known of these ... generations and have even traded with them. Like us, they are a numerous people, but seem ... beyond belief. They ... thousands of spirit beings, many ... multiple arms or are shaped like animals. How does one think of such things?

Daniel lay the packet down and rubbed his eyes, his mind trying to fill in the blank spaces. *Hell, what is this?* He then saw the note scribbled on the margin.

{*The original document is very old and badly stained in this area. Many words have been lost, and some are hardly ever attested or are probably inaccurately transcribed.*}

Oh, thought Daniel, the lacunae problem. Most ancient works suffered from gaps, either from disintegration of the manuscript or problems of transcription, which made them difficult to understand. *It could be worse* he thought, *I could be working with fragments like the Dead Sea Scrolls.* He closed his eyes again, *one thing for sure, this isn't the Dead Sea Scrolls, and unless it straightens itself out soon, I'm giving it up.* He picked up the packet again.

One day our camp was visited by ... holy man ...nude before us without the least awareness of how strange.... Our women quickly turned their eyes from him. ...... look upon a man's maleness, although Snow Pine later admitted .... He was a tall man with long white hair, and large dark eyes framed in an angular face. Never have I seen a man with so little flesh on his bones. He called himself a ...[Word not attested, meaning uncertain], and taught a .....

of great gentleness for all people and living creatures, believing all possess souls and have value. ....holy man .....spent ...life as an ascetic, meditating and fasting for long periods to gain control over his body. His only dress was a cloth over his mouth to avoid the swallowing of insects, and he continually swept the path before him with a broom so that even the tiniest creature would be moved aside, and not be stepped upon.

I remember thinking, but did not ask, what of the worms underground? But that is small of me. The holy man did seem to truly care for all living things. Often, when we sat and talked in the evenings, he would refuse to drink water for fear of accidentally swallowing .... ever-present gnats that were drawn to our fire. It is said that many of the holiest of his religion have followed the logic of their strange thoughts *'perhaps better word is beliefs'* to their natural conclusion, and have starved ..... death rather than ....life of a living thing. These are strange doctrines indeed, but not harmful. Our memories of the recent chaos in our homeland made us warm to these gentle people. Although barbarians, they were kind to us and we stayed with them for several months, gathering food and water. It was with some regret that we left, but this was not the land we sought.

Our boats sailed and drifted for several weeks before we again saw a place to land and ... *'word seems like to regain'* our supplies. The water currents of the place were wild and strong and we often feared for our lives or of being separated. Just as we thought that all was lost and we would again be swept away from land, the currents pushed us to shore. Unlike the land of the western people, this was a very dry place with no sign of villages or agriculture. I did not know whether we had found an island or a new land like our home. The first natives we saw were tiny, well formed, and black. Their diminutive size made even the oldest of them appear like children. .... no permanent homes, moving about like animals, gathering food as they went. The men hunted with bows, arrows, and spears, while the women and children spent their days picking berries and digging roots.

It was difficult to communicate with them as their language contained strange clicking sounds which were difficult to interpret or recreate, but I think they call themselves *'again a word without meaning'*...........small ones are primitive, even for barbarians, and have no written language. We never saw many of them at any one time; they travel in small clan groups, always numbering less than twenty. At first, they were very shy, but soon they warmed to us and were delighted with the gifts we brought, especially our metal knives, mirrors, and utensils. Neither the men nor women wear clothes but the climate was very warm and they seemed comfortable.

After we spent several weeks near one group, they invited us to spend the evening in their camp. We were wondering, with some concern, what we might be offered for food, as they have a fondness for small grubs and insects, when the Chief brought forward two of the largest eggs one could imagine. After a fire was started and banked so that the coals were hot, a hole was tapped in the crown of each egg. They then inserted a stick and twirled it until the egg became well mixed. A tortoise shell was ....serve as a pot and the eggs ....poured into it. The whole shell of the tortoise was then inserted into the fire and the eggs stirred until they hardened. Within minutes the meal ....the air was filled with the smell of good food. In our land we also cook eggs in a similar way, but nowhere do we have birds that lay eggs .... It is hard to imagine, but the content from the two eggs fed twenty people when combined with berries and roots the women gathered. Even today as I write this, I marvel at the size of those eggs.

The land of the little ones was not the land we sought, but for a time, we were caught up by the friendliness of our new friends and the warmness of the climate. Snow Pine especially liked the little ones, and spent many hours going with the women to hunt herbs and to learn of their medicinal value. Among these small people we felt secure and were lulled into letting our defenses wait for another day. However, this turned into an almost fatal mistake.

One afternoon, our camp was attacked by a large group of black men. These were tall men with short stabbing spears and leather shields. Although armed with the most primitive of weapons, they fought with great ferocity. It was hard to believe that they and the gentle little people with whom we had shared an evening meal could be of the same land.

Our men acquitted themselves well with few casualties, but the savages continued to press us from all sides. As the battle continued into the late afternoon, I knew we could not survive the night. Our only hope lay in retreating back to the water and casting off our sailing vessels. The barbarians contested every foot of ground as we fought our way back to the water. The way was littered with their dead and dying, yet on they came. I can still remember the frustrated howling of these dark savages as we finally floated out of their reach.

I believe that we sail-drifted for about a month after leaving the land of the black ones. Some of the group now wanted to forget our search for the land of the immortals and to return home, feeling that even if we faced the rage of Chin and died, we would at least be buried among our own. Before a decision could be reached, a sudden storm caught us and we were blown beyond our maps. We were now lost in the vast desert of the sea.

We left the land of Chin'in in three boats and had managed to stay together, but in this one fierce storm, the boat containing the family of Wang Yueming was taken away and we were reduced to two. Even now, I cannot bear the thought that I shall not see Wang again. Although not of my blood, he was truly a brother. Life is so strange; our destinies had always been tied together, even when the odds were impossible. Now, after a thousand adventures that could have parted us, he floated away in a storm. When the weather cleared, we offered a dish of rice to our ancestors and prayed for the protection of Wang and his family. Yet, even as I prayed for him, I feared we would never meet again in this lifetime, and unlike the Hindi people, I believe this is the only life that I shall have.

After the loss, we tied the two remaining boats together, choosing to share a common fate rather than go on alone. Bound together, we lost the power to maneuver and we drifted where sea and wind took us. Yet, we remained together, and that was a fair trade. If one is truly lost, any direction is equally acceptable. We lost hope of completing our quest, of finding the land of the immortals or of returning home. Our fate was now in the hands of the gods that rule the sea and wind.

We drifted for several weeks before we again saw land. Being short on provisions and water, we were forced to go ashore, and landed near the mouth of a great river. The natives we saw, and only from a distance, were a wild fierce brown people with tattoos and bone adornments. I wonder that the gods have made so many types of man. The natives made no effort to make contact with us, but we were not welcome. We made no attempt to move inland away from the water's edge, as the land was swampy and the jungle dense. The nights were terrifying and filled with strange howling which came from just beyond the reach of the light of our fire. We lay huddled in our boats, fearing what lay just beyond our sight. Fortunately the wild land was lush with fresh water and food that could be gathered nearby in the safety of daylight. This was not a place where we could remain and we quickly replenished our supplies and again set off, happy to be away from this violent, hot, wet, savage place.

I do not know how many weeks we drifted with the tides and winds but we were fortunate. We had stored adequate grains, daily we caught fish, and the afternoon rains that ran down our sails provided water. On several occasions we saw islands off in the distance, but the winds and currents always moved us away from them.

By my reckoning, we arrived in this new land on or about the Festival of the Moon. We saw no one that first day, so we unloaded the boats and pulled them into the shade of the trees and covered them with boughs to hide their presence. We learned our lesson in the land of the dark ones—that not everyone welcomes strangers, even those who come in peace.

Although completely cut off from our homeland and the traditional season of harvest, at the first sign of the moon, we gathered for the festival. The women cooked small-sweetened cakes, made from quickly gathered wild grains, which we shared. In our homeland, it is our tradition on this night of the full moon, to gather and think about family and friends who are not with us. It is a sad feeling, but in the end, it made them feel real to us again and reconnected us to our past.

Snow Pine lay curled in my arms asleep. "We can be happy here, even if we have not found the land of the immortals," I said to her sleeping form. "We may never be able to go home again, but we can be happy." Little did I know how these words would soon come back like bile into my throat? Snow Pine turned toward me in her sleep, and I was again struck by her beauty. "We can be happy here," I said again, almost as if it was a promise or vow, and I pressed my lips to her forehead.

After a time, we saw people in the distance, but they never approached—indeed, they fled when we came near. They appeared quite primitive. They wore few clothes and had few adornments but decorated themselves with mud. I thought that it would have been useful to make some contact with them, but given our experience with the fierce black men, I would rather they be too shy than too bold.

And they were delightfully shy in the beginning. They observed us from a distance for more than a moon, and then they slowly came forward, a few at a time; the men with bows and spears, the women and children staring in rapt wonder. They touched our faces, marveling at our eyes, which are almond in shape rather than round. It is as if they have never seen people like us before. The winds have blown us far from the Middle Kingdom. Snow Pine in her silks and light hair especially delighted the children; they gathered around laughing and singing as she walked among them. One child especially caught her interest, a bright eyed demon called Tan na. She was everywhere, a dynamo of energy, eyes as black as the night and raven colored hair that shone with small lights when she moved. Over the weeks she became Snow Pine's quick moving shadow. Seeing them both together, I realized how great a mother Snow Pine would be. I wondered when our family would begin.

Although underfoot and like children among us, the natives tried to help as we sought to bring order and create a space for ourselves in this new land. I assigned several of our party to learn the language and to explore their techniques for living in this place. Although barbarians, we would have to learn from them if we were to make our home here. Soon, through a combination of sign language and words, we began to communicate, and found the natives to be very helpful. They taught us which local plants were safe to eat and which to avoid. The nearby warm waters teamed with sea and air creatures which were unfamiliar to us, and they taught us how to harvest and preserve them for storage. By year's end, with their help, we felt secure in this new place. The spot chosen for our new home was on a gentle rise overlooking the sea. It offered a natural defense, a place not easily come upon by stealth.

Snow Pine was a favorite among the natives and, as her healing skills became known, they brought their sick to her for care. The ever present little Tan na became the healer's apprentice, even seeking out little animals to care for. Even the Shaman of the tribe, Holtah, appeared impressed with Snow Pine's skills.

Holtah was a tall man, with haunting dark eyes and long white hair. His totem was the bear, and he adorned himself with furs, and necklaces of teeth and claws. At first he tried to ignore what she was doing among his people, but as her fame as a healer spread, he watched her, first as if to check her skills, but later as a student of her arts. He was particularly impressed and appeared to ascribe great magic to the bone fragment needles she placed in the skin of her patients to restore the harmony of their life force. She was especially good with the children and the old ones. It is sad to note that it is this very kindness that in the end brought us down.

Slowly, in the dark days before spring, some of our companions came down with a light rash across their bodies. Snow Pine was quick to recognize the disease among us, isolating the few until the fevers and skin

Raymond Scott Edge

eruptions subsided. She warned Holtah to keep the tribe members away from our camp, but soon they too fell ill. For them the disease ran a different course than it did among us. Who knows why the gods favor some and not others? The illness came upon our new friends with great harshness.

The disease among the natives caused Snow Pine great sorrow, but the greatest pain was caused when Tan na became ill. The child's fever went up and a reddening flush spread across her face, arms, and chest. Snow Pine was frantic and bathed her with cold water in an attempt to lower the heat. Although Tan na's skin remained smooth and, unlike the others, no pustules appeared, she obviously was becoming worse and suffered great pain. Snow Pine remained at her side, singing, bathing, praying, but to no avail. The redness of Tan na's skin brightened, turned a deeper color, and then purplish black. Her skin became silky smooth to the touch and blood dripped from her nose. Nothing Snow Pine did helped: no medications, no treatment, no prayers changed the course of the disease and finally the girl's mind went and her skin sloughed off in sheets. Snow Pine could only sit, wipe the blood from her face, and wait until the end. I cannot remember ever seeing such a hopeless, haunted look upon her face as when the child died.

For most of the other tribe members, the disease followed a less dramatic and painful course, but still they died in great numbers and, even with Snow Pine's best efforts, nothing changed the process. Few of those who came down with the rash could be saved, and they only to live scarred on body, face, and mind.

It was strange to watch our people get the disease, and then regain health, even while our new friends were dying. Slowly the natives lost faith in our medicines, which worked for us but not for them. Even their attitude toward

46

Snow Pine changed, although she continued to care for them unceasingly. Their earlier smiles of appreciation became sullen looks of wariness as if they were blaming us for their illness. Blaming us for getting well while they died!

These feelings of betrayal were inflamed when Holtah, who had ceased to study the new medicine with Snow Pine, now spoke against her, insinuating that we were treating and healing ourselves but allowing them to die. Had I but known where these lies would lead, I might have prevented the disaster, but foretelling the future is not among my gifts.

In the warm light of the full spring, as the earth renews itself, the illness left our people, although it continued to ravage the natives. For those who still came for treatment, we did all that we could. A wedge had been pushed between our two peoples, but I had hopes that, once the disease was gone, our peoples could again live in friendship. We had so much to gain from each other.

On that last day, I remember thinking that perhaps the worst was over, when we were visited by a greater number of the natives than usual. They came among us smiling, and we welcomed them, attempting to mend the breach. Even that devil Holtah, who had spoken against us, was in camp smiling and eating our food.

Just as the evening fires burned low, a fierce cry went up from the natives, and they fell upon us with clubs and bludgeons. Their closeness and numbers did not allow a proper defense. I found myself fighting for my life as several came upon me at once. None of them were my equal in the martial arts, but their numbers and willingness to die took away my advantage. Across the fire, I saw Holtah rise above Snow Pine, and strike her with a club cruelly adorned with the teeth of the great bear. Even now, the sound of the blow against her skull—and the redness of

47

her blood seeping where the multiple teeth points cut her face—awaken me at night. I screamed in pain and hatred, pushing aside my assailants, but even as I moved to protect her, I was grabbed from behind. It was too late. Several other natives beat her to unconsciousness and finally she lay still by the fire.

It was as if ants were attacking grasshoppers. Around each of my men swarmed groups of the barbarians attempting to bring them down. The night was filled with savage cries as one by one we fell. Although our men killed many of the natives, their numbers were too great. In the end there was nothing to be done but to run. Piteously few of us made it to the shelter of darkness, but even there they sought us, and with each killing, a chilling, bloodthirsty cry went up to the sky above. Sometime in the night, I stumbled upon this animal burrow in which I hide. Lying in the darkness, I wept, hearing the cries of our men, and counting each outburst as one of us lost. What of Snow Pine? The blood flowing down her face fills my mind.

Around me, the cave grows bright and Snow Pine is here, dispelling the chill and dampness with her warmth and smell. Her laughter is like the small spring that bubbles from the wall. I show her that I have continued our journal. In my mind I hear her voice chiding me about the order in which I have placed events.

"Yes," I respond, "I must tell the story in sequential order so that those who read might understand." The sound of my voice echoes in the cave, and startles me awake and she is gone. "Snow Pine, how real you are, even in my dreams. How can you no longer be?" The vision of her still body lying by the fire pushes its way into my mind, and I weep without consolation. The thought of Snow Pine's death is impossible for my mind to comprehend. How can I be without her?

Chapter 5

A Time Lost in Time

Great completion must appear as if inadequate
Thus it becomes infinite in its effects.
Lao Tzu

I begin to write again. Snow Pine is right; to honor the telling, to honor our past, I must begin before the beginning, in a time at the very margins of my people's memory. Our first ancestors dwelt in the marshes of our south coast. People say that we are the first people. Unlike the barbarians at our borders who have migrated toward us, we have always been on our land. It is our people who first learned to raise animals and first prepared the soil for seeds. In all the earth, we are the central kingdom, the middle of everything. Even today we honor our remarkable ancients who first cultivated the wild rice. Not even they could have known the civilizing power of this act.

In the central highlands, others of our ancestors moved across the land in small family groups gathering food. In time, they gathered in great matriarchal clans, creating compact, self-contained villages. The main crop of these northern ancestors was millet, which they .... fruits, vegetables, ...meat of dogs and pigs. Some now say that these early people did not truly exist, that they are the creation of ancient storytellers, but I have seen the broken pieces of their ....in trenches that were once filled with water to protect them from invaders, and observed how .... dead in the earth. They existed, and it is from these early .... people come.

Damn, Daniel thought, *lacunae again.* He stared at the blank areas in the writing, trying to fill in the gaps with reasonable words. He saw a bracketed note written along the side margins.

{This section of the manuscript had many small cuts in the paper and several stains that made it difficult to read. I think it would be a useful reference to think about the Neolithic people who inhabited the Banpo Village archeological site excavated near the ancient capital of Xian. I doubt that it would be the same people, but the ideas presented are a match.}

Banpo Village, never heard of it, Daniel thought. *I'll look that up when I get back to the university library.* He then resumed his reading.

It is said that these simple clan villages, dug into the hillsides, provided the foundation for the development of Chin'in society. Early records show how these ancestors worked in metals .... protective walls and moats provide evidence that, even then, we had an unfortunate acquaintance with war. Among the fragments of this earlier time, I have found the special oracle bones that priests used to consult with the spirits of ancestors. They would heat the bones and read the resulting cracks and fissures. Did the ancestors see my story in the diviner bones? Am I now a man lost, and without a future? If cast today, would the bones defy the heat and remain without cracks?

Our histories tell us that a people known as the Shang fought their way to dominance in the land. The Shang were mighty priest warriors whose noble families were especially fierce. They built large towns protected by tall wooden walls to keep out the barbarian invaders from the northern deserts. The Shang nobles were a luxury loving people, and their bronze vessels are still prized and passed down among us. The products of their metallurgy skills are still treated with awe. However, in the end, it was foolishness that brought them down.

I remember so long ago, a lesson given by my teacher, Master Yi. "Beware the mistakes of the Shang," he said, "a people who forgot who they were and surrounded themselves with artisans, workers in bronze, jade, and ceramics. In their pride of achievement, they kept the blessings of the metal to themselves, forcing the peasants to continue scratching the soil with branches of wood. In the end they found themselves surrounded with trinkets, which they could not eat."

All civilization stands on the backs of those who till the soil. The mighty Shang forgot this truth and lost their heavenly mandate to rule. They built their foundation upon the three cardinal faults of greed, hatred, and delusion, and in the end, their failure to see the world as it truly was, destroyed them.

Our histories tell us that the Shang fell to the warriors of a vassal state known as the Chou. The epoch clash between the Shang and Chou provides our scholars and teachers with the great lessons of the dynastic cycle where good is ever pitted against evil. Dynasties fall when the leadership, through internal wickedness, loses the mandate of heaven to rule and are replaced.

I can still hear another lesson of Master Yi, "The gods favor the good, and will not suffer the wicked to long rule our land."

It is said that one can foretell the loss of the heavenly mandate from signs such as floods, famine, personal debauchery, and widespread drunkenness. Through these signs, the gods make known their unhappiness with a ruling family. Only the gods know who should ascend the dragon throne.

As a boy growing up in Chin'in, the legends and myths of the Chou were part of my education. The Chou was a great nation whose ruling family maintained power by granting large land holdings to loyal kinsmen in return for military service, tribute, and fealty. The king himself commanded one garrison; to his south and east were two other armies led by vassal lords. In this way, the Chou maintained an admirable equilibrium over their territories for more than three hundred years. However, as is often true, time and success rusted the ties between the vassal lords and the royal family. The Chou became complacent and did not notice their danger until it was too late.

Nomads from the north came sweeping out of the desert, moving like locusts over the Chou farmlands. Over the centuries such invasions occurred many times, but the great armies always gathered to punish and push the barbarians back to their desert wastelands. This time however, when the call went out, the vassal states hesitated, delayed in providing assistance, and betrayed their emperor so that the royal capital was sacked and plundered. The emperor himself led a noble last defense and paid with his life. The royal family fled and established a new capital at Loyang, where they pretended to rule for several hundred years while the once powerful Chou state cracked and splintered into small warring nations.

As Chou society disintegrated, chaos and disharmony became the rule. Great thinkers across our land attempted to explain the change in fortune. Lao Tzu and Kong Fu Zi

{Kong Fu Zi, is better known by the Latinized form Confucius}

were but two of the many famous poets, teachers, and philosophers who exhorted their princes to virtue. The writings of these great thinkers—as they attempted the valiant but fruitless effort to restore order and harmony— represent a human treasure of wisdom. However, even if fruitless, their effort has led us to call their period, the Age of Philosophers.

By the end of the fourth century of chaos, the number of warring states had dwindled to seven powerful states and fifteen weaker states upon which the seven preyed. One of the powerful competing states was known as Chin'in. In my lifetime, the word Chin'in has come to mean not only my people but all the diverse peoples of our land.

I remember that we once captured a strange wanderer from the tribe known as the Hindi. He claimed that he came from a people who lived beyond the far mountains, a people as numerous as the sands. On a daily basis, his stories became more fanciful, and one day he told us that it was a man's destiny to live one's life over and over again until it had been done correctly. I remember that Lord Chin found his story of multiple lives amusing, and ordered us to put him to death so that in his next life he could come back and tell a more believable story. Perhaps that is the nature of my tale, for me to tell and retell until it is in order. Snow Pine would be amused at the scattered nature of my thoughts.

Perhaps, Snow Pine is right, I have once again confused the telling by placing events out of order. The light that has filled the cave this day begins to weaken and I grow tired of writing. Tomorrow, I shall start anew at the true beginning, the last battle of the war of the seven kingdoms. I shall tell you how my Lord Chin became the first emperor of a unified land, and how our tragic story of love, adventure, and betrayal begins.

Chapter 6

An Unlikely Story

Daniel woke up to the sun streaming into his room. The manuscript still lay next to his hand on the bed. He had read into the morning hours and should have been exhausted but felt exhilarated. *Fantastic* he thought, *No wonder the Chinese guy had trouble with this. The part about the early dynastic history of China is true, although pretty common knowledge. But to imagine that somehow a group of them made their way to the New World after landing in India, Africa, and maybe near the mouth of the Amazon in South America...now that stretches credibility.* He didn't know whether to laugh or cry, throw the damn thing in the garbage, or to read on. He imagined the reception that the Chinese scholar had gotten when he tried to present the manuscript to the various departments. *They're right; this has to be a hoax.*

But, the story intrigued him and his first thought was to lay back and continue to read. "Better be careful," he said to himself. "If I hope to graduate in June, I need to get back into the good graces of Professor Eldredge and that means volunteering extra time to finish cataloguing the materials from the Cahokia dig." *No rest for the wicked or the weary, or for that matter, graduate students,* he thought.

He looked at the manuscript and thought about Sun Kai hiding in the cave. It would have to be on the Gulf coast somewhere. He thought of Sun Kai's description of white sands, clear water, and pine forest. It would need to be away from where the Mississippi entered the Gulf as that water is always brown, perhaps toward Alabama? He smiled ruefully wondering if what he was thinking was really true. *Two thousand years ago would the Mississippi have always run muddy, or was that a byproduct of humanity's efforts, like the river's current smell of petroleum. Was it possible that in those days it ran clear, at least in the dry seasons?* Each time he thought of a possibility, a way to fix the position of the original cave, the mental path reached a brick wall; nothing made sense. *One thing's for sure,* he thought, *it wasn't near Alton, Illinois.*

Daniel placed the manuscript on the side table, dressed, skipped breakfast and by nine was in the newspaper archive office seated at a scanner, reviewing microfiche. He was looking for a needle in a haystack, a missing person, lost sometime between the Missouri Compromise of 1820—as far back as the archives went—and the early twentieth-first century. If the guy had actually been Chinese, given the prejudice of the times, would they have even bothered to mention his name in the paper? The task appeared hopeless, and even if he found a missing person, so what? It wouldn't necessarily be the guy in the cave. These thoughts didn't please Daniel but he liked historical research, and going through the old newspapers at least allowed him to feel he was accomplishing something.

At home that night, Daniel quickly finished the evening meal, begged off from the family card game, and went to bed early. He couldn't wait to continue the story. He picked up the papers and read. "I begin again; I am Sun Kai ….."

Chapter 7

A True Beginning

The man of calling is not benevolent.
To him men are like straw dogs, destined for sacrifice.
Lao Tzu

I begin again; I am Sun Kai, First in Command, leader of the Hawk Men, and Captain of our army, Old Hundred Surnames. It is a cold and dark morning and I pull my coat tight about my ears. About me are thousands of Chin'in soldiers, and although no light is shown, and no voices are heard, I can sense their presence, smell their sweat, feel them straining against their battle harnesses. Their impatience fills me as we await the light of the new day. One more hour and this tension and impatience will turn to movement, movement to fear and rage, and finally to the ruin of the city above us as yet unclear in the dim light.

"Younger Brother, Go down the line and check the final positions," I whisper to Fan Shaofei, my second in command and best friend in this world. Although not related by blood, Fan has grown closer to me than most relatives because of shared experiences. We were boyhood friends, fellow disciples of Master Yi of the Huashan Mountain Monastery, and now serve our Lord Chin as we have for the full duration of the conquest of the Seven Kingdoms. Yes, Fan is perhaps more than a brother; he is one of the few humans that I trust with my life.

This morning is the same as hundreds of others. One more hour and Old Hundred Surnames, sons drawn from each of the leading families of Chin'in, seeing the morning light, will move forward, crest this final wall, and this war of wars will end. Above us the last capital of the warring states is about to fall; win this, and we can go home. Although the citizens in the city above us sleep soundly and securely behind their protective wall, they do so only because they do not know that Old Hundred Surnames await outside and that the priests have read the oracle bones, which foretell of today's victory.

Someone, perhaps Fan, stumbles in the darkness and curses as rocks shift and fall into the trench. My ears pick up the flapping sound of a banner in the wind. These are muted sounds, loud to those who strain to see the first light but not enough to spread the alarm or alert the guards on the towers above. This morning is like so many others. In the past we breached some walls by long siege, some by force, others by negotiations, and others like this one, by treachery, but in the end, it is always the same, the walls are crossed.

The outcome of this battle was decided before the first man moved. It is not the strength of our army that would breach the wall this day, but rather an obsession of the heart. Today's key to the breaching of the wall was a gambit in a war for the possession of the beautiful concubine Snow Pine. Two men, one a young lover, a scion of one of the first families of the city, the other, the lord of the city who could command any woman for his bed, were locked in an unequal struggle for the beautiful courtesan. The young man, in desperation, sent a messenger to negotiate his cause with Lord Chin, enemy of his city.

The young man promised that if Chin would but give his word, he would provide information regarding a secret entrance through the city wall. The asking price for this treachery was guaranteed safety of the young man and his family, and possession of the woman as his own. I remember thinking how immature to the ways of the world the young man must be, that he would betray his city for a woman, but then, I had not yet met Snow Pine. But, once again, I am losing my place in the story. Assurances were given, and, now in the darkness, we awaited the morning sun.

Even as the royal chop was placed on the document, we knew that any agreement with Lord Chin, Slayer of Dragons, Eagle Who Sees Far, and soon to be Emperor of a unified land would buy only the quick end of the defenses. "It is like a cat promising to only eat white mice," Fan laughed. The solemn guarantees given were only a matter of convenience. My Lord Chin would have this city, easy or hard, fast or slow, for it was his destiny, and the assurances only changed the circumstances of the taking. In the end, the agreements would not spare the family, nor buy the boy the woman.

As the night gave way to morning, I could make out the outline of the Hawk Men Banner waving in the morning breeze. Off to our left a light appeared at the bottom of the wall as the secret door was unlatched.

I moved forward in a vanguard of Hawk Men, the silent

warriors of Chin'in, drawn from the Huashan Mountain Monastery. These warrior monks rejected the heavy battle harnesses of the common soldier and wore only the light gray robes of their order with no adornment except the hawk embroidered over the left breast. From their waist belts hung swords drawn from the forge on Huashan Mountain and stamped with the hawk. On our banner was a profile of our Lord Chin draped in a cloak of hawk feathers. Although each hawk warrior is a weapons master, the swords they carry make them only slightly more lethal. Each was a silent killing ghost, individually terrible to fight, and impossible to overcome as a cohort. The warriors quickly gained access to the city wall, killing even those who made the way possible by unlatching the gate. Inside we moved to open the main gate and silence those watching from the city towers above.

The regular army, Old Hundred Surnames under the command of Fan who had recently been lying silently outside, came forward through the city gate. The shrill sound of trumpets, the sight of the great Chin'in army dragon banner, and screaming army, were terrifying, and what few defenders there were in place dropped their weapons and fled. Old Hundred Surnames, disciplined by a thousand battles, moved as one mind. Any city dwellers that slept through these events were now awakened by the sound of the alarm from the North Drum Tower. However, this time the drum was being beaten by their enemies, not to summon defenders, but to acknowledge the entrance to the city by the warriors of Lord Chin. The troops moved quickly from house to house, taking whatever, and whomever they desired. Our troops were hardened by a thousand battles, any resistance by man, woman, or child, led to the death of all who were sheltered under the roof.

After opening the gate, I guided our forces as they

pushed the city defenders back to a stronghold near the Eastern Tower. The remaining city forces regrouped and ended the battle with honor—they died bravely. Their desperation made them into tigers and their shield wall twice pushed our men back from the ramparts. However, even they must have known their situation was hopeless; perhaps they could hold for an hour, perhaps a day, even two, but in the end we would prevail. As I watched the valiant defenders, my heart was saddened because I could not give them time to prove their valor. My orders were clear; Lord Chin wished a quick victory. I instructed Fan, "Use the flaming arrows; we end this now, even if we lose the city wall in the fire." The massive oaken wall that the defenders had depended upon to shield them from our bowmen's arrows now became their funeral pyre. The waiting Hawk bowmen quickly dispatched any defenders who fled the conflagration. On this day Lord Chin was not to be denied.

By late afternoon, the sky turned dark and clouds threatened rain. It was as if the gods, knowing the setting our play required, prepared a dark and gloomy hour for its enactment. Flanked by his officers and priests, Lord Chin sat on a platform erected in the main city square. Our Lord was taller and larger than most of our people, with a great craggy face and black piercing eyes. Although a man of bulk, he was agile and strong; none could look upon him and see softness. He was dressed in flowing silk robes adorned with the great Chin'in dragon symbol, and looked more the nobleman than fierce warrior he'd become. Although a man given to mood swings and violent decisions, on this day he appeared relaxed and at peace as he sat chatting with his officers and spiritual advisors.

Large urns of incense burned, and the air was filled with pungent smoke and military music. Chin signaled with a movement of his hand and all grew silent as a line of defeated soldiers moved forward, piling their battle flags in a great heap before the raised platform. Chin stood, and leaving the stand, strode out upon the defeated standards. Today it was to be obvious who ruled.

Chin then moved back to the stand where the former lord of the city, captured early in the battle, was on his knees, chained like a dog. The other surviving city leaders stood in sullen silence off to the side surrounded by our troops. The families of the men were also present and held in a group. Lord Chin nodded to me to bring the family of the former lord forward. Once in place, he ordered the man to look upon his family as they were slain. As each head was taken, it was placed on a standard to stare down at the groveling man. The man's eyes were wild in desperation, an animal trapped without hope. With one quick blow from my sword, I severed his head from his body, gathered it up, and threw it among the other captured leaders. "Dogs, to your knees," I yelled as my troops drew their swords and pushed the now terrified city leaders from their feet. "No dog may look upon the face of the Mighty Chin, Slayer of Dragons, Eagle Who Sees Far, and now Lord of this city and live. All who wish to live choose now. Kowtow and swear allegiance to your master."

Each of the city leaders were hustled forward by guards, brought to Chin and thrown at his feet. The families of the men, fearing a repetition of the earlier events, keened in fear and many swooned. All prior sullenness and pride had been swept away by the rolling head of their former lord. Now terrified, each man groveled, begged for mercy, kissed the hem of their new lord's robe, and swore everlasting fealty.

After he had individually forgiven and restored each of the men to their waiting families, Lord Chin again looked to me and said, "Bring me he who gave me entrance to this city." I nodded, and the young man who had negotiated the opening of the secret passage was brought forward to kowtow in front of Chin. Although in his early twenties, he looked like a boy in his long sleeved gown. It was hard to imagine such a soft and callow youth having the courage to play such a part. His round face and soft mouth were almost feminine and carried a petulant anxious expression. His skin drew tight as he waited to see what Chin would say and do. His furtive eyes glanced across the crowd, uncertain as to what the disclosure of his role in the loss of the city would mean to his future.

"This is my son" Chin declared, "He has given me the city, and I honor him and his family." The boy's faced turned from tentative uncertainty to sneering confidence as he thought of his good fortune and imminent reward. As I looked over the crowd, it occurred to me that he would not have been so comfortable had he seen the return of sullenness to the eyes of the old deposed leadership.

As if planned by heaven itself, the sun broke through the clouds and bathed the scene in light. Lord Chin continued to smile upon the boy saying, "At first light tomorrow, you will travel with me to Xian, to bring them news of our victory. We this day have established a new dynasty which shall rule for 10,000 years." Chin gave his most benevolent smile and turned away from the boy to whisper to me. "I shall provide for him my chef and food taster for the journey to be sure that the young snake eats well and does not return. There is no crime greater than disloyalty."

I have thought many times of that day and how it did not occur to me that, at some point, I would commit the same great crime. At that moment, it was inconceivable to me that, in the near future, I would flee from the presence of Lord Chin and chose the unknown over staying with my people. I am glad that foretelling is not my gift, for I doubt I could have borne the thoughts.

My Lord Chin continued, saying "By the way, the concubine Snow Pine is yours; he will have no need for her. I leave in the morning, but you must stay as civic leader until a local administration is arranged. Keep five cohorts of Hawk Men to provide security. Do my will!" As I looked at Lord Chin's face, I knew it had been a good day. He was a master of the art of human manipulation. Our old teacher, Master Yi would be proud of his pupil; he had skillfully balanced the forces of the dark and light side of the mountain, the yin and yang forces that balance the cosmos. All in all, a good day I thought, enough violence to make the old leadership fear, enough charity to make them loyal, and enough dissension to keep them divided. Yes, a good day indeed.

Chapter 8

Hawk Men

Therefore take care that men have something to hold on to.
Lao Tzu

At first light the next morning, I stood on the tower overlooking the main gate. In the morning shadows, the land stretched out to beyond the reach of my gaze, cloaked in muted browns and grays. Deep trenches and grooves marred the landscape, and gave the vistas a worn and dead appearance. Looking at the scene, I realized that every ounce of soil around this ancient city had been repeatedly moved, pushed up, shifted, and again made low. *How many stories could you tell?* I thought to the land. *How many men like us have thought we owned you and later disappeared into your silent soils? How vain we are to think that we have made a difference?* The land of course

66

did not answer; it lay still in the early light looking used and unnatural. It occurred to me, as I gazed over the landscape that we were the cause of its unnaturalness. The land bore the unmistakable look that only humans can give a place after a millennium of use.

Below me the gates swung open, but this time to allow the conquerors out. Chin, with Fan as his driver, rode at the head of the column in his war chariot, while Old Hundred Surnames marched behind. Still further along in the caravan were the spoils of the city, both human and material goods. The war of the seven kingdoms had been a long war of conquest and intrigue. It was a remarkable time for the army of Chin'in, for it was the first time in years that they could move comfortably across the territory without wondering what would greet them over the next rise. Outside of a few bandit groups located in the vast northern wastelands, no force dared to oppose them. Yesterday's rather unremarkable battle had ended the conquest of the seven kingdoms. The morning sun was rising on a new Chin'in empire, a unified land.

During its many battles, the forces of Lord Chin revolutionized warfare. All niceties of protocol were left behind as waves of cavalry and mounted archers swept away our enemies. Under his direction, the highly decorated chariots of previous kings, more symbols of prestige than conveyances of war, were supplanted by other more terrible vehicles, created to suit the new requirements of siege and assault. Some were equipped with large shields, battering rams, and siege towers, but perhaps the most dangerous of all was an assault wagon, which most resembled a turtle but for the slits along the sides from which Chin'in bowmen rained deadly fire.

The Chin'in warrior's reputation for ferocity, discipline, and bravery was so well known that officers commanded the troops forward into battle with the cry of "Do My Will! Make Them Fear!" Everything the army of Chin'in did was conceived to produce maximum fear and minimum resistance. On many occasions, cities had fallen not because of the overwhelming force of the army, but rather because of the overwhelming fear seeded in the hearts of the defenders.

In the end, Chin was no longer just Lord of Chin'in, Slayer of Dragons, Eagle Who Sees Far, or even Lord General—he was now leader of a unified state. He had become Emperor, God Ruler, and holder of the heavenly mandate. In his very person rested the essential link between his subjects and the forces of the universe.

As I stood above the gate and watched as the army wound its way out of the city, I felt aloneness. "I shall miss you Fan, first of the Hawk Men; you have been my younger brother." Not long before, I felt the same kinship with Lord Chin, but over time his success and rise in celestial status distanced him from me. Gods are not difficult to love but very difficult to be close to. Lord Chin was still a brother hawk, a fellow disciple of Huashan Mountain Monastery, but he had long ceased to be the personal friend with whom I shared my feelings and confidences. As I watched them leave, I tried to examine my feelings in regard to this change, this loss of closeness, but I could not find a name for the difference. Perhaps, the word I seek is ... inevitable.

My thoughts bring back a memory of an earlier time when, as a boy, I stood alone above the great northern gate of Xian and watched as Chin's father, lord of our city, led his army forth to deal with a marauding tribe who were raiding local farmers and peasants. Later that morning, Chin, Fan, and I, who had been left in the care of our mothers and sisters, donned our small battle harnesses and marched about the city protecting it in the absence of our fathers. This was serious business although it only gained ridicule from our silly sisters. Even then, Chin, the oldest, was our leader.

We spent a splendid morning chasing and fighting the elusive enemy and finally came to the falcon pens where Chin's father kept his favorite birds. These were special birds trained to take their prey in flight and rip them with silver spurs attached to their talons. Chin took one of the birds from its cage. "Sun, get one of the doves!" He indicated a nearby cage of white doves, which were being raised for temple ceremonies. I remember thinking that we were headed for trouble. "These are for the priests," I said, "for the gods."

"The gods won't miss a few birds, throw one up and see how my hawk brings it down," Chin demanded. Against my better judgment, I pulled one of the doves from its cage, quickly mumbling a prayer of apology to any of the gods I might be offending, and threw the bird upward. Even then, I knew that it was easier to put up with the anger of ancestors and gods, than with that of my friend Chin.

We released several of the white doves and watched their desperate flight as the hawk pursued them across the sky. Each released dove dived and turned but in the end was not able to shake off the pursuing hawk. We each took a turn wearing a special leather sleeve, which allowed the hawk to return to our arm without its spurs tearing our flesh. However, as the game went on, Fan became careless, and his naked arm was badly cut by the returning hawk. "Aaagh," Fan cried, as he shook off the bird, further tearing his flesh. Blood ran freely from the deep cuts. I remember Chin and I also started to cry, feeling not only sorrow at the plight of our friend, but also because we knew that this adventure would now be one we must explain to our fathers. Perhaps, the gods had been watching after all.

Fan was the youngest and smallest of us and as he stood there, blood seeping between his fingers, darkening his cloak, tears formed in his eyes and squeezed from his tightly shut eyes. But he stood straight as a soldier with firm jaw and lips.

"Let me see," I said and removed his fingers to reveal the deep cuts made by the silver spurs.

"You are a brave warrior," said Chin, "and you have been marked by the hunter. The hawk is now your brother."

"Maybe we can tell them that I fell into thorns so that you will not be in trouble," Fan whimpered. Chin and I just shook our heads, those cuts were not made by thorns, and no story would fool our mothers, nor satisfy our fathers.

Chin moved forward with a young falcon in his hand and a set of spurs hanging from his arm. He quickly broke the neck of the bird, separating the head so that it bled freely upon the knifed spurs. He rapidly drew the spurs across his arm until the flesh tore and bleeding began. "I now am also a brother to the hawk, and a brother to brave Fan Shofei." Chin then handed the spurs to me saying, "Join us in this brotherhood that binds the Hawk Men."

I stood with the spurs in my hand, absolutely sure that I did not wish to cut my arm, but with my two friends challenging me with their eyes, I pulled the sharp spurs across my arms to open wounds.

"We shall make a vow never to reveal how we came to have these wounds," said Chin. "We shall tell our mothers that we fell into thorns and were scratched."

We then came together in as much of a circle as three small boys can make and pushed our arms together. Following Chin's lead, we vowed in voices somber, "We shall never reveal the secrets of the day. We are now true brothers by blood and brothers of the hawk. We shall be hawk warriors, who kill silently and without mercy." Chin

70

and I ripped our cloaks to make bandages to wrap the wounds. Somehow, the morning's events ceased to be a disaster, but rather a solemn adventure. Later in life, I would not be able to recall what story I told my mother, but would always remember and draw strength from the day that Chin, Fan, and I became brothers to the hawk.

As each of us reached our tenth birthday, our parents sent us to the monks of the Huashan Mountain Monastery for training in martial arts, discipline, and the five relationships that bind civilization. It was here that I first met Master Yi and learned the discipline of a warrior monk. Although Master Yi treated all of the boys similarly, Chin had been singled out for special consideration. At first I thought it was because he was the son of our lord, but I did not envy him, as the special consideration did not take the form of favor but rather of higher expectation. If Fan and I were required to fast for three days, Chin was made to go without food for four. When each of us were required to hang from ropes and to remain silent in the face of wracking pain, Chin's pain was made more excruciating by pulling the ropes tighter and adding weights to his feet.

After one especially grueling event in which we were held under water, Chin appeared unconscious when they drew him out, and lay unresponsive. Fearing for my friend, I questioned why he was being treated thus. "Master Yi, why do you treat him so harshly? What has he done to deserve this from you? If you continue he will surely die."

I still remember the look on our Master's face when he replied, "Do not worry little one, it is not in my power to take his spirit. I am but a simple teacher. I have thrown the oracle bones and the ancestors tell me that Chin has a future well beyond this time and place. He will surely not die today or from my hand."

As consciousness returned from his near-drowning

incident, and for weeks afterward, Chin had seizures in which his body was flung about as if attacked by demons. After each event, he would awaken as from a deep sleep and tell Fan and I of his wonderous journeys to a beautiful land with a jade ribbon river and pointed mountains so steep that no man might climb them. The stories of Chin were amazing in the telling and he was able to provide great detail regarding the scenery of the area. He spoke of floating down the jade river and seeing mountains carved into the shapes of animals and mystical beasts.

On one such occasion, Chin awoke and spoke about meeting an elderly man dressed in red and black robes. He said the ancient one led him into a cavern at the base of the mountain and pointed to a crystal wall. Across this wall, pictures showing amazing events moved, it was as if he was looking into the future. Chin told of seeing a time of great destruction as massive armies moved like locusts over the land. He saw an army of laborers building a great structure that stretched like a mighty dragon across the land from the ocean to a distant barren desert. Chin told of one scene that kept repeating itself. The wall's crystals revealed three men who looked like us but older. As the scene moved across the wall, he saw the one that looked like him pointing to a distant mountain, as if commanding the other two to go. He said he questioned the old man as to the meaning of these wondrous events, and his only reply was, "Do My Will."

As Chin's visions unfurled, becoming more detailed and complete, more and more monastery students came to listen to his tales. As they listened, they asked one another "What does this mean? Who is he? Is Chin to be a man of destiny?" As time went on, even Chin himself wondered about his fate and saw himself as a man of destiny. As these ideas took hold of his spirit, he hoped in his heart that he was the one, the celestial leader, he who would unite the land, he who would set upon the dragon throne, he who would receive the heavenly mandate and rule as a son of heaven.

Drawing upon the boyhood experience of forming the hawk brotherhood, Chin now initiated others from those who came to listen. In time, his followers would expand into a brotherhood of warrior monks, all dedicated to Chin and to the establishment of his empire.

Standing above the gate watching the army move outward, I shook off the memories of Huashan Mountain and the prophetic visions of Chin. My thoughts now came to rest on the many battles, of the hawk men that I led, and the tasks we were called upon to perform. Under the direction of Lord Chin, the warrior monks became a true instrument of terror, a silent enemy that seemed to have the power of invisibility. Often, prior to battles, we would move behind the lines of our arrayed enemies. Many encampments of our enemies awakened on the day of battle to our handiwork—leaders dead in their tents with throats cut. Following these grisly discoveries, and as the first rays of the sun came up, the earth would then become a hell. Old Hundred Surnames, with trumpets blowing, dragon banner waving in the wind, and officers screaming, "Do My Will! Make Them Fear!" would come over the crest to do battle. It was a rare enemy that would stand and fight.

As I watched the last of the troops leave the city gate, I drew my robe up on my arm to reveal the small white scars earned so many years ago. I smiled to myself, such an innocent beginning. Looking up, I saw that the Hawk Men battle ensign flew over the city. It was a rough picture of the upper torso of a Lord Chin dressed in a cloak of feathers. This ensign was carved into the gold coin that hung about my neck and also stamped onto my sword.

Hawk Men, I thought: *Warriors that kill silently, relentlessly, and without mercy.* To commemorate the great victory over our enemies, we have etched the character for 10,000, on the reverse side of our hawk men coins, signifying the number of years Lord Chin's dynasty would last.

My thoughts darkened as I thought of the many battles fought to bring about the unification of the warring states. Many of the silent warriors I had led would not be returning home from the wars. Many had joined our ancestors to assist in the building of the empire from the other side of the veil. That morning I was tired of the killing, glad to see the conquest at an end, and felt sorrow at seeing the chariot of Fan Shofei pass from my sight. We had arranged to keep in contact by carrier pigeon, but that was not the same. *Farewell Little Brother, I miss you already.*

Chapter 9

Building an Empire

If a wholly great one rules – the people hardly know that he exists.
Lesser men are loved and praised, still lesser ones are feared.
Lao Tzu

The days following the departure of the army were filled, dawn to dusk, with activity. The several hundred Hawk Men that Chin left behind maintained the security of the city but, in fact, the old families showed no desire to offer resistance. The vision of their old Lord's head rolling among them was too fresh, and few wished a repeat demonstration. The major problem that I faced was in knowing whom to trust within the city's old administration. To give me time in selecting local officials, I chose several of the most senior Hawk Men monks and charged them with the leadership of the city's departments.

All members of the Hawk Cult wore the same plain robes of the Huashan Mountain monk, with the exception that cult members had an embroidered hawk at the level of the heart, and the gold coin bearing the likeness of Chin in his feathered cloak hanging from a chain about their necks.

The selected senior monks were all cold-eyed, competent men, whose quiet stealth and fierce nature were legendary, and whose very presence made others uncomfortable. I allowed each of them to sequester teams of citizens to provide labor for their administrative sections. My only demand of them was to broach no excuses for delay, and that no family was exempt from their call to duty. "Do my will, make them fear!"

The work during those first weeks was both exhausting and fulfilling. So much needed doing. At each turn of my hand a new task presented itself: we had to repair the outer wall, water systems needed to be restored, and the surrounding farms must be brought into production again. Watching each day as the operations went forward, I selected those men from local families who would fill the administrative posts for our new civil administration. I awoke with excitement each morning and collapsed each night, content with a day's work done.

At the end of the third week the fluttering sounds of a pigeon alerted me to the first message from Fan. Eagerly, I broke the seal and spread the silk. It was a note telling of the celebration in Xian.

Dear Older Brother, our passage home was uneventful with the exception of a short raid by Praxan bandits. Our forces quite naturally put them to rout, but the effrontery of their attack on Lord Chin has brought them to his attention as enemies that will be dealt with.

Our arrival in Xian was a glorious event. The city turned out in riotous celebration, with fireworks, and dragon dancing. A huge meal was prepared in the City Square for all to eat. It was nice to meet with old friends who still live in the city. Many send you their fondest regards. I was also able to meet with those who have lost sons in the war, proud but sad moments.

I am sorry to report that the young lord who so gallantly opened the city wall for us has grown ill, and even with the best efforts of our physicians, it is believed that he will die. I am sure that this will bring distress to those who knew him well.

One can see that the mandate of heaven has truly passed to Lord Chin. His wisdom has confounded the sages and all speak his name in awe. He has taken upon himself the title of Chin Shi Huang Di (first sovereign – god ruler). It is so strange to suddenly be required to kowtow in the presence of someone with whom we played as a child. How does one deal with a son of heaven?

I had dinner with your mother, father, and sister on my first night at home. All is well – they miss you. Your younger brother, Fan.

My heart was filled with the warmth of his message. I tried to imagine the changes that Chin was initiating as he assumed reins over our newly unified land. Fan was right, the attack by the Praxan bandits must not go unanswered, they grow too bold. However, that was a matter that could wait for another day—this day our attention must be directed toward rebuilding the eastern wall and restoring the water system; the Praxan devils must wait.

It was fortunate that the area was rich in water resources; the Wei, Jing, and Ba Rivers encircled the city like glistening ribbons of silver. My problem with water came not from its scarcity, but from the fact that the passing armies had long ago destroyed whatever system was available in the past. A chore of this nature called for the talents of someone like my second in command, Wang Yueming. Wang, a fellow Huashan Mountain monk, was a man of short stature but one imbued with a relentless nature and inexhaustible energy. If I requested it, he would move the mountains. "Conscript as many people as you need for the task" I commanded. "This must be done before the rains. Do my will!"

Before the afternoon was done, conscription notices went out to all the surname families in the city. Each family was to provide 500 able-bodied men and provide them with provisions and equipment for the task. Soon, everywhere one looked, earthen projects designed to control the flow of the rivers were begun. The water projects had an immediate priority, as the system had to be in place to allow for the spring planting. The city's granaries were perilously low following the protracted war.

One afternoon Wang burst into my residence, his face flushed with excitement. He carried a stack of parchment covered with drawings of a strange device. "This you will find amazing," he said. "We borrowed the idea from the peasant farmers from the far south who use similar small devices to move water up a terraced field." When I examined the drawings, they appeared to be a system of large mechanized wheels with attached bowls. The drawings showed a group of men, treading on pedals and working levers, which turned wheels, so that the attached bowls dipped water from one level and poured it into the next holding basin. *Wang is right*, I thought, *it is amazing.*

"Look." Wang exclaimed, "With a set of these we can move water from the river to a mountain reservoir which can deliver water to the city with a force sufficient to clean and maintain our inner canal systems." This idea gained my immediate attention, as current flow through the city's canals was unable to clear the collected night soils. As summer progressed and the water levels in the canals lowered, they had become stagnant festering cesspools with unbearable smell. "How will it be powered?" I asked. "To make this work will require a crew of at least two hundred."

Wang smiled, "I was thinking that the family of the young fool would provide the labor—perhaps even in honor of his memory. They could consider it a gallant gesture as a memorial to his great service."

I smiled, as the choice was a good one. Although the boy's action of opening the city wall to Chin was universally praised and never criticized, it had made his family members pariahs in the community, and none would complain about the administration adding this additional burden to them. "A fine choice, inform them of the honor, Do my will."

With each day passing, the work within the city progressed and some level of normalcy returned. The martial law, which restricted the movement of people, was lifted so trade could again be allowed. The city itself lay on the southern edge of the Quinlin Mountains, a one hundred mile chain of lofty peaks, which provided an admirable screen from the barbarian north.

Daniel sat up and rubbed his eyes. He looked at the note written in the margin.

{The original text term was li. In order to make the

reading more accessible, I have used an equivalent miles.}

What the hell is a li, obviously *some kind of distance measurement,* Daniel thought. He reached for his note pad to make a reminder to look it up later. He then settled back, picked up the manuscript, and continued to read.

The most notable of the peaks was the statuesque Mount Huashan, known as the sanctuary; it was a beautiful area with lush valleys and hot springs. Travelers leaving the city made their way through the Tongguan Pass to the east or Songuan Pass to the west, which provided the gateways to neighboring cities.

The next morning I awoke to the sound of wings in the aviary. Fan had sent a new message.

Dear Older Brother. How I miss the opportunity to speak with you. Every day our Lord becomes more the Emperor. Yesterday he brought nine numerologists to tell his fortune. Each Lo Shu grid surpassed the one before in wondrous predictions. You will not be surprised that none of the predictions spoke of bad news. As you know, Lord Chin, Slayer of Dragons, Eagle Who Sees Far, is not one who suffers bad news. The predictions of his glorious future have been posted throughout the city for all to see.

Our Lord has long thought about the day when he would be emperor and moves quickly in creating new dynastic standards for everything from coinage to the width of roads. He recently ordered that all the fortified walls be connected into a single great wall that will span the entire kingdom's northern border. I am sure you will be receiving these orders soon.

Do not be surprised if you are released soon and can return to the capital. Lord Chin misses your counsel and your reports are well received. He has begun to send administrators out to the newly united areas. Perhaps we will be together soon.

Tomorrow I will visit your sister Mai. Until then, be well.

As I read the note, a chill moved me, and I quickly destroyed the message. Fan will need to be careful in the tone of his writing; he speaks too familiarly and openly of Lord Chin's plans. I must warn him how easy it is, for those who desire, to misunderstand careless remarks.

My dark moment passed however, as I noted that Fan intended to spend time with my sister. I wondered how long it would be before they saw how much they cared for each other. It was as if their childhood memories kept them hidden from each other. How often do we not see what is there because we do not expect to see it? Perhaps, I can assist them in the discovery.

My mind then turned to the repair of the eastern city wall we burned while capturing the city. If Chin was going to order that all defensive walls be connected, perhaps I should plan to go beyond the repairs and send the wall outward toward Tongguan pass in the east. This would provide a better shield against the bandits and make the whole valley more defensible. The problem lay in available labor for such a task, as citizens of the city were already committed to several major projects and we could not afford to move the farmers and peasants from the land with the spring planting season approaching.

By my calculations, the repair and the building of the

additional wall would take 10,000 men. It occurred to me that now might be a good time to move against the northern barbarians in order to get the needed workers. It would be good to take the Hawk Men into the field again; the months of administrative duties from dawn to candle light had taken their toll on my body and spirit. In battle everything was so clear, so simple, so quick.

Six months had passed since Lord Chin left the city. These months had seen the repair of the eastern city wall and the beginning of the long earthen wall toward Tonguan pass. Civil authority had been re-established and schools and temples reopened. The water project had moved forward to a point that the spring planting could be done. Even the wheels that move the water up the mountainside to create a great lake were functioning. The Huashan Mountain monks, who had initially dominated the city, were now acting as shadow leaders behind newly selected local administration.

The next morning, messengers arrived from the capital with news that a royal delegation from Xian could be expected to reach the city within the week. My mind winced at the news—a royal delegation to come and waste my time. *Within every crisis is found the seeds of opportunity*, I thought, *perhaps they will bring my release and I can return home.*

Although the thought of being able to return to the capital was pleasing, there was still so much to be done. As I vented my frustration at the disruption to my schedules, I knew that much of my displeasure came from a perceived lack within myself. I had spent decades of my life as a warrior monk, and whereas I felt comfortable in the company of fighting men, the thought of a royal delegation with soft manners and endless protocol brought fear to my heart. "What should I say? What would we do?"

I must have been allowing my mutterings to become audible, as Wang turned from his work at the calligraphy table. "Why don't you have the courtesan, Snow Pine, handle the meetings for you. I am told that she has experience in organizing appropriate entertainment for similar delegations for the old Lord. She is reportedly a woman of great refinement, of uncommon grace and culture." When I looked at him blankly, he continued. "You remember her, she was the one Lord Chin bestowed upon you. I understand that she continues to live in the residence of Madam Young."

In the work of the last few months, I had found little time for the company of anyone not directly involved in the building of the city. I vaguely remembered the woman, but Wang was usually wise in his assessment of assets.

"A good idea, Wang. Send word that I would speak with her this very evening. Do my will."

Chapter 10

Snow Pine

The soft wins victory over the hard.
The weak wins victory over the strong.
Lao Tzu

It is cold this morning as I awaken in my cave, this prison from which I never go. As the sun creeps in I am surprised at my condition. In the mirrored pool, I see my reflection; it is like looking at someone else. Who is this dirty person who smells of the rankness of a beasts burrow? Surely, this strange creature is not myself. No matter what happens to me, weak or strong, young or old, hurt or well, rarely has the picture within my mind fit the person I see in the glass; this image is that of an animal.

Yesterday's writings of Snow Pine brought her back, and she came to me again as I lay sleeping in the night.

Without light, I could not see her face but immediately recognized her smell, her soft touch, her warmth. I do not need the light to know her every feature and expression. It was almost like seeing her standing again at the pool in our old home. Such a warm and generous body, none were like her. Even as I lie here shivering in the cold, watching the morning sun which gives little warmth, I can feel her body against mine. It is as if my body's memory has been impressed with her and even in her absence, I can still feel her presence. Last night she appeared anxious that I tell our story, tell it correctly, and in order. I do not know why she goads me onward in the telling. But when the sun warms my hands, I will begin again.

What a fool I have become! I know that Snow Pine is gone to our ancestors—I watched her fall by the fire, her crimson blood darkening her hair. Yet, even with my knowledge that her visits are just signs that whatever sanity I possess is slipping away, I keep pushing that reality from my mind. Perhaps I fear that if I truly acknowledge her death, she will never return to me in the night. I would rather have her in my madness than not at all. I shall begin again, and tell you of my Snow Pine, and what she has told me of those days, so long ago.

As Wang Yueming surmised, Snow Pine was still living at the residence of Madam Young, and it was there my invitation found her. As she later explained, the invitation, which was to me a simple matter, was to her, the final spark that caused the simmering anger—which had grown in her for months—to burst into flame. As Snow Pine sat playing the two-stringed erdu, she was caught up in the mood of the music. Her skills with the instrument were substantial, and in her hands the music flowed forth as a human voice, first soft, and gentle, then wild and angry.

85

Anyone listening to the sounds that morning would have known that this was an angry woman.

In all of the six months since I had been placed in charge of the city by Lord Chin, I had not called upon her, and now, like a common servant, she had been summoned. Although she had no personal interest in me at the time, the very idea of my not calling, after she had been so publicly given to me, was a boil that refused to heal. "Am I to be treated this way? Does he think he can make me wait for months and then snap his finger?" she fumed. The erdu again went to a high angry register. "Who does he think he is?" she said to a waiting maid.

Snow Pine had not appreciated the casual manner in which she had been given to me—as a trophy for the capture of the city. She was Snow Pine, a consort of rare quality, and a treasure, not something to be given lightly. The idea that she had been given to a warrior monk was horrible in itself, but then I made the outrage more complete by not bothering to call upon her. Again the erdu moved upward along the scale. This morning a messenger had come, commanding her to attend my table this very evening. "Commanding me!" she fumed as she remembered the message. The attending maids winced at the erdu's shrill tone, rarely had they seen their mistress in such a state of anger.

"Perhaps, he is one who only likes pretty boys?" suggested her maid Su with a smile. "You are lucky that he has not called. I understand that he keeps no friends except those silent gray robed devils."

The gathering maids all nodded in agreement, "No real man would have kept his distance for this long."

Su added, "There must be something wrong with him!"

Snow Pine was not a woman of arrogance or false pride, but she knew her worth. As she put her erdu away and slipped from her robe, she mused to herself, "We shall see if he still likes pretty boys after tonight." She turned to Su, "I would like a massage and scented bath. Have someone prepare paper cuts to adorn my hair; flowers and butterflies would be nice. I will wear my purple robe this evening."

Snow Pine was taller, and more full-bodied than most Chin'in women and had amazingly green eyes. These differences came from her blood, as she was captured as a child from the northern nomads, those we call Praxans.

The Praxan, a northern barbarian people, had lived peacefully along our frontier for countless years. No one alive remembers when they arrived or from where they came. They maintained an existence separate from the Chin'in, living a nomadic tribal life, moving quietly with their herds of sheep and goats along our northern borders. To us they appeared a simple people with a barbarous language, strange and gross features, nomads who announced their presence with the smell of garlic, mutton, and foul cheese.

The people of Chin'in are a cultured people who live within the protective shadow of walled cities. My people could only have contempt for those who would prefer nomadic wandering, open air and tents to our ordered life of farm, family and hearth. Ours is the way of civilization, while theirs is little better than that of the beasts.

Snow Pine has since told me that her people's choice of roaming the hills and open valleys was a conscious one made centuries before. That once they lived in a mighty walled city on the edge of a warm sea. War came to them and following a great and fearsome battle, their city wall was breached and they escaped to become wanderers. When pressed on how she could know such a thing, she tells me that the stories are known by all Praxen and are told and retold to each generation by traveling singers and chanters which she calls citherodes.

Thus these wandering people had lived and prospered in the marginal northern frontiers for hundreds of years in peace and simplicity. However, the last fifty years had not been a good time for the Praxan. The wars between the Seven States had drawn them like pawns into the contest. As our armies moved across the land, the warring states had taken to capturing isolated groups of nomads and using them as slave labor to support the battles.

In the end, those remaining were forced to leave their pastoral ways. The nomad clans fell back to their mountain retreats where they in desperation joined together under the single banner of a savage chieftain born under the sign of the wolf, and named after Ascanius, the lost son of an ancient matriarch.

Under his banner, the Praxans formed into highly mobile fighting units modeled after the hero sagas as sung by the citharodes. Each unit was formed like a wolf pack, which could move and kill quickly, and just as quickly, fade into their wild mountain lairs. Soon, the areas outside the walls of our northern cities were the territories of the warrior packs, and none dared follow them into their mountain retreats. The very name Ascanius struck fear into the heart of all who lived along our northern borders. It was a name that mothers used to frighten their children. "Behave, or I shall send you away with the Praxan devils and Ascanius will eat you."

During the conquest of the Seven States, the Chin'in were too busy to focus on the Praxan problem and resorted to sporadic but non-sustained raids into the northern dry lands. It was in such a raid that young Snow Pine was captured. The army under the command of Lord Chin's father, Lord of Xian, came upon a mountain pass which led to a secluded valley. Nestled along the river were the tents of Ascanius himself. On this day however, he along with most of his men were attacking a supply train far to the south.

The army moved quickly into the valley, burning the skin-covered shelters, killing all who resisted and enslaving the others. My Snow Pine was but a child then, and was off with her younger brother Certes, catching butterflies along the river. Seeing the troops enter the valley she quickly pushed young Certes into the hollow of a tree and covered him with leaves. "Certes! Lie still and do not move!" she admonished, and then screamed and ran away from the hidden boy to draw the attention of a group of soldiers who were beating the bushes. The ruse worked, though the men quickly caught and bound her. Then with a few others who had been spared, she was brought down from the mountain. Although just a child, her captors recognized that she was going to be an unusual beauty. She, along with the other survivors, was taken to the nearest city stripped, paraded and put up for sale. Most went as slaves and servants, however, Snow Pine's height, fair skin, and green eyes brought her to the attention of Madam Young, an older courtesan, who, as a noted beauty herself recognized its potential in another.

Thus began her twelve years of study under Madam Young. Although Snow Pine remained in her heart a Praxan and remembered her true name—her Praxan name, Cassea, she was an attentive student and quickly learned the language of our people. She soon became the flower of the house and was renamed Snow Pine, for her height, paleness of skin, and grace. Always a young woman of quick mind, she had a talent for the poetic phrase, calligraphy, playing of the two stringed erdu, and singing. She soon became a favorite hostess, noted for her extraordinary musical talent, wittiness of conversation, and foreign beauty.

It is at this point in our lives that our stars aligned. Madam Young arranged several socials for the richest young men, drawn from the leading families of the city, to introduce them to her stable of young women. These were very honorable affairs, although it was hoped that the meetings would lead to future relationships. Many of the finest families contained concubines who had learned their skills under the watchful eye of Madam Young. As her prize graduate, Snow Pine was asked to mix with the guests and to entertain with music, fortune telling, and stories drawn from ancient fables. It was at one of these events that Snow Pine drew the attention of the young fool.

Although it was made known to all who attended that she was not one of the available women but was the consort of the city's lord, the young man would not listen to reason. For weeks afterwards, he showed up everywhere. Silly poems and lavish gifts appeared at her residence but were returned. At first the old lord thought of the young man's efforts as those of a smitten peasant, but as the weeks went on, he became impatient and ordered the family to restrain the son.

Having been denied, the young man became obsessive about Snow Pine. He was frustrated and desperate. In his mind he could not imagine how she could prefer the elderly lord over a young and virile man such as himself. Yet, how could he compete with the lord of the city? Why was she returning his gifts? Only a mind in this unstable condition could have seen the army of Chin as a suitable tool to win a woman. His obsession for Snow Pine grew until he came to see our presence in siege outside the city wall as his only hope. However, an invading army is too blunt an instrument for such delicate matters and his efforts in the end gained him only a poisoned meal and sent the object of his desire to the bed of another.

Now, following my invitation, Snow Pine fumed over the way I first ignored—and now seemingly commanded—her to me. *Commanded me!* she thought as she examined herself in the mirror's metal surface. Although not vain, she knew the value of her worth and felt satisfaction with the reflection. *If I know anything, I know men, and this new quiet one, who rules, and does not seem to need the company of women, is just a man. Pretty boys indeed!*

Snow Pine arrived early for our meeting and was quickly shown into my chamber by an attending monk. I remember that I was still signing documents and asked for her forgiveness, telling her that I would be but a moment. My aid then seated her off to the side of the chamber and left the room. She later told me that at first she was discomforted by the delay but then saw that this would be an opportunity to observe me without appearing to stare.

Her first assessment of me was that I was younger than she had imagined, given the position of trust that I held with Lord Chin. She was pleased to note that when I stood, I was about her height. Many of the men with whom she had dealt were shorter, and the effort to make herself seem smaller or they taller was always tedious. As a warrior, I kept my body lean and compact and with the exception of a wildness to my hair which would not contain itself into the current fashion, I was unremarkable. Snow Pine, ever kind and generous, remembers thinking that at least I was not ugly, nor did I appear uncomfortable with her presence. As she sat waiting, she wondered why I had not called on her in all this time.

When I looked up and our eyes met, Snow Pine blushed. She startled me, as I had not really looked at her as she came in. I remember smiling like a child in my confusion. What a fool she must think me. I stood speechless. She later told me that the intensity of my gaze made her feel disquieted, as a mouse might feel at the attention of a cat. *I shall need to be careful with this one*, she had thought to herself.

I finally blurted out my appreciation for her attendance to me at such short notice.

"I have heard so many wonderful things about you and appreciate your willingness to serve. Perhaps we can eat and talk of my needs?" When I clapped my hands, Zhelin the monk who had led her into the chamber returned. "Zhelin, what do we have in our unworthy kitchen? Madam Snow Pine and I will be dining alone."

After a short discussion with my aide, I asked "If it is acceptable, I have selected braised cream cabbage, fish with hot sauce, yams in spun syrup, peppery hot mutton, and white fungus soup." I hoped that she would be pleased by my selections. The dinner contained several elaborate dishes generally reserved for special guests, especially the selection of the hot peppery mutton, which was a dish that had entered Chin'in cuisine by way of the Praxans.

I am a man of long silences and some discomfort in the company of women. Yet that afternoon in the presence of Snow Pine, it was if a dam had been broken and I found myself telling her of the many projects that were ongoing about the city. Snow Pine was especially interested in the water wheels that were now half way up the mountain, and how, in the future, they would allow the city to have water delivered under sufficient force to cleanse the canal systems. I told her of my vision of a city transformed, where canals would be used like roads and where prominent fountains with cascading waters cooled even the hottest days.

It was late in the meal when I finally remembered why I had called her to me. "I apologize for bringing you here at such short notice." I said, "This morning we received word of a delegation from the capital, which will arrive within the week. While I can imagine a great city with fountains and wheels that dance up mountains, I fear that I am woefully unprepared to receive such a delegation. I would be most grateful for your assistance in this matter." Snow Pine blushed, thinking to herself that planning a social event and acting as a hostess was not the service that she thought I was going to request that afternoon. However, she was most gracious in her reply, "My Lord, I would be most pleased to serve you in this manner. I have performed similar duties in the house of Madam Young."

As the white fungus soup arrived, signaling the end of the meal, I asked about the Praxan people. Where did they come from? Had she ever met Ascanius? How many were they? How are they organized? Although I was to learn later that she remembered the Praxan leader well, at this time Snow Pine claimed no memory of knowing him, having been taken from her people at an early age. Seeing an erdu in the corner, she sought to change the direction of our conversation to other matters and suggested that she sing some of the Praxan folk songs that she learned as a child.

As I sat back upon the pillows, she told me that these were songs sung by traveling citharodes who wandered from village to village and acted as the people's collective memory. Her first song was of a city lost, a golden kingdom, a culture of grace, and an age of heroes. One especially poignant character she sang about was Cassandra, daughter of the city's ruler, who, although gifted by the immortals with the ability to foresee the future, was cursed by an inability to convince others of her visions.

As Snow Pine sang, her voice and the erdu became one, and the legends of the Praxan people became alive in the telling. These were epic songs, stories of an earlier age, tales of an ancient people who lived lives of culture and power. Their home was a mighty city whose ships reached out and traded with the world. The city had possessed a most fearsome weapon of liquid fire, which could be sprayed from bronze tubes onto forces below the walls, horrible fires not quenchable by water. The songs spoke of whole armies being swallowed up in the conflagration.

She sang of nobles so fair and wondrous, that even the immortals who ruled from the high mountain were made jealous. She sang of a kidnapped queen, whose beauty launched a mighty armada sent to avenge the disgrace, and how in the end, a lesser people of silver and brass had come to besiege the mighty city of gold. Even with the foretelling of Cassandra, and the help of heroes descended from the immortals themselves, the city wall had been breached by the treachery of a false gift.

She sang of the night the golden city fell, when, with enemy soldiers rampaging like wolves, Aeneas son of the true king, had fought valiantly. He could hear the screams of women who were being dragged from their places of hiding and abused. Finally, when he knew all was lost, he carried his father Anchises from the battle, gathered the remnants of his family, Cassandra his sister, his wife Creusa, and son Ascanius and attempted to flee the blazing ruins. However, unkind fate struck again, and in the turmoil of that dreadful night, Creussa and Cassandra became separated from Aeneas, and Ascanius and were forced to escape alone.

Snow Pine's final song told of how Creusa, and Cassandra were borne away by allies from inner Asia, and how they crossed the land of the fire breathing Chimera who make their homes among the vents of gas and flames that emerge from the ground.

After years of wandering, this remnant of the people arrived in the mountainous valleys where they chose to live the peaceful lives of nomadic herders. It was a conscious choice borne from their grief of a mighty city lost. Only Cassandra, who saw the future, knew their days of peace were but a short respite, but as always the curse held, she went unheeded.

When she had finished the singing, Snow Pine laughed self consciously. She had been caught up in the telling. "I am so sorry that I went on so long, with my silly stories." I assured her that her singing was lovely and the stories wondrous but given the hour, we must end our meeting. I clapped my hands for Zhelin to attend me, "Please see Madam Snow Pine to her residence safely. Do my will!" I then turned to Snow Pine, "When you have plans prepared for the delegation, send word to Zhelin, and we will meet again."

I sat in silence after she left that evening. It was obvious to me that Snow Pine remembered more about the Praxan people than she would admit. I would need to talk with her again on the matter, perhaps those nomads were more formidable than I supposed. I also thought long about the woman herself. Why had she made me feel so nervous, something that I had not felt since childhood? My nervousness had taken the form of my telling her about my plans for the city, as if she were someone I needed to impress. *I shall need to be careful with this one.*

Chapter 11

The Praxan Incident

If there is no place to flee it is fatal territory
Sun Tzu, The Art of War

The morning following our meeting, Snow Pine awoke early, quickly dressed, and went into the garden. Over the years she had maintained clandestine relations with her Praxan family and on that morning she expected an important visitor. On the far side of the garden, in a shaded alcove, she sat down in the grass to wait. The familiar voice of her brother, Certes, came from the branches overhead. "It is good to see you Sister," he announced and jumped down beside her. "It has been a long time."

Snow Pine looked quickly around to be certain no one saw the arrival of her brother; as she anticipated, the sheltered alcove offered a screen from curious eyes. The two sat and talked of current events. Certes brought news of her family in the hills; all was well, but Ascanius was now requiring more and more of the men for his raids against the Chin'in devils. He told her Ascanius had gathered the citherodes from all the clans and spent days questioning them about a strange fire weapon that was described in several of the old saga songs. According to the legends, the weapon at one time made the Praxan invulnerable. "They will fear our fables; we shall sing our enemies to death," Certes laughed. "At times I worry about Ascanius and his visions." He also told Snow Pine that he was interested in one of Ascanius's daughters but had not gotten the nerve to approach her or her father in regard to his feelings. "Why is this thing that is so natural, so hard," he said with exasperation? In this, Snow Pine felt the expert, and gave him advice on how to approach and please the lady.

Snow Pine then related the details of her meeting with me the previous night, how I appeared to be an honorable man, and how she had sung the epic songs. She told him that my intentions toward her had been honorable, and that I asked her to prepare a welcoming ceremony and banquet for a delegation that was expected any day from the capital.

"He is a Huashan Mountain monk devil!" Certes blurted. "Remember who you are, and that your name is Cassia." Snow Pine choked down a retort. She could hardly forget, given that he reminded her all the time. In her heart she knew what she knew, that she was both Cassia and Snow Pine, that she had enjoyed the evening before, and that I was not as cold or blood thirsty as believed by my enemies. Shortly thereafter, it was time for Certes to go. Snow Pine embraced him and pushed some coins into his coat; he quickly pulled himself onto the branch above and crossed over the garden wall.

At her brother's departure, her mind returned to our meeting. She later related to me that she had been most taken by my excitement in regard to building the city, and that my excitement became her excitement to see the plans unfold. She began the mental preparations for the welcoming events and banquet. She saw in her mind my pleasure at receiving the accolades from the appreciative visitors, and the thought pleased her. Her excitement might have been less had she but known the import of her earlier conversation with Certes.

For me, the morning following the dinner with Snow Pine was brighter, although I could not put my finger upon the reason for my inner excitement. The evening had gone well and Snow Pine had been everything that had been said of her. My mind endlessly toyed with the melodies that she sang. *Perhaps the young fool who had opened the wall was not as foolish as I had supposed*, I thought. *I wish I were better with women. I seem never to have anything to say to them.* This thought had no more crossed my mind than I remembered how I had practically drawn for her a map of the city and stuttered in my eagerness to explain the changes we planned. *I hope she was not too bored, or thought me a fool.*

My mind then turned to our discussions regarding the Praxans. It was obviously the one subject about which she was reticent. Her singing of the ancient saga songs was both beautiful and intensely personal. It was obvious to me that she still had emotional attachments to these wild northern people. It was always wise to understand those whom you might someday oppose; perhaps Snow Pine might prove the key to these barbarians. I would need to discuss them further them with her. Yet, was it the Praxans that I was interested in or did I simply wish to continue the discussion with Snow Pine? I smiled at the thought.

By mid-morning the next day, Snow Pine sent a message that she had preliminary plans for the upcoming occasions and was prepared to meet at my earliest convenience. I quickly dispatched Zhelin to bring her to my chambers. I tried to work as I awaited her arrival; how difficult it was to remain focused on the task at hand. Something about her disquieted me and intruded upon my thoughts. As she came into the room, I rose to greet her. "I appreciate your kindness, and thank you for your assistance with this matter."

"It is my pleasure to serve" she replied and sat where I indicated.

She then outlined her plans for the delegation. It would begin with formal greetings at the gate of the great city wall, and continue with a series of activities moving inward toward the city center, concluding with a welcoming banquet and entertainment. As I listened, I was again impressed with her quickness of mind and the manner in which she made the simple, elegant. I also noted with appreciation that her planned activities would show our last few month's work within the city in a most positive light without appearing to focus on my achievements. She understood the thousand rules that were a mystery to me. As each event was discussed and decided, I gave my aides the appropriate orders and sent them away with the familiar "Do my will!" to make the invitations and oversee the preparations.

We talked late into the afternoon, and I ordered eight-treasure tea to be served. Although we were essentially through with our business, I was loath to end our meeting. "It is such a perfect afternoon; perhaps you will stay and dine with me?" I said. "Perhaps you would be kind enough to continue your beautiful singing."

I was rewarded by her smile and an indication that, yes,

she would indeed like to dine with me and continue the singing. "My lord is too kind," she said.

I find it strange how the minute details of that meal, taken so long ago, seem so clear. As we moved to the table, hot towels were brought to refresh our faces and hands. We continued to talk of the upcoming events and dined on the initial cold meat and vegetable dishes that were placed before us. By mid meal, a great many serving dishes covered the table, each filled with slices of meat or vegetable, and small bowls contained an array of sauces both dark and light. I felt enchanted by her, her grace, beauty, and wit. Even the manner in which she used the eating sticks was graceful and sensual. The main entrée was a pepper hot, spicy mutton dish, which I selected in deference to her. I was rewarded by a warm appreciative smile as she lifted one small slice of meat and pepper into her mouth. Her smile warmed the room. We concluded the meal with a selection of sweet fruits, followed by a subtle squash flower soup.

As the dinner ended we moved to a more comfortable seating area, and Snow Pine again picked up the erdu to sing. Her selection was drawn from the ancient Chin'in fable known as the Tragic Butterfly Lovers. The story is one of two young lovers, each from a noble warring family. The hate between the two families threatens to keep the young lovers apart, but an ingenious plot is put in place to allow them to overcome the objections of their fathers. However, in the last hour, the plan is discovered and the lovers must part. Rather than be separated, the lovers choose to die together. Realizing what their hate had done, both families are grief stricken and gather together to honor the love of their children at a shared tomb. Seeing the families together, the spirits of the young lovers come forward as butterflies and dance among the flowers brought to the grave.

The beauty of the song and singer that late afternoon transfixed me. *"You are a true treasure,"* I said and reached to touch her arm.

"My lord is too kind," she replied. Later Snow Pine was to tell me later that I was not the only one confused by the moment. She had leaned into my touch and as my hand left, we both stood for a moment neither knowing where this was to take us next. *Think!* she thought, *This is what I do, how can I be confused by such a man?* Snow Pine again attempted to move the conversation forward, "I am so pleased that you like my singing," she said. *Oh,* she thought as her mind rushed to think of something further to say. Somehow, *I am so pleased that you liked my singing,* was inadequate for our situation.

Nothing had been said or done that indicated a special relationship with this woman, yet I knew my world was changed. I turned toward her, taking her into my arms. We stood silent and still for a long moment and I motioned her to sit beside me on the couch. It was time to explore these new feelings.

As she moved to be seated, we were distracted by Wang Yueming, who entered and requested an audience. "My lord, I bear grave news, it appears that Praxan bandits have attacked the delegation as they came into the valley." All thoughts of dinner, singing, and what to say next were instantly lost in the gravity of the moment. How could a royal delegation have been attacked? The very audacity of the action made the assault seem unreal. Wang went on to relay that a single survivor escaped and brought news of the attack. I clapped my hands and a gray clad aide appeared. "Take Madam Snow Pine to her residence." I turned to Snow Pine and expressed my regret that we needed to end the evening's conversation, and that her assistance with the delegation appeared to no longer be needed.

Later she was to tell me that I had frightened her that evening as my face transformed from fond affection to a frozen coldness. The man who had dismissed her was not the Sun who stuttered slightly in his haste to tell her all of his plans for the future, but rather a warrior monk filled with deadly resolve.

I then turned to Wang, "Lead a cohort of Hawk Men to the site of the battle, and send a second to Songguan Pass. If we are lucky, perhaps we can engage them before they slip from the valley. Return to me with news, Do my will!"

Wang Yueming quick-paced his cohort toward the battle scene. It was hard to imagine that a royal delegation had been attacked, much less destroyed. Each traveling delegation carried with it a unit of "Old Hundred Surnames," men hardened by many battles and not easily fooled or defeated. How could such a thing have happened? Upon his arrival, a grisly scene confronted him. Not only had the Praxan destroyed the delegation, but they had also taken the time to desecrate the bodies. The bodies had been stripped of all clothing and mutilated. Both men and women suffered the same indignities and now lay with their bodies sliced open and their intestines stretched out across the bushes as if to decorate them. It was evident that in the hours following the battle, carrion eaters had feasted upon the now swelling corpses.

Wang moved quickly among the bodies attempting to identify those that he knew. "Each body is to be reassembled" he commanded, "nothing is to be left behind."

The importance of body integrity in burial is important among our people; one would not want to go into the world of the ancestors incomplete. Although personally shaken by the scene, Wang allowed no emotion other than confident anger.

"Today is theirs, tomorrow is ours," he vowed loudly.

As he moved about the scene of battle, Wang could see that this had not been a chance meeting, but rather a matter of planning. The Praxan had camped and waited for the delegation, and attacked at the moment when they were vulnerable and strung out along the trail. This troubled Wang. How would these bandits know when a delegation was going to pass? How did they know?

Once all prayers had been said for the slain and the bodies buried, Wang assigned the cohort to his second in command

"I need to report this to Brother Sun," he said, using the familiar family title common among the Huashan Mountain monks. "Take the cohort and reinforce the second that is on the way to Songguan pass. If we are lucky, we may still have an opportunity to deal with these devils before they escape. Do my will!"

Wang watched the cohort move off before he began his run for the city. As he ran, he began the meditation learned from Master Yi, allowing his body to take over the mechanical processes of the movement, and free his mind to review the details of the event. He was troubled at the completeness of the destruction of the delegation. Why had they allowed the one survivor to escape?

As I waited in the city for Wang to send word, the hours became bitterly long and sleepless. It was almost with relief that I welcomed Wang into my apartment at seven that morning, as any news was better than not knowing. He quickly described the massacre. The manner in which they desecrated the bodies struck me as being purposeful, yet, what purpose could they have in seeking to outrage and offend? The fact that the Praxan had lain in wait for the delegation was also troubling, "How could the Praxan have known they were coming?" I did not know the answer to either of my questions, but did know that if they wished a fight, we were going to comply. "Their actions will not stand unanswered."

Shocked by the destruction of the first delegation, I was shortly to receive even more troubling news. At ten that morning, the cohort of Huashan Mountain warriors that had been sent by Wang to reinforce the second group sent to Songguan Pass, returned to the city. They reported that they had quick-marched to the pass only to find that our troops had also been ambushed and destroyed.

The description of the scene at Songguan Pass was so horrible in detail that I decided to escort a fresh cohort to the battle area. To have a royal delegation become lax enough in their discipline to be destroyed as they entered the valley, unaware of a waiting enemy, was without precedent, but thinkable. The idea that a cohort of hawk men in the field, who were aware of the presence of an enemy and could still have been trapped and destroyed— that was not in the realm of possibility!

The battle scene that confronted me that morning, a place filled with broken and charred bodies, was like a dark dream from the nether world. Reading the signs of battle, I deduced that the cohort came upon the Praxans as they were leaving the valley. Upon the sighting, the barbarians had broken ranks and run as if to escape over the pass. As the cohort gave chase, they unwittingly entered an ambush. The fleeing enemy suddenly moved to a defensive position above them and a larger group of barbarians closed off the passage below. The cohort then moved itself to a defensive position beneath a rock overhang and prepared its defense. This was standard battle order and one from which they should have been able to hold off an enemy five times their own size.

It was what came next in the battle that most confused

me, for it appeared as if the rock overhang under which our troops had sheltered had not only been chosen by them but also by the Praxan. As the cohort gathered below in defensive positions, the Praxan unleashed a terrible weapon of fire and destruction from above. Balls of fire covered with a sticky material burned and exploded as they came off the hill. The fire burned with a smoky sulfur smell and the heated balls had the consistency of pitch. As the balls exploded, they covered the area with a burning substance that could not be put out by water nor scrapped off. Those caught in the path of this terrible weapon were consumed and cremated.

I crouched and studied the scene before me; this was not a chance engagement, the Praxan had prepared for the battle. Perhaps even the desecration of the bodies of the imperial delegation had been nothing more than bait to draw a cohort of Huashan Mountain warriors to them. The battle plan had been simple in its implementation and terrible in its effect. The cohort, as it sheltered below the rock outcropping, had entered fatal territory, a place they could not defend nor from which they could escape. I commanded that our brother hawk men be buried at the site of the battle. "Also, gather what you can of the sticky material that has not completely burned, Lord Chin must hear of this. Do my will!"

Chapter 12

The pledge!

The man of calling gives himself away and his Self is increased.
Lao Tzu

U pon my return to the city, I found it awash in fear and confusion. Rumors of the fire weapon abounded and became more terrible with each telling. Farmers and peasants fled their fields for the safety of the city wall. Their flight swelled our already crowded streets. Fear and rumor ruled the day, as small groups of frightened men gathered throughout the city casting their eyes about as if the Praxen were hidden within. In several instances mobs had chased and beaten those they identified as being foreign, only later to discover they were but harmless traveling merchants. Of all the petitioners, the merchants were the worse, hounding me, following my every step, and demanding protection for caravans along the trade routes. It was as if all the work we had accomplished in the last year was unraveling before my eyes. I quickly ordered fresh cohorts into the field to close off the mountain passes and isolate our valley. I needed to assure my self of no more surprises as I turned my attention to the city's needs.

The mobs in the city grew careless in their identification of Praxan and foreigners. Some of the most recent killings and beatings appeared to be opportunistic settlements of past grudges. Gathering my shadow administration around me, I knew that we had to respond to the confusion and disorder. The people could not be allowed to wallow in their rumors or soon they would be chasing us down the streets.

"Impose a candle light to sunrise curfew and allow no unsanctioned public meetings of five or more people," I said. "The people must feel our presence at all key points within the city. Make them fear! Do my will."

By the next morning, gray clad, cold-eyed Huashan Mountain monks were seen at every corner of the city, and calm was restored.

Thankfully, in this period following the initial disasters, I had little time for anything beyond restoring the city to calm, certainly not time to explore my personal feelings for a woman. As I went about my duties, thoughts concerning Snow Pine would attempt to intrude but were quickly pushed aside, subsumed among the myriad tasks that occupied my mind.

Dealing with the city's problem gave me a brief respite in which I avoided the questions that played at the edges of my mind, but as calm returned, the issue of the initial attack pushed itself forward to confront me. How did they know the delegation was coming across the pass? Yet the question that really troubled my soul was: Could the woman have betrayed me? Are the feelings I feel, only mine? Once, while touring the city, I thought I saw her on the street but if she saw me she did not acknowledge it, and quickly turned and entered a merchant's shop.

For Snow Pine, the news of the Praxan victory also brought mixed emotions. It was a strange quandary, and initially it was as if both Cassia and Snow Pine wrestled for her soul. How should she feel? In the end, it did not matter to her whether the Chin'in or Praxan had won the battles, what mattered was that in her conversations with her brother Certes, she had betrayed me. This matter troubled her heart. Although she knew that the betrayal had not been her intent, would I believe that she provided the information in innocence? Should she tell me and risk my anger or worse? Not able to divine her own feelings, she decided to allow the matter to unfold based on my actions. She then waited for my call with both longing and fear.

News of the loss of a royal delegation and defeat of a Huashan Mountain monk cohort spread like wildfire across the northern frontier. It soon became obvious that Ascanius had planned the two Praxan victories as practical demonstrations of the vulnerability of Chin'in power. He gathered to him the war leaders of the various northern tribes and enlisted them in his cause. Ascanius told them of his warrior's quest into the desert and shared with them dreams and visions gained by fire and fast. He described how the gods had opened the future to him and taught him rituals whereby warriors purified through ritual could be changed into packs of human shadow wolves, terrible in battle and impervious to the weapons of the Chin'in. In his dream vision, he spoke of a time when the Praxan and Chin'in would again live in peace. However, this time would come only when each learned its true nature. The Chin'in are frightened rabbits that lived in warrens, and prey of the Praxan, the northern wolves. The fact that the Praxan had not lost a single warrior in the two initial battles appeared to confirm the dream's claim of invulnerability. Inspired by his visions' of power, thousands of young warriors left their tribes to perform the rituals and become members of tight wolf packs that harassed the northern travel and trade routes.

I soon received orders from the capital in regard to the new Praxan threat. The message was clear, my Lord Chin wanted decisive action.

You are to suppress all border conflict by whatever means necessary. I am sending you the army of the south and west and placing them under your direct command. Fan Shaofei shall act as your second. Capture and destroy this dog Ascanius, and his wolf packs. All members of the dream cult are to be interrogated as to the nature of the new fire weapons and then immediately put to death. Make them fear! Do my will!

The thought of action in the field pleased me. The order was unambiguous and direct, not filled with the doubts and hesitations that had of late controlled my mind. The idea that I would soon see Fan again also lifted my spirits. Perhaps, with action soon to be underway, it was time for me to have that conversation with Madam Snow Pine. She had been reticent in talking about the Praxan but perhaps in the questioning I could divine her true feelings. Her true feelings-the words echoed in my mind and tasted hollow on my tongue. Do I really want to know? One must always be careful what one asks the gods to give. I turned to my aid Zhelin, "Please send a message to Madam Snow Pine. I request her attendance. Do my will!"

Snow Pine later told me she also was in a state of

confusion in the weeks following our last meeting. Once, she had seen me on the streets, but had moved quickly into a shop, to avoid conversation. While she knew that, at some point, she would need to see me again, she had not made her decision as to what she would say. Should she tell me of Certes? If I did not ask, should she tell about giving the information? When my invitation arrived, neither the message nor messenger provided her with information to guide her choice.

You are requested to attend Lord Sun in his chamber at five this afternoon for dinner. Please advise the messenger of your intent.

As she read and reread the note, she could not gain from it the feelings of its sender. "Please advise Lord Sun that it will be my honor to attend him this evening," she said as she dismissed the gray clad monk.

For weeks she had been waiting for this summons and now it was here? *I am the Snow Pine,* she thought to herself in mantra fashion. *He is just a man. This I can do.* As she thought these things, a small fear crept into her mind. *What if he hates me?* She pushed this from her mind and turned to her maid.

"Su! Make ready my bath and prepare my purple robe."

I remember that afternoon as she entered my chamber; it was as if the air itself had withdrawn from the room. There was tightness in my chest and although I had prepared for the meeting and rehearsed my lines, I found they could not be brought forth. My resolve regarding this woman splintered, and in that moment, I knew I did not care about information regarding the Praxan, the only important issue was—had she betrayed me?

Although not a word was spoken as she had entered the

room, the look on my face told her this was the time to choose. There would be no small talk in regard to events of the day; no words could be parsed for later examination for meaning, no need for cleverness or wit. It was the time; she must choose truth or deception.

"My Lord," she began but the words faltered as she recognized which path her heart had taken. Even if this were the last time I would ever look upon her with affection, she would tell me the truth. This mental resolve made her gait unsure and as she came forward, I reached to steady her. Our closeness washed away the last of our reserves. As I held her to me, her words asking for forgiveness and understanding quickly dissolved in a liquid wetness of incoherence as if her very soul was being harrowed.

I could not stand her pain and lowered her to the couch, comforting her until she regained her composure. Her closeness, softness, and vulnerability made my body ache with a need for her, but this was not the hour. That time would come, but not today, not at a moment of confusion and mutual weakness.

Once she ceased crying, she told me of her meetings with her brother Certes and how she had shared the information regarding the delegation but not with the dreadful intent that had befallen them. I put my finger to her lips.

"We shall speak no more of this."

I lay there holding her in my arms as she gradually relaxed and slipped into a light sleep.

In the middle of the night, Snow Pine awoke to find herself in my arms. She told me of her life as Cassia, daughter to the clan singer. She told me of that morning long ago when she was captured and of her new life with Madam Young. She spoke of the training, and how she became the courtesan, Snow Pine. She told me of her many contacts over the years with her family and of the morning she last met with Certes. As I listened I knew that these meetings were not those of a spy among an enemy people, but only of someone holding on to the past and those she loved. It also became apparent she had passed up many opportunities to return to her people.

Even now, such a long distance from that time, I remember the following few days with clarity. Knowing I had several days before Fan could arrive with the troops, I turned the administration of the city over to Wang so that Snow Pine and I could spend time together in the countryside. In the nearby foothills was an area with pavilions, pools, and paths where in the past a noble family had built their summer palace. The area was beautiful and peaceful, and the natural hot springs provided mineral pools for exercise and relaxation. I had previously selected one of the residences for summer use and it was there we retired to spend this brief time.

Although as her lord I could have commanded her to my bed, I chose instead to allow our relationship to grow naturally without pressure. As we prepared to retire that first evening, I selected a bedroom that faced the warm springs, and as the air cooled, I watched the mists rise toward the stars. I was somewhat startled by the sound of footsteps at the door and reached for my sword, which was always near. As the door opened I could barely see the outline of the person, but relaxed as I caught the soft rustle of silk and smell of her perfume. She said not a word as she came to the bed. I again heard the rustle of silk as her garments fell to the floor. As she entered the bed, I lay with breath suspended. She pushed my garments apart so that our flesh touched and gently took my hand placing it to her breast.

"Snow Pine?"

Her hand immediately came to my lips asking for silence and then caressed my cheek. I took her hand from my face and kissed each finger in turn. My hands explored the warm silken curves of her body. Snow Pine was unlike any other I had been with in that she was more full bodied than most Chin'in women. I then explored her body with my lips, first the shell-like structures of her ears, the tip of her prominent nose, the long curve of her neck. Her lips were sweet, and as we kissed she turned toward me and nestled closely. Our bodies fit together as if contoured by a god. It occurred to me then, and many times afterwards, this was the one woman for whom I was made. Her breathing became more languorous and she pushed toward me turning me onto my back. She moved astride me and gently made love to me with her hands and body. Her hair came lose and hung to her waist, and it moved across my chest in the rhythm of our bodies. My senses filled with her. She loved me with more tenderness and knowledge than I had known possible.

When I awoke the next morning I found her awake and watching me. I smiled and pulled her to me. She took my face in her two hands looking directly into my eyes. "I swear I did not know," she said. "I swear"

I took her hands and brought them to my chest. Taking the gold hawk man mcdallion from my neck, I placed it around hers. "Different paths have brought us together but from this day our path is one, and I pledge to you, never to doubt."

She then placed her hand upon the coin and repeated my words, "From this day our path is one, and I pledge to you, never to doubt."

Snow Pine came again to my cave last night, I do not

know if my memories of those early days called her or if she came because I was too caught up in telling of us. She was always a very modest woman.

Anyway, I shall begin again. Let it be sufficient to say that those early days were the happiest of my life. We spent the mornings walking and exploring the gardens, while in the afternoon we would slip into one of the hot pools for relaxation and talk. It was here that Zhelin, Wang, and Fan found us.

As the three men came through the gate, I recognized them immediately, slipped into my robe, and rushed to greet and embrace Fan. "Little brother, it is so good to see you again. You must tell me of the news from the capital."

Following our quick embraces, I turned to introduce Fan to Snow Pine. Fan smiled, "Ah yes, I remember you, you played such an important part in the capture of the city." As he spoke, he looked at our faces and his smiled increased. "It also pleases me to meet the woman who has captured my friend. This has been too long in coming. I wish you joy."

The men took seats in a small grotto and Snow Pine left to bring tea. When she was beyond hearing, Fan told of the events at the capital. Lord Chin was enraged over the Praxan wolf pack depredations and of our forces seeming inability to deal with the situation. With each day, wolf packs were appearing more numerous and bold. There was concern in the capital that if these raids were not stopped soon, the whole northern frontier could be destabilized and perhaps even the great silk trade route itself endangered.

In his frustration, Lord Chin shifted his attention among his advisors to find the most direct response. This was not a time for reflection but rather for action.

"Our Lord Chin is no fool" Fan said, "He has

surrounded himself with a wide diversity of advisors who, in their different approaches, provide him with balanced and free options."

Having said the good and loyal, Fan went on to express his concern that, though the emperor had adequate advisors to suit anyone's needs, three groups competed for his ear.

The largest group was the Confucian scholars who taught that a nation must be ruled as a father rules a perfected family. Our Lord Chin liked the image of being the Father to all of the people but felt constrained by the detailed rules that ritualized daily life.

Fan laughed as he spoke of the second group of advisors, the Taoists, who taught that the perfect ruler was the one who does nothing. These advisors claimed that one could divine the way of government from the study of nature, from watching the breeze move the cloud, or the mountain stream finding its way to the sea.

"Although he is frustrated and thinks their political views crazy, he is very interested in their ideas of immortality," Fan told us. "Since he has become the Son of Heaven, he has begun to fear his own death. He cannot imagine us without him."

Fan related that the emperor had gathered around him several senior Taoist monks, practitioners of the Dark Learning, and set them to the task of finding the keys to immortality. Under their tutelage, the Emperor had begun a series of meditative and ascetic techniques designed to produce long life. He had ordered the monks to find the ingredients of the elixir of life, a fabled drink, supposedly used by the mysterious and capricious immortals that were thought to live beyond our southern sea. Many of the monks had delved into the ancient alchemist manuscripts for the secret potion that brought long life. Several of these had even brought back ingredients they claimed would bring the desired effects, but which in the end, had been found wanting. These advisors quickly found that one does not have a second opportunity to fail a Son of Heaven.

The group of advisors that were most in tune with the emperor's current thoughts was the legalists, led by Minister Li Si. These advisors appealed to Chin's impatience with delay and desire for action. The legalists argued that the lands' period of disorder could be put to an end and harmony restored, if the emperor followed the simple formula of punishing incompetence and disloyalty and rewarding those who served him well.

"I can tell you that since the Praxan event, the emperor has moved firmly into the legalist camp," Fan said. "Last week he put forth a rule that the peaceful border nomads are to be moved inland and forced to become farmers. Any caught away from their village area without a travel permit are to have their ears cut off." Fan smiled, shaking his head, "You should see them farm. The Legalists may talk of rich rewards for those who serve, but they are stressing punishments. I have even heard they advise that all non-practical books be burned. I fear that our Lord not only wishes to control all action but all thought in his land."

As we sat, Zhelin, Fan, Wang, and I considered which books should be included in the practical and non-practical lists. Given the emperors recent obsession with immortality we were all sure that any books containing an *"elixir of eternal life"* formula would be spared. Our creation of lists seemed hilarious, made up mainly of the texts we studied at the monastery, but had we known the future, it would have brought us to tears.

Snow Pine returned with a beautifully carved teak tray fashioned into the shape of a living forest. Concealed within the tray's curves were the miniscule cups needed for the tea ceremony. Following the traditions she learned while living with Madam Young, she artfully preheated the cups, allowing the water to flow freely over the surface of the tray and precisely measured tea. As water splashed over the tray, the rich smell of tea filled the grotto. The tea selected was a single stem tea that was strong to the taste. As we watched, Snow Pine presented each cup of tea in a manner both efficient and graceful.

We concluded our refreshment and Wang announced that he had prepared a special treat for the occasion. Knowing his great love for street theatre, it was no surprise to see the actors enter the room. For Wang, an aficionado of the art, any time was right for street opera. These folk artists were very popular among the people, and the groups traveled across the countryside in highly decorated wagons, presenting small dramas through song, dialog, acrobatics, and dance. As each of the painted performers came forward, Wang told of their place in the drama. Today's performance was the story of an aging Chou general and his favorite concubine. Although presented as a tragedy, the singing, dancing, acrobatics, and fanciful swordplay fully delighted us that evening.

"We should have them perform each time we are here," laughed Snow Pine.

That evening, the five of us bathed together in the heated spring waters. In the soft flickering evening light I observed Snow Pine standing nude at the edge of the pool and was again captured by her beauty. In the light, her full body and alabaster skin radiated an inner glow. Taking my eyes away, I whispered to Wang that I was going to ask Snow Pine to stay at the residence during my absence. "She will be safe here away from the city. Perhaps you can have a sculptor come from the city and do a statue of her at the pool."

We continued to talk into the early hours of the morning. Fan had much to tell about the changes that were occurring in the capital.

"You may be lord of the city for a long time," he said. "Our Lord Chin has initiated a new policy which he calls Weakening the Branches – Strengthening the Trunk."

At first I did not understand the reference but as Fan explained, the wisdom of the actions became clear.

"He is ordering all the old ruling families from the Warring States to attend him at the capital and is using his trusted lieutenants to govern the various provinces. In this way, he can watch his old enemies and can reward his friends."

At one time, this news about a policy that would keep me away from the capital would have been bad news indeed, but since I'd met Snow Pine, the urgency of my return home had disappeared.

Now that the field forces had arrived from Xian, it was time for me to leave Snow Pine and assume command of the operation against the Praxan. Although it would mean a several month separation, I asked Snow Pine to stay at the country villa until I could return.

"You will be safer here than in the city. Fan tells me Lord Chin wants immediate action and I am to lead our forces."

As I looked into her eyes, I could tell she was troubled by my news. I held her tightly to me and promised that although I did not know how the conflict would turn out, that I would deal with her people honorably, and if possible look after her family.

"Look after you," she replied, "you are my family."

Within days, the army of the West and South moved forward away from the city to deal with the Praxan. Having seen the results of their fire weapon, I moved the troops cautiously, never placing Old Hundred Surnames in a situation where they could be surprised from above. The

118

army was provisioned for a six-month campaign and moved with confidence over the mountain pass and into the vast northern wilderness.

Although I had prepared the army for many contingencies, I was surprised by the events that transpired over the next several months. No army of barbarians came forward to meet or challenge us. Instead, each time we saw a band of the northern warriors, they kept their distance. The smaller wolf pack units always managed to fade away as we approached; it was as if we were fighting ghosts. Given the vastness of the territory and the size and structure of our forces, we could not take the barbarians by surprise nor could we contain the smaller, more mobile units. After several months of chasing shadows, our once proud army was in disarray, not from defeat but rather from disuse.

One evening I brought the commanders of each of the units to me. Each told the same story, *"These devils refuse to stand and fight but still attack our merchants."* I knew each of the officers personally: they were brave, loyal soldiers; each had given me the best they had with no results.

But in exasperation I shouted at them, "Do not tell me what I already know, I need an answer! Make then fear! Do my will!" Each man before me looked down, and refused to make eye contact; they had given their best, our army was too blunt an instrument for the task at hand. We were being defeated by a thousand small cuts.

Finding no solution to the problem, I resolved to bring the army back into our valley and once again close off the mountain passes. I then broke the army into smaller units to convoy the traders between cities in order to halt the raid on commerce. This strategy led to an immediate and substantial decrease in raids on our merchants, but it did not solve the Praxan problem. While the new policy was a

Raymond Scott Edge

better utilization of our forces, it was essentially a losing
strategy, for it allowed the enemy to chose the time and
place for battle. Remembering the charred bodies of the
cohort of Huashan Mountain monks, I knew that the time
and place would be chosen wisely by our enemies, and
waiting would not do.

What I needed was something that would make the
Praxan come forward and fight. But what? Perhaps my
goals in the last several months, of attempting to defeat
them on the field, had been wrong. I did not need to find
the men but rather their wives and children. If I could
threaten their loved ones, the men would come to me, and
on that day, I would crush them. This strategy however,
was not as easy as it sounded, as the Praxan were a nomad
people without established towns or cities. Just as the wolf
packs themselves seemed to appear and disappear into the
vast wilderness, all news of the Praxan women and children
had vanished.

Over the next several weeks, small bands of Huashan
Mountain monks were sent to discover the hiding place of
the women. The Praxan devils, however, are a wary people
and a suspicious prey. Many of my men were found out,
and the few that returned did so without the information I
sought. *What I need is invisibility,* I thought, and a plan
grew in my mind that would allow my men to hide in plain
sight.

Turning to my aid, "Find Wang, and Fan and ask that
they attend me at the hot springs. Do My Will."

I rushed home to see Snow Pine and to prepare a
demonstration of my plan. That very afternoon, when
Wang and Fan arrived at my mountain residence, Snow
Pine greeted them.

"It is so wonderful to see you again," she said. "My
Lord Sun will be with you shortly." To Wang she said,

"You will be pleased. As I have promised, we will be entertained by a traveling troupe of players. My Lord has asked that you be entertained and made comfortable until he can join us."

With that, Snow Pine seated the men and served them tea, cold fruits, and sweet cookies. Once they were comfortable, she clapped her hands and a curtain was drawn to reveal a group of players. Wang recognized the play as the tale of the ancient one known simply as the God of Agriculture, a legendary figure who had roamed the earth tasting all available plants and recording their effects upon his body. It was a wondrous story, as the effects of each of the plants eaten were played out in both humorous and tragic scenes. In the end, as always in these morality plays, virtue triumphed and a pharmacopoeia of useful plants was given to our ancestors which would serve as the basis for our foods and herbal medicines.

As the play concluded, I joined the actors for the last encore. We were appropriately rewarded by enthusiastic applause. It was a strange sensation, standing there in the presence of my friends with my face painted the traditional red and black, and not be recognized by them. It is a truth that we often see only what we expect. Both men went back to their conversations and did not look up until I greeted them.

"My brothers, it is fine to see you again."

Fan gasped in recognition, "Sun is that you?" standing to embrace me.

I then told them of my plan. "We will send out dozens of these traveling wagons to perform in the countryside villages both in the northern territories and in the lands we control. Each troupe of players will have a mixture of true actors and Huashan Mountain monks who will play only minor parts." I could tell by their faces that I had confused them.

"Why would we do this?" Fan questioned.

"The wagons are a part of every day life throughout the empire, welcomed in both Chin'in and Praxan territory. Just as you failed to recognize me because you did not expect to see me, the Praxan will fail to see the Huashan Mountain monks. Our spies will be hidden in plain sight."

Finally both Wang and Fan shook their heads in understanding. "It is a great idea." Wang said, "Each wagon will be our eyes and ears and can move freely through enemy territory. In this way we can watch and listen and find where these devils are hiding."

Wang looked quickly to see if Snow Pine was following the conversation. Seeing his concern, I called her to me.

"Yes, she knows about the plan," I assured him. "In fact, it was she who helped me put on this make-up. I trust her with my life."

Wang and Fan smiled their acquiescence, although from their expressions I could tell they still questioned my wisdom about trusting this Praxan woman though they were willing to let their distrust pass for the moment.

The next several months at the hot springs were busy but happy ones for me as we put small contingents of Huashan Mountain monks through their dramatic paces. Although unfamiliar with the craft of street theatre, each monk possessed acrobatic and sword fighting skills that were always a dramatic and popular part of street productions.

By early spring, all was ready, and the wagons were sent out to cover the territory. As I predicted, the very nature of the wagons made them instantly welcomed in the various villages. It is a rare individual, regardless of tribe, Chin'in, or Praxan, whose face does not light up like a child with the arrival of street players.

Soon a flood of information regarding Praxan movement filtered back toward the city. Many of the reports held nothing but sightings of small warrior groups, revealing nothing about the fire weapon or where the families of Ascanius were finding shelter. As the months passed, it became clear, however, that the staging ground was somewhere near the headwaters of the Jing River. It was a vast area of high mountainous peaks, known for its rugged beauty and vast underground caves. There were rumors that the fire weapon itself was being made from minerals mined in the caves.

As is true in many cases, the very volume of information received both clarified what was happening in the field and yet hid it from view. It was also evident from the messages that I was receiving from the capital that Lord Chin had begun to chafe under the period of inaction, and desired us to move forward to conclusion. As I reviewed the month's reports, I came to understand that the very volume of information was keeping me from seeing the truth. "Too many pieces to the puzzle," my mind stated silently. "The only way to learn the way forward is to see for myself,"

Having decided on this course of action I ordered my aides to prepare for a trip that would allow me to view the scene personally. Once the plans were underway, I went to explain the decision to Snow Pine. This would not be easy as I knew she would be less than pleased.

The idea of going into the field myself was exciting and lifted my spirits. "It has been too long," I told myself. Traveling to our residence, I rehearsed my words to Snow Pine, knowing she would focus more on the danger to me than the potential for information. Approaching the residence, I noted that the outer gate was open and no servant was present. *I will need to talk to her about this*, I thought. Although the danger was minimal, caution was always rewarded. Upon entering the family enclosure, the head servant ran forward. "Madam has left, and we know not where!"

Chapter 13

The Queen of Troy Knowledge

Daniel fell asleep in the early hours of the morning, his dreams filled with a beautiful concubine in an exotic land. It was a restless sleep; he could almost see them: Sun the Asian warrior, and Snow Pine the Eurasian beauty. Often in his dreams they appeared to him side by side, smiling and waving to him, but as he approached them, they always faded away.

His mom allowed him to sleep in and miss breakfast so it was nearly noon when he came downstairs. He went to the pot and poured himself the last of the morning coffee. His mom looked up.

"What's got you burning the midnight oils?" she asked.

"Oh, nothing," Daniel replied, "just some manuscript I'm reading that has me bugged. I can't seem to figure it out. Mom, do you remember a historical character by the name of Cassandra having to do with the fall of Troy?" Although not formally educated, his mother had filled her life with books and was a devoted fan of the History Channel. He often wished that his professors were as prepared as his mother. She turned toward him wiping her hands on the kitchen towel. "Cassandra, of the Troy legend? The one that could see the future but couldn't get anyone to believe her? Is that the Cassandra you're thinking of, dear?"

Daniel shook his head, "That's probably the Cassandra I'm looking for. Do you know of any evidence that people from Troy went anywhere else after they lost the city?" His mother shook her head. He continued, "I think maybe I'll spend the day in the library. I need to know more about the fall of Troy and what happened to the people afterwards."

"You might look in the mythology section" she advised. "Although I can't remember reading that they went anywhere, they must have gone somewhere, not everyone could have been killed." She then smiled at him, running her fingers through his hair before returning to her work. "You're just like your father, he'd get an idea in his head and worry it for weeks until he could make sense of it and put it away."

Later, when Daniel arrived at the university library, his mother's comment comparing him to his father came to his mind. *That may be true, but I can't afford to spend too much time on this project or Eldredge will have my skin.*

He thought about the time he'd spent at the Alton Democrat. A waste; my man in the cave is not going to be found in the paper's archives. That mystery will need to wait for another day to solve. He knew that he should be working on his assignments for Eldredge but he supposed that the cataloging could be put off for a few more days,

126

skin me or not. He smiled remembering the Credo of the Procrastinator: 'Put off until tomorrow what you can do today, after all you got away with it yesterday.'

Having made up his mind that he could put off the work for Eldredge for at least another day, Daniel decided to investigate the Greek-China connection in the manuscript to see if it was even chronologically possible, and then tackle Chin'in dynasty material to see if any historical record supported the Sun Kai story. He opened his notebook where he had jotted down the reminders to look up an archeological site known as Banpo Village, near Xian, and to check the relationship between some ancient Chinese measurements and the modern counterparts.

The early Greek history section of the stacks contained a wide selection of myths, tales, and histories, which he thumbed through. He had picked up a number of books for further examination when he saw Lauren Caurcas, another graduate student from Eldredge's class, sitting at a small reading table. She looked up, saw him, and smiled a greeting. "I thought I was compulsive," she said. "You working on the class assignment?"

Daniel smiled sheepishly and sat down, "Naw, something I came across is really bugging me and I'm trying to make sense of it. If I was in my right mind, I would be doing class stuff."

"What's it about, maybe I can help, " she suggested.

"I doubt it," Daniel said, "unless you know something about early Greek legends surrounding the fall of Troy."

"Well you just happen to be talking to the Queen of Troy knowledge," Lauren laughed, her smile open and warm. "My grandmother, Angelina Caurcas, came from the Anatolia area of Turkey. When I was little, she used to tell me lots of stories about the city. She once told me that her grandmother actually knew the archeologist, Schliemann, perhaps even had a thing with him. They say he was fond of young Turkish women. Anyway, ask me, I'm a font of useless knowledge about useless things. I think it was my grandmother's stories that influenced my choice of majors, first history, and then archeology."

Daniel sat back, not knowing where to begin. It was nice talking to someone who loved what he loved. He understood the fascination/self-deprecation feelings common to history and archeology majors. You went into the major because it fascinated you, but you were always fearful that it was so arcane you would never be able to put it to some commercial use. Like make a living. *It would've been nice to have been born rich*, he thought.

"OK, Troy Queen, what do you know about the fall of Troy, the royal family, citharodes, and Greek Fire?"

As it turned out, she knew a great deal about the fall of Troy and the royal family. She told Daniel about the fateful morning of the ninth year of the siege of Troy when the Trojans awoke to find the Greek fleet gone. On the plain where the army had been encamped the day before, only debris and a gigantic wooden horse remained. Scouts were sent out to examine the strange beast and returned telling of an inscription on its side offering thanks to the Goddess Athena in return for granting a safe journey home.

Daniel watched her face as she told the story. Lauren knew her stuff and was soon caught up in the magic of the time, her face illustrating the emotions of the events. It was obvious that this daughter of Turkish immigrants was even now fully committed to the Trojan side. She went on to tell how King Priam of Troy gave the order to remove a section of the wall so the large statue of the horse could be brought into the city. Greek soldiers who had hidden in the horse crept out in the night to allow free passage for the army which, under the cover of darkness, had sailed back to the

Trojan shore. Before the Trojans understood what was happening, the slaughter began. It was an orgy of rape and destruction.

Few of the Trojan leaders survived the night. King Priam saw his son Polites cut down before his eyes and was then himself slain. Even the baby son of Hector, who was at first taken alive, was subsequently thrown from the city wall. Only Antenor and Aeneas of the city's leadership remained. Aeneas saw King Priam fall and knew all was lost. Taking his son Ascanius by the hand, he attempted to flee the city with his wife, Creusa. Somehow, his wife was lost in the confusion and turmoil. Aeneas returned to the city to find his wife but they were permanently separated.

"Ascanius?" Daniel broke into the telling. "Ascanius? Wow! You *are* the Queen of Troy knowledge, but can you tell me where they went from there?" Lauren smiled, happy to tell this part of the story.

"Well, it's traditionally believed that Aeneas left Troy with his father Anchises and the child Ascanius and landed on the mainland of Italy. We Turks believe that it was Aeneas who took Rome to glory." Lauren paused to see if Daniel believed her story.

He was staring at her in rapt attention. "Do you know anything about whether the wife, Creusa survived? Did she go anywhere?"

"Well, now you're beyond the Queen of Troy Knowledge," laughed Lauren. "Tell you what though, I'll spend some time researching it for you. Can't have my font of knowledge tested and so easily found wanting. Besides, I love this stuff." She grinned at him with excitement.

Daniel looked at his watch and then at Lauren. "Perhaps we can do lunch? Can't have the Queen become faint from lack of food. How about pizza?"

Lauren continued to smile. "I'd love to, and then maybe

you'll tell me what this is all about. What are you researching? This can't have anything to do with Eldredge's Early Pre-Columbian American Civilizations class."

On the way to the pizza parlor, Daniel explained that he was reading something that indicated that some survivors from Troy had made their way to Asia and had appeared on the northern border of China during the Chin'in dynasty.

"Really? How marvelous," said Lauren. It was now her turn to look in rapt attention. "China, how fun!"

With that, Daniel relaxed a bit. He had feared that once he told her about the Troy/China connection, she would think him a fool. He couldn't explain why but suddenly her approval meant something to him.

Over pizza, they chatted about citherodes and Greek Fire. Apparently, citherodes were singers who carried the oral traditions of the Trojan and Greek people. As for Greek Fire, no one apparently knew exactly what was in the formula, but it was used in Greece, and then later during the Byzantine empire, to destroy Turkish ships.

"You'll have to let me see this thing you're reading. Anything that deals with Troy, Greek Fire, Citharodes, and China all in the same document must be extraordinary," Lauren laughed.

He looked at her face to be sure her laugh was not at his expense; after all, it did seem pretty farfetched. He was relieved by her expression, for what he saw was just someone genuinely excited by an idea. He liked her laugh, in fact he liked just about everything about her.

Lauren's face turned serious and she reached for his hand. "Daniel, I probably shouldn't ask you but it's all over the graduate student gossip line that Eldredge was less than pleased with your class presentation. Did you really tell his archeology class that a local Native American petroglyph was actually Chinese?"

Daniel stiffened and for a second didn't know whether to confirm or deny his problem with Eldredge, then laughed and chose the former. Shrugging his shoulders, he gave her his best John Wayne smile. "Au-au yep, little lady, I did indeed." He went on to explain that the material came from an abstract he had written with the hope that Eldredge would allow him to present it in a graduate seminar. How he had grown up around the Piasa and had always thought it looked like a banner, and when he thought about what banner that might be, it seemed very similar to the Chin Dragon Banner. "But, you're right, Eldredge wasn't impressed, in fact he hated it." He lowered his voice several registers until it mimicked the deep tones of Dr. Eldredge's voice. "Daniel, a hint suffices the wise, but a thousand lectures profit not the heedless."

Lauren laughed, tickled at the imitation of their instructor. "What do you suppose he meant by that?"

The smile grew tighter on Daniel's face. "Well if I had to guess, I'd say Eldredge was telling me to give up on the China-Piasa connection if I want to stay in his good graces and have a future with the department."

"Well that's not fair!" Lauren protested, "Some people have speculated that the Chinese were but one of several groups that came to Pre-Columbian America. It could be true."

"I know," Daniel agreed, "but without proof, he's right, I'd be laughed out of the department if I tried to present my ideas, and I shouldn't have taught it in class as real information. I think that's what Eldredge has on his mind. He's not being mean, just protective of the department's reputation and his poor misguided graduate student. I suppose I should be appreciative. Anyway, Eldredge has made it pretty obvious that he doesn't want my name or his department attached to crazy, China Discovers America pseudoscholarship."

"Well, protective or not, it's still not fair." Lauren moved to Daniel's side and hugged him. "I heard Josh Green went a little weird about the SCA. Did he?"

Daniel looked at her. "Yeah, I wasn't sure what to do for a second, he was pretty tense."

She hugged him again and laughed, "Well, whether Josh went weird, or whether Eldredge liked your class, I'll bet you did a magnificent job."

He smiled in appreciation for the support, "Well, it probably wasn't really magnificent, how about great, or maybe OK? Anyway, thanks, oh by the way have you ever been out to see the Piasa Bird? "

Her blank look told him she was not a local. "The petroglyth you were talking about? Is it near here?" she asked. "I'd love to see it."

He told her a little about the Piasa and that perhaps one warm morning during Winter break, he would take her out to see the thing. He knew he should be careful about what he showed her out at the bluff, but he couldn't help noting how attractive she was and a trip to the Piasa would be a fun trip.

After the pizza, they talked for a bit longer and agreed to meet again the next afternoon. Lauren promised that in the interim she would attempt to look up any information regarding Creusa surviving the fall of the city.

Daniel gave Lauren a lift to where she worked as a part-time waitress. He was humming as he drove home. He had found out more than he could have hoped and met someone with whom he could share his thoughts and ideas. None of the information he had gathered proved anything about the manuscript, but at least it still left open the possibility that it could be true. One thing that troubled him however, was the fact that Sun, the Huashan Mountain monk society, and even the Praxans, were not found in any of the texts that he had reviewed.

When he arrived home, he went directly to his room to continue the journal. He couldn't wait to find out what had happened to Snow Pine.

Chapter 14

The Search

*The demands that Great Man makes are upon himself;
are those that Petty Man makes upon others.*
Confucius

The servants reported to me that when they awakened that morning, Snow Pine was no longer in residence. They first thought she had gone for a walk but, as the morning passed, they became alarmed and sent searchers to find her.

I was stunned by the news, what could have happened?

"Double the searchers, she must be found. Do my will!"

With that command I knew the servants would put all their efforts into finding Snow Pine, and, if she were in the vicinity, she would be found. I then went to the residence to await news, trying to push my worst fears and doubts back from the center of my mind.

As the evening came, search parties returned, but none with news of Snow Pine. *Where could she have gone? Where could she have gone? Where could she have gone?* The question became an echo that I could not shut off, endlessly repeating, but finding no answer.

Later that evening, I sat by the pool near the newly carved alabaster statue of Snow Pine. In the flickering light of the candle, the seeming nearness of her standing nude by the pool heightened my sense of loss as I remembered other nights not so long before. I moved to the statue, almost willing it to be her. "Where have you gone?" As I reached the statue, I noticed her morning robe lying at its feet and a small gold coin hung about the neck. I leaned forward and retrieved the gold coin necklace that bore the unmistakable hawk man symbol. I recognized it immediately as the pledge coin I had given her, the one she always wore about her neck. The coin in my hand gave me cold comfort as my mind raced to explain its presence. Why had she left it? Was its abandonment a message? If so, what did it mean?

A thought came unbidden to my mind. *What if she has returned to her people? What if she left the coin to free herself from the pledge?* My fist closed about the coin with a tightness that bit into my palm. The dark thoughts brought me to my knees before the statue, and my body shook from a tension that could find no release. Opening my hand, I took the red string upon which the pendant was hung and placed it about my neck. Although alone by the pool, I shouted to the statue.

"Different paths have brought us together but from this day forward our path is one and I pledge to you, never to doubt!"

The next morning found me still at the statue as if willing it to life. It was a madness that filled my mind with doubts, even as my mouth screamed my pledge of faithfulness. I knew that the servants could hear, but none came forward for fear of what I might do. Out of desperation I chanted the seed sound as taught by Master Yi. He had said it held great power, sounds capable of balancing the universe. Surely my world and universe was in need. "Om mani padni om—Om mani padni om—Om mani padni om" Slowly that morning, the balance returned but I knew that I must get away from the residence if I were to remain sane.

That very day I returned to the city and prepared myself for a tour with one of the traveling theatre troupes. The activity was welcome as it allowed me to push my thoughts of Snow Pine aside, and with enough activity and discipline, keep her from dominating my thoughts. I knew that if I lost focus and thought of her, Snow Pine's loss would preclude all other thoughts. Within the week our troupe was made ready and we headed toward the headwaters of the Jing river basin, which, reports indicated, was the center of Praxan activity.

The first day we passed through Chin'in controlled territory and although the villages we passed through bid us stay and perform, I pushed the troupe forward. As our wagon entered Praxan territory, we came to a small hamlet and were surprised to find the camp of another troupe which was heading back toward Chin'in territory. I instantly recognized the Huashan Mountain monk assigned to the group, as my aide, Zhelin. The thought of spending some time with him lifted my spirits and I eagerly sought him out.

After our initial greetings, Zhelin motioned that he needed to speak with me in private. The first words from his mouth chilled me and threatened to overcome the mental barriers that I had so painfully erected.

"I saw her last evening," he said. "She was riding with

a group of Praxan; I believe that one of them was the devil Ascanius himself. My Lord, I am sorry to bring you this news."

I did not need to be told the name of the she to whom he referred. Zhelin went on to tell how he and the troupe had been preparing for a performance when riders approached. He immediately recognized Snow Pine but did not think she saw him. The group passed closely by but did not stop, then moved on until he lost them from sight.

"My Lord, I do not wish to offend, but she did not seem in distress and appeared comfortable with her companions."

Instantly I wished to be away from Zhelin as passionately as I had previously desired his company. A great wave overcame the mental barriers that I had built and I raised my hand in a feeble attempt to stop further words.

"My Lord, it is good to see you," he said, noting my distress.

The best I could manage was "Goodnight, my Brother," and I stumbled away.

As I left him that evening, my face had already revealed my thoughts. Behind me I heard him swear, "If I ever get another chance, I will kill that woman. Once a Praxan, always a Praxan."

I stumbled away into a nearby wood, my stomach turned, and I vomited the remains of an earlier meal. Nausea overwhelmed me as I lay in the grass, curled into a tight ball. For a long time I lay unmoving, dimly aware of my surroundings. *I am a fool*, I thought. I then reached to touch the golden coin about my neck. "I pledge to you, never to doubt," I said through gritted teeth. The air around me grew thin, and my vision blurred. It was as if my heart was stopping in my chest, and darkness filled the space around me.

When I regained consciousness, it was the hour of morning promise. I steeled myself from the feelings that had immobilized me. Using techniques learned from Master Yi, I consciously gathered my thoughts of Snow Pine into a single chamber, and closed the door to the area. How long I could keep this resolve, I did not know. Although this could never be a permanent solution, it would give me the needed respite to concentrate on other matters. After cleansing myself in a shallow stream, I again sought out Zhelin to give him a message for Fan.

Dear Brother – I need you to return to Xian and report to Lord Chin. I believe that we are on the verge of finding the hiding place of that devil Ascanius and his fire weapon. I will proceed on into the mountains to ascertain its exact location. I have with me several doves, which will return to your aviary when released. I will use these to get word to you as to my findings. If I locate them, it will be important that we have immediate support from units of "Old Hundred Surnames." Please inform my commanders that they are to regroup and await orders. Do my will.

I recommend a visit to my family. I am sure that they will be pleased to see you, especially my sister Mai. Tell them that I think of them often and always with great pride and joy.

I watched the wagons of Zhelin's troupe leave the village and move beyond my sight. Returning to my own troupe, I packed, wished them good fortune, and set out alone to follow the trail that Zhelin indicated Snow Pine had taken. At first the trail looked to be one that great groups had taken, for the ground had a beaten look. As those I followed had several days lead, I moved quickly along the trail. A few miles from the village, however, the trail turned into the mountains and almost disappeared into the rocks. Continuing upward along this lesser path, I prayed that the scratches and marks along the way were truly those I sought.

The mountain area grew wild, as I preceded upward toward dragon teeth ridges. The area grew more rocky and vegetation lessened, and the marks along the way became fewer and less clear. That night I cold camped and in the morning again set out upon the trail that was less and less sure with each mile I traveled. By midmorning, I found myself entering a box canyon with no apparent path forward. My heart sank, I had lost them. Looking down, I realized the scratches that guided me had vanished.

The canyon was a wild place with a stream running its center and steep walls on three sides. As I faced the end, it was apparent that no trail could continue over the forward wall. A mighty waterfall came crashing down its rocky surface to explode on the rocks below only to gather again and form the mountainous stream.

This could not be the way, I would need to go back to the village and begin again. My thoughts darkened my mind as I recognized the truth of my failure. Following the scratches had after all been a fool's errand. Whoever or whatever had made the scratches must have backtracked out of the valley and was gone. I moved upward off the trail into an area shaded by an overhanging boulder to eat my meal and contemplate what to do next. As I finished my meal, I allowed the horse to eat the grass while I stretched out on the warmed rocks to rest. Having lost the trail put me into a mental stupor where it seemed pointless to move forward.

As I lay there drowsy, near sleep, I was brought alert by the sound of a horse. I saw a small Praxan wolf pack of less

Raymond Scott Edge

than a dozen men entering the valley along the path from which I had come. These wild warriors moved with the ease and grace of the animals they emulated. I moved quickly and quietly to still my horse and knew that I was in the hands of fate. There was no place to hide, no place to retreat, and if discovered, no way to win against the warriors moving along the path below me.

I stood watching their approach, knowing my only hope was that they would not look up and see me. My desire was to watch their every move, but I feared that by watching them intently, they might feel my presence. Shifting my focus, I looked not at them but at the waterfall at the far end of the valley. I could hear their quiet banter as they approached and moved below me. Had any of them looked up, I was standing in plain sight, but this was not my day to die—the horsemen moved on toward the waterfall.

I stood as if frozen as they passed below, and they slowly moved forward until they once again came into my line of vision. Somewhere near the middle of the valley they left the trail and were now making their way along the stream. My mind raced trying to think of where I might hide, for surely they must return along this path when they found their way blocked by the waterfall and sheer cliff. I watched them as they became lost in the mist at the bottom of the falls and for a moment felt as if my eyes were playing tricks, for they disappeared into the falling waters. Minutes went by and they did not reappear. It was as if they had been swallowed by the mists.

After a few minutes, when nothing moved in the small valley, I led the horse to a more sheltered place, away from the trail. That afternoon, I saw two small wolf bands move into the valley, and like the first, leave the trail to ride along the stream and disappear in the mist. There was obviously a trail under the falls, but I dared not investigate in daylight.

140

As the sun fell behind the mountain walls, I left my horse and approached the falls. I climbed among the rocks above the trail so as not to be seen by anyone on watch. Evening came quickly and, as shadows made the rocks black in the darkness, I sat and watched the spot where the warriors had vanished. One place along the bottom of the falls was illuminated as if someone tended a fire behind the water.

I waited until the stars indicated the hour was near midnight. The illumination behind the falls died down but still gave a pink glow to the water. Cautiously I approached the point where the water seemed to glow. When I moved behind the falls, I could see a cavern that extended into the mountain. I moved through the curtain and slipped between the rocks along the side. It was there I almost fell over the sleeping guard. The fellow stirred as my foot touched him, and he turned onto his side. I stood, knife in hand, frozen at his side, willing him to back to sleep, and he did not move more. My eyes gradually adjusted to the darkness. The air in the cave was heavy with a strange acrid odor that I could not immediately identify. Across the trail someone shifted and coughed. Apparently the trail had two watchers. The ancients had blessed me with the one less diligent.

I saw a series of lights that illuminated a trail into the mountain and I made my way toward them. Following the lights I slowly made my way deeper into the mountain, until in the first hours of morning, I came to the other side. Here the cave opened into a truly closed off valley with sheer walls on four sides. It appeared that the only egress from the valley was the passage I had just taken through the mountain. This was a large valley and spread out before me were thousands of tents, each with their own low burning campfire. I had found them, the place where the Praxan hid the women and children.

I made my way slowly backed toward the waterfall entrance feeling that nothing further could be accomplished this night. The watchers were not prepared for someone coming from behind and presented no problem as I skirted their positions and left the cave. Returning to my camp I walked my horse to the valley entrance and freed him. I then returned to move my belongings into a sheltered place further away from the trail. The sun had begun to clear the valley walls as I took a bird from the cage.

Dear Brother – I have found their hiding place. Bring five cohorts of monks to the village where I met Zhelin, he knows the place. Also shift Old Surnames troops forward. We may be able to end this soon. Await my word. Do My Will!

I watched as the pigeon circled the valley and flew from sight, then pulled my robe about me to sleep the day. I would need the rest if I was to reenter the cave that evening. Although exhausted, sleep evaded me as questions whirled in my mind. What of Snow Pine? Was she there? Finally in desperation, I repeated my pledge as a mantra, over and over to clear my mind. "From this day forward, our path is one. I shall not doubt."

Chapter 15

A clear duty

*Time goes on and on like the flowing water in the river,
never ceasing day or night.*
Confucius

I awoke with a start, having slept the day away. Fearing a fire, I ate cold biscuits and contemplated my return to the hidden valley. Tucking several days of water and food supply into my pack, I moved toward the sound of the waterfall.

Approaching the entrance, I sat and waited in the darkness until I could discern the position of the guards. Once again, I made my way behind them and, without their knowledge, entered the cave. I was again struck by the acrid odor within the cavern as if some great beast used it for a personal toilet.

Attempting to move slowly and silently in the near dark, I made my way along the rocks just off the lighted path. Periodically I came across various side passages and rooms that went off the main trail. I saw no other beings and, as I moved further into the cave, the silence was broken only by the sound of dripping water. Approaching the entrance to the hidden valley I noted, in the half light, that some of side rooms were being used to store supplies while others appeared to be lighted workshops. It was almost dawn when I reached the entrance to the hidden valley. Prior to entering the valley, I made my way into one of the storage rooms, and found a place to hide my gear and sleep during the day. When I again came to the cave entrance, the dawn light was just beginning to illuminate the valley cliffs. Looking over the valley, I saw a dark cloud come out of the sun, dipping and moving in the light. The cloud caught my eye as the rest of the sky appeared clear. As it approached the cave entrance, I saw that the cloud was made up of thousands of bats returning to the cave to sleep the daylight hours. Their numbers were so great that it appeared as if waves and waves of black curtains were making their way into the cave. The mystery was solved; it was not a great beast but thousands of tiny ones that gave the cave the acrid odor. After the bats cleared the entrance, I made my way back into the cave to find my hiding place and, like the bats, sleep the day.

I awoke in the late afternoon, at first confused; it took several seconds to remember my situation. The storage room in which I was hiding was filled with bags. Cutting small holes in several revealed they were filled with minerals such as the yellow sulfur, which our physicians use to heal wounds; others were black charcoal, and quicklime. Several Praxan men moved into my view at the front of the room. My position in the back allowed me to watch their activity and yet remain secure from their sight. I watched from the dim shadows as they carried some of the bags from the storage area to one of the side workshops. After they left the area, I retrieved my view glass from my pack and moved to a higher position on top of the stored minerals so that I might remain unseen yet ascertain what they were doing.

In the lighted workshop, three men were involved in grinding and mixing something. I could see they were using the charcoal, quicklime, and sulfur they had taken from the storage area. They mixed the dry powder with what appeared to be bat soil, along with a thick slippery black water substance which I have seen seeping from the ground in many places. Once the mixture became a paste, they packed it into gourd-like jugs. I could only imagine what the purpose of the mixture could be, perhaps medicine, fertilizer, or even the liquid fire weapon.

Whether medicine, fertilizer, or weapon, its identity would need to wait, and I settled back into the darkness until I could safely enter the hidden valley. Soon the men took several of the jugs and moved toward the cave entrance leading to the hidden valley. When I was sure they were gone, I moved from my hiding place, and in the early darkness, went out into the valley. The air was heavy with the smell of cooking fires and garlic spiced mutton. The people were completing their evening meal and many began moving toward a central fire. Needing a disguise, I entered one of the empty tents, and finding a robe with a hood that would hide my face in shadow, stepped out and quickly blended into a group moving toward the central fire.

I found a place somewhat to the back and away from the others, and sat to watch. Within minutes Ascanius himself came from one of the tents near the fire and with nine others, mounted a stand. One of the nine, an old and feeble man, needed assistance. Once in place, Ascanius lifted his arms for silence and started to speak.

"My people, it is with great joy that we come together, for that which was lost to us has returned. My brother and voice of our past has returned from a great illness." He pointed to the old man.

"Tonight we have Cassia to thank for his recovery. A daughter's love is remarkable medicine." He then pointed into the audience where Snow Pine stood.

My heart and breath stopped as I looked upon my love. Somehow, I had hoped she had been captured or brought here under duress. Yet there she stood, receiving the acclamation of these people. On this night, she was not a prisoner. I stood watching from the shadow of the hood, as Ascanius continued.

"My brother has not been fully restored so we must wait to again hear his voice sing the songs of the ancients. Yet his flesh has been returned to us and I have asked Cassia to sing in his stead."

Snow Pine made her way to the stand and, moving to her father's side, and began to sing. Her clear voice filled the evening and all listened with rapt attention.

The emotions that filled me were almost too much to bear. Thousands of thoughts flooded my mind: remembrances of our first meeting, her singing the ancient saga songs, and our many evenings spent at the hot springs. Who is this woman? How much of anything has been real? I held my heart in check and watched as she finished the singing and helped her father off the stand. The two were joined by a young man with a strong family resemblance, who was several years younger than Snow Pine. He helped support the old man as they made their way back to the tent village. I followed them in the darkness until they reached their tent. Snow Pine went into the tent with her father and soon she and an elderly woman came out to sit by their small evening fire. The young man who I supposed was her brother Certes, made his way back to the center fire.

Sitting in the shadow of a nearby tent, I watched as the two women sat quietly talking. After about an hour, Snow Pine went into the tent and came out, assisting her father. She guided him through a series of exercises, which I recognized as Qi Gong, the powerful healing technique of our physicians. Even from a distance I could see that she was not here under duress but was fulfilling the duty of a loving daughter. As the man gradually tired, Snow Pine ended the exercise and lovingly aided him in returning to the tent. I watched for the remainder of the evening, hoping that I would again see her but she did not return to the outside. Even if she had, could I approach her? Would she welcome me, or would she sound the alarm? As the dawn brought pinkness to the cliffs above the valley, I returned to the cave to sleep.

My rest was troubled because I kept reliving the scene where Ascanius greeted Snow Pine as his niece. Was our whole time together a lie? Finally, in desperation and exhaustion, I uttered the pledge mantra, "I shall never doubt. I shall never doubt," but it was more exhaustion than comfort that brought sleep that morning.

It was late afternoon when I came awake. Taking my view glass, I climbed to the top of the stacks and again watched the workers in the opposite caves. In the workshop, the men were still grinding the minerals and filling the gourds. I could see that in other chambers, people were storing supplies. One great room off to my left appeared to be a treasure room. It looked to be filled with goods taken from the merchants and diplomatic trains that had fallen to the wolf packs: stacks of gold, silk, and porcelain, the wealth of a kingdom. In a side room I could make out the armor taken from several units of our army. How low these proud symbols of our military had fallen. *This shall not stand*, I thought. *This shall not stand!*

That night, I again donned the stolen robe with heavy cowl and joined the Praxan at the central fire. I found a place toward the back where I could observe the group with my view glass and climbed into the branches of a tree. From this vantage point I had a clear view of the stand and the surrounding area illuminated by the fire. Neither Snow Pine nor her family was in sight this evening. As I sat watching, five small cages, barely large enough for a human, were brought forward to stand at the outer edge of the illumination. My heart froze! Within each cage was a Huashan Mountain warrior monk, still wearing the face make-up of a traveling theatrical group. We had been discovered.

The evening began much as the night before, with Ascanius taking the stand, calling a citherode forward to sing one of the saga songs. Then he exhorted his people.

"My people, once again, the ancients have come to our aid. The immortals from our sacred mountain have again joined us in our quest. Soon it will be Chin'in women and children who hide. Although they are as numerous as rabbits, soon it will be they who will run before our warriors. Shortly we take the field, and they will know our power. The hour of the promised vision is near." Ascanius then turned and gestured toward a man who had been standing behind him. "This afternoon we have been joined by our brothers from the vast northern wastelands who have come to take up our banner. I give you Timiltuk!"

Timiltuk grunted his acknowledgement. He was a short man whose face, burned by endless days of wind and sun, seemed but an iron wedge pulled from the blacksmith's fire. His eyes were cold as that of a hawk and standing there with his furs pulled against the night air, he appeared more feral, more animal of prey than man.

The name Timiltuk stirred a memory from an earlier time. Once, many years before, while on patrol, I had come across an army unit dealing with a local village leader by that name. They had charged the village leader with arrogance for attempting to hide grain needed by the army. In punishment for this theft of omission, they had taken his left hand. When his wife had screamed and tried to come to his aid, they had laughingly taken her ears and cut the noses from his children. The village leader had been forced to watch the humiliation of his family. Weakness had unmanned him and he had begged them to stop, crying at their feet, promising to give all. Could this be the same man?

The man standing before me now wore the clothing of the nomadic peoples who lived beyond the border of our land. Periodically they have become emboldened enough to raid our outer settlements, but always faded back into the wastelands when confronted by our army. The presence of any of these chieftains with Ascanius was ominous, as it meant that the Praxan leader had support among the numerous desert tribes, savage and cruel people forged by the harshness of the vast deserts.

Timiltuk stepped up alongside Ascanius and spoke in a voice as quiet and dry as his homeland.

"For hundreds of years these soft yellow people, regardless of the name they used, have ruled here. Any one of my warriors sitting his horse is as good as ten of them."

The crowd leaned forward to hear his words.

"But the soft ones never allowed for such a battle. Always it has been a hundred to one, or the devils have hidden behind their walls. Only in the most favorable of conditions have they been willing to fight and in the end, it has always been my people who have been rounded up and forced to live in work villages, supplying the labor for the yellow devils' massive walls and canals."

Timiltuk turned to contemplate the man who had addressed him as brother. "Ascanius calls me brother, and tonight it is truly so. Yet I answer his call for my people, a people who need more land, a people whose young men need to be tested by war, a people who remember past suffering and have lived on bitterness."

He raised the stump of his severed left arm: "By this I swear, Yes, we are brothers," he said to Ascanius. "And this brotherhood will soon be felt upon the land."

My mind swirled at the sight of his severed arm. It was him, the village leader who had cried that day. Looking at him now, it was hard to imagine anything that would cause him to show weakness. We had created an implacable enemy. Ascanius grasped Timiltuk's good arm with his own, thrusting it high into the air.

Upon a command from Ascanius, a group of warriors brought forward a number of devices that looked somewhat like wooden and bamboo insects, and arrayed them at the other end of the field across from the caged humans. At first I did not understand the intent of the devices, as their design was unknown to me. The Praxan warriors then placed jugs, like those I had seen in the cave, within the basket–like arms of the devices, and slowly cranked tension onto the ropes. My mind froze in sudden understanding and dread; these were throwing machines.

The crowd before the stand became silent as if waiting for a signal. It was not long in coming. Ascanius lifted his face to the sky and began a wolf howl that caused the hairs on my arms and neck to involuntarily stand.

"Aaaaawwwwooooooooooollllllllll" The note hung in the

150

air and repeated as it bounced against the cliff walls of the enclosed valley. It was a primal call, not that of a male calling to mate but rather that of pack leader calling his pack to close in on a kill. With that call, the men next to the devices put fire to a fuse on the jugs and released the tension of the arms. The jugs flew skyward and moved gracefully in an arc one hundred yards down field toward the enclosed men.

Shit, that's the length of a football field, Daniel thought, and then saw the margin note.

The text uses the word zhang for the distance the jugs flew. Although the zhang is a unit of distance, it is impossible to know the exact measurement. The term was used in several dynastic periods, but not describing the same distance. I have used the term yards to make for easier reading.

Daniel picked up his notepad thinking to jot down a reminder to look up the meaning of zhang. *Why bother, he thought, if they can't agree to its meaning, why should I care?* He put down the pad and continued to read.

On the first barrage many of the jugs fell before and aft of their targets, yet several found their victims, filling the cage with an explosive sound and liquid fire. The caged men had little time to scream as they were engulfed in flame. The screams of pain quickly turned into a non-human keening, like a high wind through trees.

The crowd lifted their faces to the sky and picked up the cry of the hunting beast. *"Aaaaaawwwooooollllll, Aaaaawwwoooool, Aaaaawwwooollll, Aaaaaaawwwooolll"*

The men at the devices were busy refitting the

machines to throw additional jugs. In the cages down field, the remaining Huashan Mountain monks, now understanding their fate, watched in horror. I saw several removing the coin necklaces from about their necks, kissing them, and beginning the ritual of those about to die. Their bravery in the face of this horror made me proud for them, but the fact that soon they were to die as animals in a cage brought rage to my heart, then tears to my eyes. It was everything I could do to stay in the tree and watch. My body shrank from the horror below, yet I kept my eyes on the scene to honor their dying. I waited, not moving until the last of my brothers went to our ancestors.

That night as I made my way through the camp, my duty was clear. I must warn the others. I must prepare for battle. I must do my duty. I could almost hear my Lord Chin's words as I reported this tale. "Make them fear! Do my will!"

I no longer had time to watch for Snow Pine, hoping and fearing that we might meet. That hour was past; it was time to leave the valley and report. As I moved in the darkness toward the cave entrance, I found myself again in front of the tent Snow Pine shared with her family. Several garments that I recognized as hers were hanging to dry. I moved quickly to one, and placed within its folds the coin necklace she had left at the poolside.

I then made my way back into the mountain cave, pausing only long enough to pick up my pack and two of the fire jugs. I feared that they would be missed but hoped that the Praxan warriors, confident of their security, would not worry about an exact tally. I found myself in the outer valley, making my way to my hidden cache of goods, just as the sun rose.

I hurriedly wrote a note and quickly freed my last pigeon.

Brother. Recall all theatrical troupes immediately and send no more. I shall be with you in the small village in two days time. Prepare the men to move forward within the week. Do My Will!

Chapter 16

A Daughter's Duty

It is cowardice to fail to do what is right.
Confucius

The last few weeks had been a blur of confusing activity for Snow Pine, a time of mixed emotions during which she did what seemed right but always with a feeling of dread and doubt. Her crisis had begun when she took early morning tea at the mountain residence she and I shared. As mistress of the residence, she loved the early morning hours before others awakened, a time for herself, a time for undisturbed personal thoughts and reflections. She had taken her tea to the pavilion and was sitting near the hot spring, examining the newly carved nude statue of her, posed as if entering the pool. Remembering the many evenings that she and I had spent there, she experienced warm feelings. She smiled as she looked at the statue, which appeared to her a bit more rounded than she saw herself, but she knew that I was pleased with the depiction.

Without warning, she was surrounded by a group of men who, by their dress, were easily identified as Praxan. She recognized the leader of the group. "Certes," she cried, "how wonderful to see you but you shouldn't be here, it is dangerous for Praxans."

Certes waved her concerns aside. "Cassia, father is gravely ill, you must come!" He pulled from his bag a set of riding clothes and gave them to his sister. "Put these on. We are risking our lives to be here with you."

Snow Pine's mind raced with the news. What should she do? She could not leave without telling me and yet there was no time; for the safety of her brother she had to leave immediately. If her father was ill, she had no choice but to go.

"Move away and let me dress," she said. She then moved to the side of the statue and removed her light robe, letting it fall in folds at her feet. She fingered the gold coin that hung about her neck suspended on the red string. Where I am going this cannot go, she thought and leaning over, she placed the string about the neck of the statue. *Sun, please forgive me for this, and understand.*

Stopping only to get a medical kit, Snow Pine rejoined the others and crossed the wall that enclosed the residence. Horses were tethered nearby so the group mounted and moved quickly across Chin'in territory, following paths known only to goats and those that herd or hunt them.

The group skirted the towns and farms until they cleared the pass and entered an area dominated by Praxan. In the late afternoon, after Certes called the group to a halt, Snow Pine and the men rested in a small grove of trees. Certes was obviously anxious and set men at watch.

155

"What bothers you my brother?" Snow Pine asked as Certes continued to move restlessly about the camp. It was unlikely that Chin'in forces could surprise them even if it were a cohort of Huashan Mountain hawk men.

"Be still and see," he replied. "You will like the surprise."

By five that afternoon a cloud of dust appeared on the horizon. As she watched, the cloud became discernable as a large group of riders, winding their way along the trail toward them, first seen and then hidden by the trees. As the horses approached, Snow Pine understood the anxiety of her brother; the banner that came in view was that of Ascanius himself.

Snow Pine was shocked at the sight of her uncle. Ascanius was no longer the laughing giant of her childhood memories but more the wolf in winter. It was as if he had been returned to the forge and refired into a harder darker metal. He came to her smiling, but the smile did not quite thaw the frost that lay deep in his blue eyes.

"It is good to see you my niece. It has been too long."

Snow Pine moved forward into his embrace. "Yes, my uncle, it has been too long. I am honored that you have come. Tell me of father."

Ascanius put his hands to her face, looking deeply into her eyes. "He is not well and we fear for his recovery." Ascanius' face grew darker, "I miss his voice among the citharodes, his spirit and advice at my counsel fire. Perhaps the sight of you will bring him back to us."

The thought of her father not singing was almost more than Snow Pine could endure. Some of her strongest memories of childhood were the sound of his voice singing the ancient sagas. It was the memory of that voice that she used to put herself to sleep when all else failed. It was that voice and those songs that had kept her from losing her

Praxan self these many years.

"With your permission, my Uncle, I would waste no further time here. May we leave now?"

Although Snow Pine was completely familiar with the Praxan, she had never before seen a wolf pack. Each man sat easily in the saddle, and although relaxed, appeared coiled as a spring, ready for action. Each pair of eyes constantly searched the trail before and to the sides. The pack seemed unaware of the wind that unfurled their banner and flared their cloaks to reveal the short horse bows and long double bladed swords sticking above the right shoulder of each man, through a slit in his cloak. Snow Pine chilled looking at them, with the recognition that these were hunters, not prey.

The trail moved upward toward the high mountains. In the late afternoon they came to an isolated mountain village. As they passed the town center, Snow Pine saw the brightly decorated theatre wagon and performers preparing for a show. Although she recognized Zhelin as one of the players, she gave no sign and was not sure that he had seen her. Ascanius had ridden directly through the village without pause and soon it was lost from view behind. An hour later, he called a halt in a secluded copse of trees where, after eating, the group made camp for the night.

The pack moved forward again before dawn the next morning, ever higher into the mountains. None spoke; the only sounds were the creak of harnesses and the sound of hooves hitting the ground and displacing rocks. As the contingent moved ever upward, the air thinned. Snow Pine noted the change in trees, as those that lose leaves in winter gave way to evergreen and evergreen to bare rocks.

As they crossed the highlands, some of the riders went to the back of the party, dismounted, proceeded on foot, and swept away the evidence of their passage. The group then crossed a high pass and dipped again into a sheltered forested valley. Off to the left, a deer startled and bolted away with white tail flashing.

As they came down into the valley, Snow Pine saw the waterfall at the valley's end and the stream running its center. Once in the valley, Ascanius led the group off the trail and into the cold stream, which rose to the horse's flanks. Small trout which darted away from the horses' hooves appeared as flashes in the clear water. As they moved upward toward the waterfall, Snow Pine wondered at the destination since she could see no way forward beyond the overhanging cliffs. It was not until the leaders in the group entered the mist and disappeared that she understood.

Coming out into the light on the far side of the mountain, Snow Pine was awed by the tent village that lay before her. On this side of the mountain, the Praxan had ceased to care about covering their trail and the ground had the trampled look of a gathering. The aroma of garlic and spiced meat clung in the afternoon air, mixed with the smoke from hundreds of cooking fires. Praxan women and children moved freely among the tents, secure in the isolation of their secluded valley. *It is the place where we have hidden the families,* she thought, thinking of the invisible waterfall entrance. *A safe place, a small group could hold the valley entrance against an army, and if the Chin'in ever find this place, they will probably need to.*

Certes led Snow Pine to one of the tents located near the council fire. As she entered, she gave words to a prayer that she would not be too late. Her mother sat on a blanket off to the side; the look on her face told Snow Pine that all was not well. The tent exuded a warm odor of illness, and the man lying on the robe was slick with sweat. Her father did not acknowledge her presence as she approached. A shaman sitting at his side slowly sang the song of wellness while brushing him with a fan of hawk feathers.

The man was a noted healer among the people, one who could enter the spirit trail of those who approached death and could often lead them back from the nether world. Watching the man chanting and brushing her father with the feathers, Snow Pine had trouble containing herself as each moment became an eternity, because she no longer believed in the spiritual or healing power of chants. Illness called for healing techniques, not spirit quests.

In her anxiety over her father's health, Snow Pine did not take time for the courtesies required when dealing with a shaman. Pushing the man aside, she began questioning her mother and brother regarding her father's illness, complaints, and symptoms. She took her father's wrist in her hands and placed her three fingers to take the pressure pulses that had recently been introduced by Chin'in physicians as a form of diagnosis. Then she placed her hands on his chin and opened his mouth to examine his tongue. Her mind raced over the many times that she had assisted the healers called to cure one of the young women who stayed in the house of Madam Young. Even as a child, she had helped the doctors who came to the home and over time, her curiosity had borne the fruits of skills.

The shaman complained angrily and rose to leave the tent.

"Who are you to interfere? I will take this outrage to the council!" Yet as he left there was a look of relief on his face; at least now he would not be blamed for the singer's death.

"Ancestors, help me remember," she pleaded under her breath as she tried to think of all the techniques she had watched the physicians employ. Snow Pine followed the diagnostic steps she had seen other doctors use: looking, hearing, smelling, questioning, and touching. Within these would be the answer to her father's disharmony. It was like a great puzzle—if she could but figure out the cause of disharmony, she could then assist him in returning to balance.

Her father was listless and weak, and his hands were cold and clammy to the touch. Even lying there at rest, he was short of breath. As she examined his tongue, she noted that it had a deep central crease all the way to the tip and appeared purple with a few dark spots. His pulse in the first position felt like an erdu string, tight and wiry. She again questioned her mother and found that her father had been complaining of heart palpations and chest pain that radiated toward his left arm. These symptoms had been made worse with exercise and excitement. Her mother also related that her father had been in poor emotional health of late because he felt guilty for the use of the liquid fire. It was he who had found the formula deeply hidden in one of the ancient saga songs. Ascanius had rejoiced in the finding, but this use of music to kill others, even Chin'in, had devastated her father.

Snow Pine feared that her abilities were insufficient to the task and that her only hope lay in the memories. Her father's emotional state had depleted his heart Qi and in turn led to heart yang deficiency. A physician had once told her that anxiety was *"stored in the chest."* In his feelings of remorse for discovering the killing weapon, he had internalized his remorse, and this had led to heart yang deficiency and stagnation of the blood within the chest. If he was to get well, she must somehow restore the flow of Qi and bring the yin and yang back into equilibrium.

Snow Pine was thankful that she had thought to bring the medical kit from the residence. She gave instructions for the brewing of an herbal tea—a gentle stimulant—that could be taken several times each day. Following the pattern shown on the kit's acupuncture manikin, she placed the needles and burnt moxibustion to transfer the heat to the internal meridian channels which would assist the movement of the Qi and blood from his chest.

That night she did not leave his bedside, and by noon the next day her father's condition had improved enough so that he recognized those around him. To see him so weak and wasted brought her to tears. Her gentle father, a man whose voice could soar like the wind, and yet enter and swell the smallest heart, lay before her as weak as a child.

Under her watchful care, he began a slow recovery. Once he could take nourishment and walk, she coached him in light Qi Gong exercises to assist him in gaining strength and to focus his energy. These gentle maneuvers, which emulate the movements of animals, are a form of physical meditation, which Snow Pine knew would not only assist him in gathering his strength but also allow him to relieve the emotional stress he felt over the liquid fire.

Chapter 17

The Immortality Temptation

When the people do not fear what is terrible,
then the great terror comes
Confucius

When I arrived at the village, I found that my messages had been received and Fan awaited. He informed me, however, that instead of moving immediately against our enemy, I had been ordered back to the capital. Lord Chin himself wished to take personal command of the forces. It was obvious that our Slayer of Dragons, Eagle Who Sees Far, was tired of waiting.

Fan and I selected two of the fastest mounts and set out immediately for the capital. The capital, Xian, is unlike any place on earth, especially in the dawn light. At certain times of the year a pall of fine dust from the desert produces a quality of light, both gray and yellow. The light is breathed almost as much as seen, and its effect is that of bringing some vistas into sharp focus and blurring others. The city upon our arrival stood out in the morning light, perfectly displayed, unique, at once sharply focused and yet hazy. The illusion gives one the impression of both new beginnings and ancient times.

We passed a great earthen wall construction project that was snaking its way across the valley. Thousands of peasants, minorities of the empire and slaves taken in battles, swarmed like ants across the surface under the direction of several units of Old Hundred Names. We stopped for a moment to watch the workers. The wall was twenty feet tall and wide enough for a chariot to move along its top. Watchtowers were placed along the wall so that archers could defend against an enemy from the security of the towers. As I stood watching, an elderly man making his way to the top of the wall missed his footing and fell to his death accompanied by his load of bricks. Others in the line continued to move upward as if nothing unusual had happened. Soldiers at the bottom ordered several slaves to pick up the body and throw it into the earthen structure where it was to be covered by the earth and brick façade. Shaking my head, I realized that I was looking at the longest cemetery in the world. *I hope this is worth the doing,* I thought. It would have been nice to have the time to talk to the officer in charge but our duties in the capital did not allow further delay. When we entered the great city wall, I was confronted by a sea of change. The streets teemed with people, everywhere building projects were underway and everywhere there was tension in the air.

Fan and I first stopped at my home to bathe and change into silken gowns; one did not meet the Son of Heaven in the simple gray garb of a warrior monk. My sister Mai beamed in happiness at my arrival—or perhaps Fan's. Within the walls of my childhood home, the air was warm with feminine affection as the women scurried about attending to our needs. Even my father, the firm taskmaster of my youth, was unable to hide his joy in my station. It was wonderful being in the presence of my family; they looked well but even at home, just below the surface, I felt an unspoken tension.

Leaving the residence of my family, we went immediately to the new central palace that had been built for our Lord Chin. It was a massive city within a city surrounded by parklands and great red walls. In the distance the red ochre walls and gold tile shone in the morning sun. The parklands surrounding the palace were a place of singular beauty with white stags, fallow deer, gazelles, and roebucks grazing on the hillsides. Squirrels of wide variety played in the overhanging branches. Throughout the area, scattered pagodas and sweeps of shining water combined to create a breathtakingly exquisite picture. When we passed through the palace west gate, which is reserved for military, I saw in the distance the Hall of Supreme Harmony. It is said that the four seasons merge here, wind and rain are gathered in, and yin and yang are in perfect harmony. It is here, at the very center of the universe, where our Lord Chin, the Son of Heaven resides. In the distance, we could hear the sound of gongs and jade chimes which announced the movements of our Lord. The air was heavy with the smoke from incense burners cast in the shape of bronze cranes and tortoises symbolizing long life. Within this inner city there were fewer people, yet the same sense of strained tension prevailed, as if everyone was holding his or her collective breath in expectation.

There was no time to explore this sense of unease, however, as our lord himself summoned us. We found, upon entering the palace complex, that we were not to meet with our Lord Chin but rather with his minister, Li Si, into whose chambers we were quickly ushered. Li Si was senior spokesman of the legalist advisors. Fan had been correct in his estimation of who had the ear of our Lord.

Minister Li Si was a small birdlike man whose body contained no extra flesh beyond that needed to cover his frame. He wore the traditional silk gown of our people with long flowing sleeves. Although courteous to the point of unctuousness, there was no firmness to his hand or warmth in his eyes. His predatory-like bright eyes flashed as we entered, like a bird assessing our food value.

"Report, that I might relay your messages to Lord Chin," he demanded.

I was somewhat taken back by his lack of conversational niceties, normally a hallmark of Chin'in courtesy. This man was not an advocate or friend.

"Lord Chin has requested a personal report, please advise him of our presence," I snapped. "Our words are for Lord Chin alone, not those he commands. Do My Will."

I placed the familiar military command in the sentence to let Minister Li Si know that General Sun Kai was not a man to be intimidated. Although I could sense his anger, he chose a wiser path, suddenly smiling and showing us to seats.

"I will advise Lord Chin of your arrival," he said. "Tea?"

As Minister Li Si left, Fan gave me a warning glance as if to say that this was not someone I wished to have as an enemy.

"I know, I know, he pushed too quickly," I said.

It had been a long day preceded by several longer days. It was hard to shift from action to diplomacy in such a short span of time, and I was almost too tired for the effort.

165

"Follow my lead in the presence of our Lord Chin," whispered Fan. "Things have changed since you were last here."

He then went on to explain the formal approach that all now went through when meeting with Chin. This involved kneeling three times and, after each kneeling, to cast oneself forward into a kowtow position where the head touches the floor.

After twenty minutes Minister Li Si returned and indicated we were to follow him.

Daniel saw the side note written in the margin.

In this area, the text uses the term ke for the measurement of time. I have replaced the word ke with minutes to assist in the understanding. The two measurements of time while similar are not exactly the same.

Now what? thought Daniel. *Twenty ke? What's a ke?* He picked up his notepad and wrote a reminder to look up ke, zhang, and li. He then went back to Sun Kai's story.

Leading the way, he ushered us toward a small side chamber off the Hall of Supreme Harmony. "Our Lord pays you great honor in meeting you privately," Li Si said through a tight smile. Stopping at the doorway, he waved us forward into the room. The sound of a gong gave advanced notice of our presence.

Our Lord was sitting on an elaborate chair before an ornate table at room center and, although no one else was visible, the rustle of side curtains told us that we were not truly alone. Fan and I entered bowing and approached Lord Chin. We kept our faces down, finally remaining in full

166

kowtow before our Lord, awaiting his notice. A swish of a fan, and a voice I immediately recognized bid us forward.

"First Brothers to the Hawk, approach." The emperor was going to recognize our common shared history as children as well as our current titles. "It pleases me that you have come."

Lying with face to floor I could not see the face of my old companion. Yet when he beckoned and we arose, his visage came as a great surprise. Cragginess and strength, which had previously characterized his features, had been replaced by florid skin which hung in folds on his face. It was less than a year since I last saw him but the transformation was breathtaking. We spoke first of earlier times, battles won, and of our childhood together as the emperor performed the duties of a host honoring the requirements of a Confucian gentleman. Although I knew he would soon come to the point of the Praxan, at least for now, we talked as old friends.

After a few minutes, Lord Chin seemed to lose his train of thought and began to ramble on about the earlier visions that he had on Huashan Mountain when we were novices. He said that he was again having the recurring dream that showed the three of us on the mountaintop with him pointing away as if to direct us to leave. As he recounted the dream, he became agitated, drool appeared on his lips, his hands twitched in minor palsy, and his voice cracked.

"So long ago, so long ago," he mumbled.

After a several second pause, our lord again spoke, but this time it was in regard to traitors.

"They are everywhere! They poison the people with their filth! I will burn them and their damn books." He laughed a high giggle as if contemplating an inner vision. "The Confucian's are the worst," he said. "They would dare even to counsel the Sun of Heaven with their dammed five relationships."

In mid-sentence he suddenly stopped talking and stared into space, drooling spit down into his beard. I glanced at Fan to see if he shared my concern in regard to the mental state of our master. The time stretched forward several minutes as our Lord stared into space with an unfocused gaze—as if he was suspended in a trance. A wizened, elderly Taoist monk came forward silently with a tray upon which rested a series of vials and two drinking goblets.

"Sire, if you will, it is time," he said and mixed the vials together in the goblet.

The mixture filled the room with the sweet smells of fresh garlic and sage, however, I was startled to see that the final vial poured contained the silver metal that never hardens. The monk took the first goblet on the tray and drank the draught in a single gulp. He then took the second and handed it to Lord Chin. The drink had an immediate calming effect on our lord whose hand tremors ceased and eyes refocused. The monk left without an explanation, Lord Chin said nothing about his potion. He now appeared more like his old self with a focus on the matters at hand.

"Sun, tell me of these Praxan devils!"

I quickly told him of finding the hidden valley, of the waterfall cave entrance, the hidden village, and of the liquid fire weapon.

"Sire, we now have the information we need to make them fight. All the options are now ours; they cannot hide the women again. We can now select when to threaten their women. They will come to us."

Chin sat watching my face as I made the report. I finished with the details of the cave complex, the making of the fire weapon, the cache of treasure and uniforms, Timiltuk and his warriors, and finally the killing of the captured monks. I told him of my bringing several of the jugs from the cave.

"We must have our alchemists evaluate these materials," he responded. "We must have its secrets, perhaps improve upon it."

Suddenly as if he had not changed the conversation, "Was your woman among them?" He leaned forward watching me intently for the answer.

"Yes." I could not break eye contact with him as he pondered the meaning of my wife being in the enemy camp.

"I brought you here to hear your answer to that question, and to have you answer a second. Can I still rely upon you to serve?"

I was trapped, confronted by the question I had avoided asking myself. "Snow Pine has chosen," I said, "And I chose long ago. I serve my Lord." Even as I said the words, I knew they were true. I would hold to my pledge not to doubt my wife or her intentions, but I could not blind myself to the truth that, for reasons I did not yet understand, she had chosen to follow another path. My hand went to the coin hung about my neck and felt the impression of the word etched onto its reverse side, 10,000. I had pledged myself to the establishment of a dynasty that was to last 10,000 years, and I must play my part.

Lord Chin's face relaxed with my confirmation of loyalty.

"Of course you are loyal, my friend, I never doubted. Now let us reason together to see that these insects no longer bedevil the harmony of the empire."

He clapped his hands, bringing servants forward with tea for the three of us. I noticed again the unusual practice of having more cups than guests and that the servers themselves first drank before serving. Our Lord Chin had ceased to trust even those within the palace walls.

Alone with us again, Lord Chin spoke of a plan of battle to capture the hidden valley; he had obviously given the matter long thought. My report to him had only reinforced his knowledge of the situation. He wanted a decisive end to the Praxan question. Following their defeat, the Praxan would not be allowed to return to their pastoral ways, they were to become extinct, a part of the great wall he was building along the northern border. As we spoke of the upcoming battle, it became clear that our lord had no desire to lead the army himself, but had brought me to the capital to hear my answer to the one question. Shortly thereafter, a gong signaled that our interview was over. As Fan and I left, the sound of Chin's parting command filled the night. "Do my will! Make them fear!"

As we left, Minister Li Si met us again. This time he was all graciousness and smiles. He stood rubbing his hands together as if absent-mindedly dry washing them. His manner was unctuous to the extreme. One could not imagine our earlier confrontation; it was as if he had arranged the meeting himself. Every alarm signal for self defense that had been built up from a life of military service sounded as we said goodbye. Li Si was not a man of virtue; what he said had nothing to do with what he felt or what he would do. Truly this was a dangerous man. Fan had been right in urging caution.

Making our way home that night, I understood the unease, the strained tension that I had felt everywhere since entering the city. I felt it myself in the presence of Lord Chin, a sense that we were on a fine balance and that the scales could be tipped in a multiple of uncertain directions. Our Lord had become erratic. Slayer of Dragons, Eagle Who Sees Far, was unwell. It was the uncertainty of what might come next that produced the unease.

I was unsure how to broach the subject with Fan but it

was he who began. Looking about to assure himself that we could not be heard, he said, "In the last six months, our lord Chin has not been well. I did not wish to tell you about the changes until you could see for yourself." Fan continued, "He no longer trusts anyone, even in his own family. I have heard that he selects a different woman for his bed nightly and they are brought to him nude so as to assure that they carry no weapon. He even has his aides sit by the bedside to record all events in detail so that any claims to future paternity can be verified or refuted."

"I care not who our Lord brings to bed," I growled. "Tell me of the medications. What disease does he battle?" It had been alarming to me, the changes I had seen in Chin, and how scattered and wild his thoughts had become.

"It is not a disease," Fan said, "He seeks the elixir of immortality."

Chapter 18

A Choice Made.

If I have to take a single phrase to sum up the Three Hundred Songs, I would say, 'Let there be no evil in your thoughts.'
Confucius

For Snow Pine the time in the hidden valley was both wonderful and dreadful. It was wonderful to be back with her family and to see her father gather his strength. It was dreadful to come to know that she had changed and could never again feel comfortable in the home of her childhood. She was no longer Cassia, she was Snow Pine, mate to Sun Kai. While she loved these people, she felt a distance from them which she could not breach, words she could not say, thoughts she could not share.

The next morning she found the coin I had left in the

pocket of the garment. Both hope and fear struck her simultaneously; her heart leaped in her chest, making it difficult to breathe. Was this the one she had left on the statue? If so, where was Sun? Why had he not made himself known? She quickly looked about hoping and dreading to see me. But, what if this is not from Sun at all, but has been put there as a test of her loyalty? She looked about to see if any watched. *This is crazy*, she thought, *be calm, and don't make a fool of yourself.* She quickly slid the string about her neck, dropping the coin beneath her clothing. Her mind raced as she tried to think of its source. Feeling it against her skin, her mind rehearsed the words which gave her strength. Our paths are one, I shall not doubt.

Later that day she assisted her father in his exercises. He was regaining strength and his face had lost its gauntness.

"Papa, you are doing so well, soon you will not need me," she laughed, and patted his hand.

He stopped to look at her, "Have you decided my daughter? Is the time near?"

She smiled at him and nodded, tears welling from her eyes. Yes, even without realizing it, she had decided, soon it would be time to go. But for now it was a joy to sit with her father, the one member of her family who could communicate to her heart wordlessly. She loved this man dearly, her brave father whose heart was too gentle for this time of wolves.

She watched as he went back to his exercises. He had mastered the five animal play movements which imitate in order: the tiger, bear, deer, ape, and bird. Qigong exercises had been popular for a thousand years and their restorative powers were legendary. Though simple in nature, the exercises had a powerful healing effect on her father and would in the future ease his stress and help him prevent further illness.

That afternoon they sang together around the fire, their voices joining and blending in a harmony rare outside of families. Yes, it was time to leave, but not today, not this hour. This hour was for her father and for her to drink in the joy of being at his side and listening to his voice. The song was of an ancient hero who was invincible in battle and had almost saved the golden city. Following his great victory, he died at the hand of the Greek hero Achilles.

Boldly he entered the battle
His enemies fall as his prey
This is the hour of our victory
This is to be our day

He chased them back to their ships
He was terrible in this wrath
None could stand against him
Only death lay in his path

Our city wall was unbroken
Noble Hector had saved the day
Only Achilles came forward
To challenge him that day

Don't go all of them pleaded
He is part immortal they say
But Hector heard the challenge
And came forward as if in play

Noble Hector fought like a lion
But this was Achilles' hour
His sword flashed in the daylight
And Hector fell before its power

Our hero has entered his heaven
Among the immortals he's King
We earthbound still remember that battle
Of our terrible loss we sing.

As they sat singing by the fire, Snow Pine looked up and saw a procession beginning to form at the other end of the valley. Fear gripped her as she recognized the colors of a unit of Old Hundred Surnames engaged in an exercise. There was no mistaking the banners, battle harness and armor. She thought to raise an alarm yet, as she looked, she noted that her uncle and the elders were standing at ease watching the mock battle.

"It is only practice my daughter. Do not be afraid," her father said as he came to stand with her to watch. "It is our young soldiers, wearing the dress of our enemy. We are still invisible in our valley." As he said the last, he looked into her eyes. "Our place here in the valley must never be revealed, regardless of your choice."

She nodded in agreement to his unspoken question and he looked away satisfied with her answer and promise. He was right; her choice was a personal one, not one that would obligate her to bring death upon her family.

When her brother Certes returned for lunch that afternoon, he was flushed from the excitement of the military maneuvers and still wore the battle harness of a Chin'in soldier. Snow Pine looked at her younger brother and was saddened at the changes that had occurred in him. The warmth of his ever quick smile now rarely touched his eyes; the war had made him into a man, but what type of man? He had the lean wary look of the animal about him. It was an attribute that defied expression, a look that was both wary and aggressive, both trapped and free. It was hard to imagine that this warrior was the same young boy with

175

whom she had chased butterflies.

"Soon the devils will feel our swords," Certes boasted shadow dancing with his saber. "They will be cut down like grain for the herds. Lord Ascanius has promised a great victory."

The sword swished through the air again, and it was all that Snow Pine could do to keep from shuddering as the blade flashed. Her mind's eye saw a distant battle between Chin'in and Praxan, with dead and dying lying in heaps.

"Please forgive me my brother, but I am suddenly tired and would rest."

Snow Pine rose and made her way into the tent. The thought of young men dying, be they Praxan or Chin'in, weighed heavily on her heart.

That evening at the central campfire, she and her father again chanted one of the ancient sagas accompanied by the lyre. The story was one oft told, the history of a noble people, who when forced from their golden city into exile, had chosen peace in a new land but in the end had again found war. The audience was appreciative and swayed to the music, knowing each story and delighting in the retelling of the glory that had once been theirs. Her father's clear voice rose and fell in the night air. None told the stories quite as well as he; none was as beloved by this people. He had been restored to his place as the lead citherode, chanter of the ancient sagas, but due to his heart weakness he had removed himself from the council of Ascanius' advisors.

Following the singing, Ascanius took the stand. He lifted his arms for silence, and again shared his vision. Ascanius called upon Hecate, goddess of the darkling moon, to seal the realm of the dead so that no Praxan warrior might enter. He then called the young men forward and began the ritual of purification that would give them invulnerability in battle. Each man kissed the three-faced statue of Hecate, the goddess who ruled over the deceased and the spirits of the night. Snow Pine shivered as she saw Certes raise the statue to his lips.

"The hour of our victory is close at hand," Ascanius promised. "Even now our forces assemble. Soon our enemies will hide in their burrows, trembling in fear of our mighty warriors. There will come a time when we will no longer hide our women and children. Praxan arise, our time has come again." As he spoke, his charisma and powerful vision awed and hushed the people.

That night, unable to sleep, Snow Pine again returned to sit by the tent fire. She looked into the night sky to find the constellations Cepheus and Cassiopeia, whose positions in the heavens she had taught me when we were first together. Where is Sun tonight, she thought. Does he look into the heaven and see the ancient ones from my homeland? What must he think of my absence? She stared into the evening coals with a new resolve. Soon I will make my way to you. Soon. Not today, perhaps tomorrow, but if not, soon. In her mind a plan formed that would allow her to leave this place. "Soon, my love, I promise," she whispered, and pulled the blanket tighter about her shoulders against the night air. "Soon."

It was several weeks before Snow Pine could put her plan into action. On the final evening, she packed her belongings in preparation and lay in the darkness waiting for her family to settle in sleep and all activity in the camp to cease. *Night must be nearly half over,* she thought as she rolled from her sleeping furs and picked up her shoulder pack. Moving quietly so as not to disturb her family, she made her way from the tent into the awaiting darkness. She stood for a moment looking back, calling upon the ancients to protect her family and restore her father to full health.

She then adjusted her pack and moved toward the cave entrance. She had little to fear of discovery, as the focus of Praxan security lay near the tents of Ascanius and at the other end of the cave leading to the outside valley.

She moved quickly along the dark path within the cave and stopped only as she came near the outside entrance, pausing to listen for signs of the two guards that were posted there. Snow Pine knew that she must get beyond the guards and find a place to hide in the outer valley before first light. Finally, both guards shifted in their positions, telling her what she needed to know, and allowing her to move silently between them.

She walked into the outer valley and made her way along the stream. The water was cold and refreshing against her legs. She looked up and saw the pinking of the ridgelines indicating a new day. She moved from the water into a copse of trees and rocks to seek shelter and security to sleep. It would not do to have a group of Praxan find her now. As she lay waiting for sleep to overtake her, she wondered when her family would discover her gone and if they would give an alarm. She awoke in late afternoon and made her way back down the canyon toward the provincial capital.

The next morning Snow Pine made a cold camp along the ridgeline, slept for a few hours, then continued toward the nearest village, hoping to secure food and a horse. Her memories of the next several days were a jumble of high ridges, long forested valleys, days baking in the sun, and nights of bone shaking cold. *Winter is coming early this year,* she thought. It was with great pleasure that she topped the last ridge and saw the small hamlet in the distance. This was still Praxan territory so she approached with care.

In the village she was able to replenish her supplies and to buy a horse. This allowed her to move quickly toward the mountain pass that marked the boundary between Praxan and Chin'in territory. As she made her way along the trail, she rehearsed the words she would say to me when she returned. She hoped against hope that I would understand and agree with her choices.

Crossing the mountain pass, Snow Pine came to the area where the cohort of Huashan Mountain monks had been trapped and destroyed. She shuddered to think of the terrible liquid fire weapon that had been unleashed that day. Late that afternoon she approached the first of the Chin'in villages. Entering the village she saw a small contingent of Chin'in warriors also approaching the town. This seemed fortuitous to her, perhaps she even knew the officer, as many of them had been welcomed at our table. *Even if I do not know this particular officer*, she thought, he *would surely offer me assistance and protection in my travels.* Either way, she felt secure as she urged her horse forward so that she could travel with the soldiers.

As she rode through the troops to the command position, thoughts of our future meeting rushed into her mind, filling her with dread and anticipation. She brought her horse to a halt next to a young officer who appeared in charge. As he turned toward her, she recognized him immediately. Brother and sister exclaimed in unison: "You!"

It was a non-smiling Certes who dragged her from her horse and ordered her bound. "Bring her along; I will deal with her later," he said. "This night we begin the end for the Chin'in devils."

Chapter 19

The Winter Winds

Behave in such a way that your father and mother have no anxiety about you except concerning your health.
Confucius

Following our interview with Lord Chin, Fan and I spent several days in the capital making preparations and meeting with our families. My sister Mai, having grown tired of waiting for Fan to notice her, came to me as her older brother to intercede on her behalf. She had grown into a lovely woman, and I knew that Fan had secretly cared for her from when they were children. Perhaps a small push would be all that was needed.

I wanted to spend some time with my father who had begun to slow with age. As master Yi taught, age in parents is both joy and dread. The time was short but I thought that

I could persuade him to move from the capital to live closer to me; I explained to him the benefits. However, father was resolute in his desire to stay at the capital where he had his friends for morning exercise, games, and gossip. He had grown old in the comfort of the place. My mother, ever the wise woman, kept her peace. She would not intervene between her mate and first son. We men would need to work this issue out ourselves. Nothing that I could say moved my father from his position and, after a time, Master Yi's words returned to my mind:

"In serving parents a man may gently remonstrate with them, but if he sees that he has failed to change their opinion, he should resume an attitude of deference and not offend them; he may feel discouraged, but not resentful."

At least with the matter between Fan and Mai, I was successful. It had required even less than a push for them to see each other as if for the first time. The joy in their finding made them radiant. Fan would be a blessing to the family, and for me, a great younger brother. Although the time was short, the two families came together in the traditional feast of marriage: round balls of sweetened rice to symbolize a life of harmony, chunks of sugar cane for a sweet future, squirrel fish to signify abundance, and finally date soup in hope for the early birth of a son. Following the joining, Fan and Mai went south to Guilin, to spend a week together before returning to work. Guilin is a fanciful place of great beauty; its Li River resembles a jade ribbon curled around pointed mountains. It is a favorite of Chin'in couples to float the river in a boat and recount the creatures and animals one sees carved into the wild rocks. It is said that even the great Taoist philosopher, Lao Tzu, when in exile from court, made his way to Guilin.

The next morning after their departure, I began the homeward trip, protected by a small cohort of monks. I missed the company of Fan but knew he would join me once he and Mai had their time together. I moved the party to the base of Huashan Mountain and made an early encampment as I had one more visit to make before leaving the area. Above the camp nestled into the mountain was the Sanctuary, home to the Hawk Cult, and residence of my teacher Master Yi. Leaving the group, I made my way upward along the carved path that I first walked as a child. Even then, Master Yi appeared as old as the mountain, and now I wished to see him again before he joined the ancestors. As I approached the courtyard of the monastery, I saw the master working with a new group of novices. I was struck once again by his immense age, yet he seemed the same as that first day so long ago. He was a small man, gnarled and bent as polished wisteria root, who once having reached full maturity, defied the aging process.

Finishing the lesson, he dismissed the boys and moved toward me.

"Ah, I had heard you were back. I am pleased you have taken the time to visit this old man," he said and ushered me toward a garden bench.

I pulled from my pack a small book of poetry, which I presented as a gift.

"No trip to the capital would be complete without some time with my teacher," I said as I made him comfortable on the bench and placed myself at his feet.

For a period of time we spoke of family matters, the marriage of Fan and Mai, and my failure to convince my father to move to my residence. Master Yi nodded his approval and his eyes crinkled with pleasure as I spoke of my decision to honor father's desire. He patted my shoulder, saying: "Dutiful sons in this day are those who get enough food for their parents. Yet even dogs and horses are well cared for to the same extent. If you fail to show respect to your parents, where lays the difference between them and the animals for which you care?"

Following this discussion about my family, a period of silence followed as I waited for the opportunity to broach the question for which I had come. Master Yi sat quietly while I organized my thoughts. He knew that I had come for more than a conversation about family, but he waited for my lead. I remembered his admonition, given when I was a boy chattering on about something of small merit. "Unless one can improve upon silence, one shouldn't."

There was no appropriate way to bring up the health of the emperor indirectly or discreetly, so I blurted out my concerns, praying it would not sound disloyal or forward. I related the story of my recent visit, his drinking of the mercury potion and my fears for his health.

Master Yi frowned as he listened. "Tell me my child, when you observed our Lord, did he appear nervous and irritable? Did he have shaking movements in his hands? Did his mind seem unclear in its thinking?" When I nodded in affirmation at each question, he went on. "The metal that is liquid is powerful medicine but also poison. True, it can give visions but if taken wrongly can lead to early death. The metal that never hardens is dangerous, even for a son of heaven."

"What must I do then master?"

Master Yi stroked his long wispy beard, and shaking his head, he advised caution. "Hear much, but maintain silence regarding doubtful points and be cautious in speaking the rest, then you will seldom fall into error." He again paused. "Remember, however, that even the gods have limits to patience. The ruler who guides the people by regulations, and keeps order by punishment, may cause the people to avoid wrong, but they will lose their self-respect. If you guide people by moral force and keep order by ritual, they will keep their self-respect and come to you on their own."

He paused before saying more. "My child, that is the best advice I can give for this time. Not until the weather turns cold do we realize that the pines and cypress are the last to lose their leaves. I believe the winds of winter will come early this year."

He laughed when concluding this last statement as if telling a personal joke. As always, I was somewhat unsure as to the full meaning of the wisdom of Master Yi.

Later, the Master and I made our way up the mountain to a place where the monastery and its adjoining farms could be seen in the afternoon light. We watched as a fog developed in the river valley below and made its way up the mountain gorge, hiding everything in its path. Soon the encampment of my soldiers, then the fields and monastery, all disappeared in the gray shroud.

Touching my arm, Master Yi leaned toward me, "Remember this," his voice a low whisper, "everything you hold to be solid can be made to disappear. You must make a choice and hold on to those people, values, and ideas that you hold dear and not waiver in them, even when your senses tell you they are gone."

I leaned forward and kissed the old man's hand in appreciation. One rarely gets better advice in uncertain times. These were strange times and indeed, the winter winds had begun to blow. I made ready to go. He walked with me for a short time, then turned toward the monastery. Somehow it was important to watch him go out of sight. His was a great spirit; I doubt that I would meet his equal again in this life.

Later that day as I continued my return trip home, I recounted Master Yi's advice. Given the emperor's inclination for reward and harsh punishment, I understood my teacher's hesitation in disagreeing or involving himself in such a private matter. I wondered if my teacher's advice, which was always firmly based on Confucian principles, was still being requested at the palace. The emperor was more in tune with the legalism philosophy of Li Si than with the more gentle Taoists or orderly Confucionists. Master Yi was right, the emperor's health or way of managing his empire was not within my ability to solve, and I would better spend my time on dealing with my own life and the pressing Praxan issue. Even in his ill health, Lord Chin had been very specific and clear in his desires regarding the Praxan.

As my party crossed the mountain pass into the valley, we passed the site where the imperial delegation had been attacked. It seemed so long ago. So much had changed since that day. The plan I was working on was now clear in my mind. My knowledge of where the Praxan women and children were hidden would allow me to set the time and place for the decisive battle. The Praxan were brave warriors but their numbers were limited and would in the end succumb to the forces of Chin'in.

As much as I resisted, the closer we came to home, the more Snow Pine pushed into my consciousness. *What of her? Would she be among the killed or captured?*

As we neared one of the outer villages that ringed the provincial capital, the advanced scouts of my party came rushing back to the camp. "Lord it is gone! The village has been burned, even the crops destroyed." Calming the scouts, I listened to their report and ordered the accompanying troops into defensive positions as we continued toward the village. When we arrived, it was as reported: the village was burned, crops and granaries destroyed, and no one left alive to tell what happened. There was a sweet stench of death to the place.

Moving on toward the provincial capital, I found the same pattern of burned villages and farms and the people missing. Village after village, it was always the same desolation, and horrible stink of death. It appeared to me as if the farmers in these small villages had offered little resistance. I could find no one left alive who could tell of the events; as we again moved forward, however, we found several peasant farmers who had hidden in their fields. The tale they told was unbelievable. The villages had been attacked by Chin'in troops. The villagers had opened the gates to greet the troops and then were attacked.

My mind refused to accept the reports. "Nonsense! Impossible!"

I moved the party quickly to the next village, and found it much the same. The story, if it was to be believed, was that Chin'in troops had arrived and commanded the gates be opened. Once the villagers complied, they were set upon, all being killed and structures burned. The only survivors were those who had been away from the village at the time and were able to hide themselves and observe the events from a distance.

I then moved the party west of the capital, to a military camp that we were using as a staging ground for the upcoming offensive against the Praxan. I looked forward to seeing my aide Zhelin who I had left in command to gather the troops and prepare for my return. I felt confident in his security as it was hard to imagine that any outside force would have prevailed against such a fortified position.

Upon my arrival, however, confidence fled and my worst fears were realized; the camp was in flames. In this case, the signs of resistance were everywhere, but the liquid fire weapon had overcome them, with many being cremated as they manned their posts. The Praxan were no longer in hiding but were moving in force across our valley. Whatever battle plans I had designed before were now obsolete given the new situation. For the time being, we were not going to be the aggressor but would be fighting for our lives.

Outside the command center, I found Zhelin. Perhaps as an example, the Praxan had paid special attention to the commander of the fort. Zhelin's body had been crucified and broken on a wheel, then used for target practice and left for dead. If we had arrived an hour later, the enemy would have gained the silence they desired as to their identity and methods. However, a spark of life still remained, and Zhelin awakened at my voice. As I held him in my arms, he reported how a large contingent of what first appeared to be "Old Hundred Names" had appeared at the gate and commanded entry. Thinking that I had returned, he rushed to open the gate. The joy of reunion vanished when he saw that these were not our troops at all but Praxan dressed in the armor of our people. He quickly ordered the gates closed, but it was too late and while his defenders had fought well, in the end they were overrun. Beyond the horror at the loss of men and the fort were his last words as he lay dying in my arms. "My Lord, she was among them."

How could she be among them? Sitting there with my dead friend I lowered my head into my hands, overwhelmed by loss. For any who feel that I have done them wrong and wish me ill, this is your hour! Finally I shook my head to clear away the thoughts that held me in stupor. It would be easy to wallow in confusion, for I had too few answers to the many questions in my mind. But today, I could not afford the leisure of confusion; today I must deal with immediate problems and leave questions of a personal nature for another time.

Leaving a contingent to secure the fort and honor our dead, I gathered the men and made my way toward the provincial capital. Each farm hamlet we passed had been burned and granaries destroyed. Reaching the capital, I found the city in a state of turmoil. Although the enemy had not attempted to breach our walls, they had concentrated their attacks on the provincial granaries, managing to destroy them, and had also broken the city water system, which supplied water under pressure to our homes. Potable water was not really a problem, as we had access to the river systems, but the loss of the granaries was of grave concern, especially given the destruction of the surrounding villages and farming communities. I knew this was a cruel move to reduce our resources as we entered the winter months.

The words of Master Yi came once again to mind. *Not until the weather turns cold do we realize that the pines and cypress are the last to lose their leaves. I believe the winds of winter will come early this year.* The thought came to me that indeed the winter had already begun.

Turning to an aide, I gave the order to have the senior Huashan Mountain warrior monks assemble in my chamber. "Do My Will!"

I thought back upon the battle plan that had formed in my mind during my return trip. How confident I had been, planning for battle in isolation from the enemy. My mind had moved our forces here and there on the map as if the enemy had no will of its own. I closed my eyes, overcome with the understanding that my fault was not overconfidence, but arrogance and stupidity. My plans had been overtaken by events. Today I was facing not an invisible enemy who would hit and run, but an aggressive enemy on the move, one that was determined to cut our food supplies as we approached winter. In quick decisive strokes, the forces of Ascanius had scorched a ten-li swath about the city and had emptied it of people and resources that I would need if we were to carry the battle to the enemy. Our positions suddenly were reversed and I now played the part of a pawn reacting to their plan rather than having the advantage. If they seized control of the two mountain passes leading into our valley, they could hold off the imperial relief forces until late spring.

As the senior cadre of Huashan Mountain monks gathered in my chambers, all knew that the city itself needed to be stabilized before we could take the offensive. I turned to my second in command, Wang. "Place troops at every corner, gather any additional food supplies from the family storehouses, do an inventory and prepare a rationing plan for the winter. Do my will!"

As the men took their assignment and left, I was again struck by the competence of the monk warriors. The men would do as ordered but was it enough?

On two occasions I sent armed parties outward with news of our desperate situation, requesting relief. Both groups were ambushed before they had reached the mountain passes. Ascanius taunted me and tried to sow fear in the city by returning the headless bodies of the warriors tied to their horses. I then sent several Huashan Mountain monks out to see if just one individual could get through the enemy's grip, but this also failed. The pigeon sent to Fan in the capital explaining my situation, was now the only hope for communication before spring again opened the mountain pass.

I stood on the great city wall that evening and the night sky was filled with the glow of a thousand fires. The Praxan were burning the wheat fields in a swath around the city. The air was filled with acrid smoke that burned the eyes and throat. Standing alone in the night, I was overwhelmed by the feeling that irreversible change had been set in motion. We were now in a death struggle with these barbarians, a struggle of history from which only one people would go forward. How could she be among them?

Chapter 20

A new discovery

Daniel awoke, stretched, and smiled. Today was a day that held real promise. Lauren had agreed to a picnic and had taken the evening off so that they could be together. It amazed him how quickly his affection for her had grown. He had never met anyone who quite shared his odd passions the way she did. Name a favorite tune, she liked it. Movies that made him cry, her too. Favorite books? Why, she even knew that Madam Murasaki had written the world's first novel, and better yet, she had actually read it and could even quote from it. She was amazing! Besides being one of the smartest people he knew, she was also interesting, more beautiful than cute, and seemed low maintenance. A person could get lost in her eyes.

He thought of his recent experiences with Donna. Donna was popular and cute but during the entire time he had known her, he couldn't remember any conversation that didn't begin and end with Donna. *Talk about high maintenance* he thought. *Donna's idea of a good time was shopping at the mall. Her idea of a sensitive male was one who applauded.*

Lauren, on the other hand, didn't seem to think about shopping or popularity at all. Her whole focus was on doing those things that interested her and made her happy. He wondered if she even knew how beautiful and unique she was. He was dazzled by her love of life and ability to be totally caught up in the moment, and her laugh; she had a killer laugh. She didn't even seem to care that he was a poor graduate student, in a major that offered very few opportunities outside of academics. They had even talked about how much fun it would be, after graduation, to volunteer for one of the international digs where you worked for free. Money didn't seem to be a priority for her at all. He began to wonder what his mother would think of her. *How scary is that,* he thought. *I need to be very careful with this one.* As mom always says, *two can live as cheaply as one but only half as long.*

Although he had not intended to take her into his confidence so quickly, he surprised himself by blurting out the whole story during their second meeting, even the details of the skeleton in the Piasa Bird cave. He made her a copy of the transcript, which she was reading. Somehow it felt natural and right that he should tell her everything and that they should be working together.

It had only been three weeks since he had first talked to her in the library. Since that time, they had met several times and she had filled in lots of information regarding the early people of Troy. In regard to whether Creusa and her son might have escaped the night Troy fell, she told him that history was silent on that matter. It spoke of Creusa getting separated from her husband, Aeneas, and of him later founding Rome, but nothing of her.

Daniel smiled as he remembered Lauren's comment, "Just like male historians!" But if history did not say they escaped that night, it didn't say that they had been captured or killed either. Creusa had simply vanished from history. *Maybe they did make their way to China. Why not,* he thought?

As for the Chin part of the story, Daniel had a better background than Lauren. In a broad sense, the story could be true. Chin had been the first emperor of a unified China. The Chinese had produced three great philosophical positions in regard to ruling: Confucianism, Taoism, and Legalism. Unlike their Confucian counterparts who insisted that good practice came from the result of teaching right principles within the five relationships, or the Taoists who claimed to follow nature, the legalists concentrated solely upon results. For legalist advisors like Li Si, the key was punishment of failure and reward of success. Every action of the Emperor was a signal to the people, therefore, every action must signal strength.

Chin had been an advocate of a rather draconian form of legalism that focused on punishments and rewards to control behavior. In his excesses, he had buried Confucian scholars alive and burned their books.

Lord Chin had become increasingly erratic as a result of taking an elixir of life but also more malleable. Advisors like Li Si had used these periods of paranoia and fear to press for increased personal power. In the name of rewards and punishments for perceived achievements and failures, they silenced those who opposed their view before the emperor.

Chin's obsession with immortality was also well recorded, especially after several attempted assassinations. The ancient documents revealed numerous occasions when Chin had sent emissaries outward searching for evidence of the immortals. The records were silent in regard to any of the voyagers returning, although it is thought that at least one group reached and settled on the mainland of Japan.

It was also a commonly held belief that Chin died from an overdose of mercury poisoning while reviewing work on the Great Wall. The mercury was part of an elixir that he drank to extend his longevity. It was a measure of how greatly the emperor was feared that no one was willing to announce his death. A wagon of fish was hastily brought in and placed behind his closed carriage so that the smell of the fish rotting would hide the odor of his decomposing corpse. Daniel smiled, thinking of how fast the delegation must have returned to the capital.

The end of Chin signaled the end of his empire. The emperor's advisor Li Si had manipulated the eldest son into committing suicide, and then became the power behind the throne as the second son became the Chin'in emperor. What neither man fully understood was how truly hated Lord Chin had become. Li Si, for all of his cleverness, was not Chin and soon the bitter fruits of legalism ripened into rebellion. The son, a weak leader without vision, was soon pushed aside. The mandate of heaven was withdrawn and another family quickly formed the new and longer lasting Han dynasty.

Daniel closed his eyes thinking of all the possibilities. So much of the story was true. Yet, nowhere in the history was there a mention of Praxan people, no mention of Huashan Mountain monks, and no mention of Sun Kai. He was still wrestling with the problem of the missing pieces when he heard the doorbell ring downstairs. The problem of the missing pieces would have to wait.

After his mom answered the door, he could hear Lauren's voice. She had noticed his mother's amber collection in the kitchen and was admiring it. The window wall was covered with open shelves filled with the odds and ends of amber objects she had collected. It was an eclectic collection of antique fishing buoys, chunks of raw amber, and vases with the only criteria for inclusion being that they be amber. Over the years, it had become every member of the family's duty to be on the lookout for anything that could be added to the wall. One of his favorite memories as a child was gathering in the kitchen and literally being bathed in a golden light as the sun passed through the pieces. This joy, plus his mother's great cooking, may have been the secret to the family's love of the kitchen.

Coming downstairs, Daniel could now see the two women talking. He could tell from his mother's animation that she was enjoying the conversation. Lauren had made a friend already, with her appreciative comments about the amber collection. Daniel heard her say that she especially liked the chunks of raw amber, many of which contained fragments of ancient leaves or insects.

Daniel and Lauren spent the next few minutes talking about the day, and gathering the daypacks for the Piasa bluff picnic. She had taken off from work so that they could spend the entire day at the site and then work together on the puzzle of the skeleton that evening. Daniel had already cleared it with his mother for Lauren to spend the night in the spare bedroom. They could then go into SIU together in the morning. Daniel knew that if he was ever going to bring the story of the manuscript, the coin and the skeleton, to Dr. Eldredge, he had to come up with something coherent. So far all he had was pieces, and most of them didn't seem to fit together.

On the short ride to the Piasa site, they talked about the transcript. He promised that he would not tell her about what was coming next and would allow her to read the story herself. The Asian warrior and his beautiful Snow Pine intrigued Lauren. "I can't wait to read how it turns out," she said. "It all seems so real."

Daniel agreed but shared his concern that it might be an elaborate hoax; after all, many of the major characters were not mentioned in any of the histories they had reviewed.

"That's true," Lauren replied, "but that doesn't really mean anything. Until they dug up the Terra Cotta warriors in the 70s outside of Chin's tomb, nobody knew anything about them either."

Daniel nodded. She was right. No one could have imagined that Chin had placed eight thousand, seven-foot warrior statures outside his tomb complex, each with its own identifiable face. Yet it was true. The statues laid hidden in the earth for over two thousand years, only coming to light when a farmer found them while digging a well. Most of the statues found had been smashed and burned years before they were discovered, but once pieced back together, they formed an amazing archeological treasure.

"You know, it may have been that Chin was so hated by the time he died that people avoided writing about him," Lauren suggested, "Or in the case of Snow Pine and Sun Kai, maybe in the end he hated them enough to try to erase them from history, like he tried to do with Confucian writing."

Daniel turned into the parking lot that served as the jumping off place for the path to the Piasa Bird. He and Lauren gathered the ice chest and day packs and began the ascent to the bluff face. In a few moments they came to a flat area under the petroglyph and stopped to view the painting. It had been raining earlier that morning which had soaked the cliff face, and now the dampness accentuated the colors. The image was massive, maybe sixteen feet long. The dark demonic-like face stared down on them with its elongated fangs, and red horns. The wings expanded to the right and left of its head. The tail was at least fifty feet long, wound three times around the body, and tipped with a spearhead thrust backward through its own hind leg. Seeing the great creature above her, Lauren laughed in wonder.

"Wow, that is amazing. Are you sure that this is ancient? It doesn't look Native American at all."

Daniel explained how the original cliff carving was first seen by white men in 1673, but that even then it had been considered ancient by the local natives. The original picture, which had been somewhere along the bluff, had been destroyed in the late nineteenth century, but the one above them was supposed to be an accurate rendition.

"Who do you suppose painted the original?" Lauren asked rhetorically, "and even more important, why?"

"I dunno," replied Daniel, "but it is magnificent, maybe even a bit scary. Perhaps that was the point."

They spent the next hour eating and talking about the manuscript and the ancient painting. Even in the winter, this part of Illinois was beautiful, the rugged cliff face above, the large caverns dug into the hillside, and the river below. Lauren leaned back against him, and life for Daniel, at that moment, was very good indeed.

She turned her head and looked into his eyes. "Snow Pine and Sun Kai, they really loved each other didn't they? How great it must be to feel that way." Daniel gently put his arm around her. *Oh, yes, it would be great*, he thought.

Later that afternoon they completed a trip into the cave. They took pictures of the skeleton, and piled up rocks to form a low wall closing off the alcove, so that it would not be in plain sight should anyone else enter the cave. They placed another sign near the wall cautioning against falling rocks. Hopefully the signs and wall would keep the skeleton safe until they could figure out what to do with the site.

Once they had completed the wall and signs, they canvassed the side passageways for any artifacts that Daniel might have overlooked in his earlier trips. They also spent time scanning the walls with their flashlights looking to see if any further pictures had been drawn or for signs of earlier cooking fires. The cave appeared empty. Along one wall, an area was darkened as if by soot from a fire, but if so, it had been a long time ago. Lauren made a diagrammatic sketch of the cave, indicating the wall painting and position of the small alcove that held the skeleton. It was important that they treat the area as an archeological site, especially if they decided to enlist the aid of their major professor Dr. Frederick Eldredge.

That evening after dinner, they sat at the kitchen table and wrote up a short paper outlining the knowns and unknowns of the skeleton in the cave. They listed all the pertinent research findings they had in regard to the transcript, and bibliographical citations of where they had looked. If Eldredge was going to be brought into the search, they needed to have all the jots and tittles in place. He was not someone who approved of graduate students coming to him with questions they should answer for themselves. It was nearly midnight before they completed the work, after which Daniel showed Lauren to the guest bedroom.

Daniel lay in his bed thinking of Lauren and the strong connection that was developing. He had never been very good with girls, never quite knowing what to say to them. As a result, he had become somewhat shy, and felt more comfortable with books and dusty artifacts than people.

Let's face it, he thought, *you're a nerd.* In his mind he saw himself with pants pulled up, a goofy grin, and a plastic penholder sticking from his pocket. *Ok, maybe not that bad,* he thought. However, what others saw as nerdish, Lauren appeared to find charming. He had even thought of inviting her to his room that evening but had decided that perhaps it was too early in the relationship. *This is one that I don't want to screw up,* he thought. He was reminded of the T.S. Eliot poem, **The Love Song of J. Alfred Prufrock** where the man reaches out to touch the woman he desires—only to be told, "That's not what I meant at all." These words were swirling around in his mind as he drifted toward asleep when his door quietly opened. "Daniel," she whispered, peeking in cautiously. He smiled and lifted the edge of the covers.

Chapter 21

Incubating seeds of dread; A season of waiting

Even the ancients hesitated to give their thoughts utterance; for fear that they might be in disgrace if they failed to keep pace with their actions.
Confucius

I awake with a start, feeling cold and cramped and for a moment, lost to time and place. Finally the darkness, dampness, and dripping sounds orient me to the cave. How real the dreams, even the sad ones which I am loath to give up because they take me to a time when I was alive and possibilities were before me. Lying here in the darkness, I again test my leg to see how far it can be straightened. The injuries have begun to heal. *Perhaps I will walk again, not run, but perhaps limp with the assistance of a stick.*

How long has it been? I no longer know, as the time has become a blur measured out in light and dark cycles. At first I marked the wall to tell me how many days had gone by, but sometime in the past I forgot, and now the marks only remind me of what I do not know. Of late my dreams have been troubled by memories of the past, vivid images of a time when everything was hushed as if waiting for the battles to begin. I remember that night on the city wall when the horizon was aflame with a thousand fires. The enemy's army had moved against us and now controlled the valley. Only the city remained under my command.

The arrival of Timiltuk's people and their alliance had brought to Ascanius a valued new potential, a fast moving cavalry. These men of the desert tribe, so small in statue, so insignificant, were extraordinary horsemen who could fire short bows at full gallop with deadly accuracy. It was just what the Praxan needed to overcome the numerical superiority of our forces. They had blocked off the mountain passes creating a no-man's land around the city and the forces of Chin'in. Now, it was a contest of wills, could we hold out until help arrived, or would we like starved rabbits, be forced from our warrens?

As the sun warms the cave and fills it with light, I take the brush and continue the record. I think again of those dark days. The situation in the city became clearer. If we started rationing immediately, the food supplies would be adequate to survive the winter. The forces available would be strong enough to hold the city and if opportunity afforded itself, perhaps even mount a campaign beyond the city wall. Although the tide of battle had shifted to my enemies and they now howled outside the city, it was just a matter of time before the full power of the empire was brought down upon these barbarians. The spring season would open the passes and the irresistible forces of Chin'in would sweep away all those who contested for this land. Waiting through the winter months would be difficult for me, but even if one cannot know the hour for action, the gods favor those who at least know the season.

Snow Pine has told me that this winter of waiting was a dark time for her. When recaptured by her brother, she had at first lost all hope, as she watched all the improvements we had brought to the valley swept away. The water projects, the farm improvements, the storage facilities were all smashed, as if by the vengeful hand of god. The acrid smell of smoke and glare of fires burning gave the impression that the world itself had been set aflame. The tribes swept out from the desert vastness, destroying, raping, looting, and killing until nothing of the old order remained. The great valley was filled with the warriors who had answered the call of Ascanius and now only the stronghold of the regional capital was in Chin'in control. Had there been tears left to shed, she might have shed them, but that was done weeks before.

At first her brother Certes had kept her tied and near him, laughing as he forced her to watch the horrors unfolded about them. However, as the weeks stretched into months, he tired of the game and no longer kept her bound, as now there was no place to run.

She told of how she had attempted to escape on several occasions but had been quickly found and brought back. With each recapture, the beatings had drained her body of reserves needed to try again. She recalled how her brother taunted her, saying he would break her like a horse and that soon she would relearn what it meant to be a Praxan woman. But, whatever the hour, however low she fell, she knew that she was no longer Cassia the Praxan, she was

Snow Pine, mate to Sun Kai.

These thoughts sustained her and gave her resolve. *Our paths are one. I shall not doubt.* Tears again ran down her cheeks and neck, as if to water the coin emblem that hung between her breasts from its red string. Certes, seeing the tears, might have taken them for weakness had they not been matched by a steely resolve that had returned to her eyes. They might beat her, but they could not change who she was or what she must do.

I now lie in the dark thinking about those times, as clear to me as if yesterday. Had I made other choices, could Snow Pine have been spared her pain? "Yes! No! Maybe!" The walls echo my cries but they do not answer.

Chapter 22

Unkind Victories

The rule for fighting on contentious terrain is that one who yields will gain, while one who fights will lose. Draw him by pretending to go off. Set up flags, beat the drums, and move swiftly toward what he loves.

Sun Tzu – Art of War

A fluttering of wings from the pigeoncote announced the arrival of a bird. I quickly removed the leg band and retrieved the note.

Dear Older Brother – Your message was received and conveyed to our Lord Chin. The good news is that a unit of Old Hundred Surnames has been dispatched to open the pass and bring you relief. Be of good cheer! Help is near.

The bad news is that our Lord has decided to begin a policy of controlling both actions and minds. He has ordered all histories and writings of philosophers brought to him to review for usefulness. It is said that he intends to end history!

This has resulted in the burning of copies of the Confucian Analects and other works that seek to advise the emperor in regard to government. I spoke to Master Yi about this and he broke down and cried. Once he composed himself, he advised me to discuss this with no one else. He said that he would gather a conference of Confucian scholars to discuss the situation. The Emperor's first son seems to be in sympathy with the scholars. Perhaps he can counsel with his father and get him to change this order.

On the best note: Mai is with child. She is so happy and sends her love and gratitude to our older brother. If it is a boy child, we shall name him Kai.

There is a piece of me that wishes even now to return to your side but unfortunately with the coming of the child and strange actions at court, I cannot leave. Know that when the spring comes I shall be at your side and that you are always in our hearts. Your younger brother, Fan.

Sitting there reading his note that day I did not truly understand the consequences of the forces set in motion by the emperor's actions. The capital was always a place of intrigue and court politics. Chin had become even more suspicious of everyone since several attempts had been made on his life. His circle of trust was growing more narrow and tight by the day. *Not even our Lord Chin can erase the past,* I thought. I smiled at his audacity and hearing the words in my mind brought me calm and assurance. *Only the Gods can end history!*

The thought of a unit of Old Hundred Names on its way to relieve us was one that brought both hope and concern. They would reach the mountain passes while they were still steeped in snow. I turned to my aid, "Wang! Prepare our forces. We must march to the pass; we cannot have another imperial force ambushed."

I left Wang in charge of the city with sufficient troops to hold the walls until I returned. Once my forces joined with those of the relief party, we should have sufficient strength to no longer fear attack from the Praxan.

It was with confidence that I set out early the next morning. The troops were drawn from units of Huashan Mountain monks and regular army. The monks with their gray robes and hoods presented a sharp contrast with the battle harnesses of the Old Hundred Names contingent. All were well mounted and ready. While not a match for the full Praxan army, if we moved quickly enough before they gathered, we were more than adequate for any small group we might encounter along the way. *A rapidly moving force has no flank*, I thought, repeating an axiom found in Sun Tzu's **Art of War**.

Passing through the burned out areas, I understood the true devastation the Praxan brought to our land. Everywhere there was a silence, a deathly hush held the land in its grasp, and I feared even the spring would not bring relief. We moved quickly, pausing only to rest the horses, for I did not wish to engage the Praxans until we reached the reinforcements. The air was crisp, cold, and clear. The coldness pushed its way beneath our hoods, causing each man to shrink within his garments, attempting to offer less of his body to the cold. About ten that morning our scouts reported seeing horsemen in the distance, but they were moving away from us and represented no challenge. The enemy would need to report and group before they could come against us. I planned to be out of the area before a true counterstroke could be organized.

It was night when we reached the foot of the high mountain pass. The land was held in the hush of winter snow; only the sounds of the horse harnesses and muffled sounds of hooves told of our upward climb. As we approached the top, it became apparent that we had reached the pass prior to the arrival of the reinforcements. As I was about to call a halt for the night and find shelter among the rocks, the air brought the smell of a wood fire and spiced mutton to my nose. I raised my hand and the group halted, frozen in silence, as our eyes sought to probe the darkness ahead to find the source of the smells.

There was faint light around the next turn of the trail. I motioned for several of the monks to dismount, and join me on foot. Drawing knives, we moved silently forward. As we approached the last turn, we saw that we were approaching a small campfire. I wondered: Who would be out here, surely not friends? Praxans? Perhaps a group stationed to watch the mountain pass and report any attempt to enter the valley?

We stopped prior to reaching the bend, and I motioned four of the monks to move forward and silence any sentries they might have posted. Almost as quickly as the monks moved, they were lost from sight in the darkness. Minutes passed as I stood straining my eyes and ears to hear any sounds from the path before. No sound came back, nothing. Where were they?

Without even the slightest crunch of snow, two of the warriors slipped through the night's curtain and were suddenly at my side. They signed that the sentries had been silenced, and that the camp contained about two dozen men—a wolf pack, watching the trail ahead. I cautioned them to save at least one of the enemies for questioning, preferably the leader, and then moved our forces forward. As we approached the enemy gathered about the fire, I heard quiet laughing, a casual joke among comrades who would soon be faced with terror.

It was over almost before it had begun; the Praxan had little time to react as the monks were among them slashing with their knives. As requested, one of the Praxan was captured rather than killed. Although bloody from the fight, he was still struggling between the two warriors who held him tight. Grabbing his hair, I twisted his face upward and found myself staring into a face convulsed with hatred. It was the face of Certes, brother of Snow Pine.

"*You!*" he cried, and struggled harder against his captives.

For a long moment I stared into his face, seeing only my beloved. Finally, pushing her from my mind, I turned to two of the more experienced and senior monks. "Brothers, we must know why these dogs were out this night. I will await your report. Do my will!"

The struggling boy was moved out of the light into the shadows. Once away from where he might hear, I sent another monk with the message that under no circumstances was Certes to die in the questioning process. Turning to my second, I commanded "Put sentries out along the path to watch both before and behind. This night has held enough surprises."

Within minutes the bodies were pushed away from the fire into the darkness and fresh snow was used to cover the tell-tail signs of the recent deadly encounter. The smell of the spiced mutton, which still awaited eating, reminded me of my hunger. I nodded to the men to serve themselves. My personal hunger, however, was quickly extinguished by cries of pain that arose from the direction where I had last seen Certes. At first the cries were those of anger, defiance, and pain, then pain alone with no rebellion, and finally, in the end, hopelessness and despair. Before morning I would have my report. I prayed for the boy's sake that he begin talking sooner than later. I knew from experience that in the end, all men begged to tell what they knew.

It was a long night. I stared into the fire and thought often of Snow Pine. Wherever she was, each cry of pain coming from the nearby woods was sending her further from me. "I shall not doubt." I sat fingering the coin about my neck and chanted the mantra that held me to sanity, but my words were drowned out by the cries from the woods. About dawn the monks returned to report that the boy had broken and told them all he knew. Upon my questioning I found that, as promised, Certes was alive although unconscious. I thanked my ancestors; even if I should never see Snow Pine again in this life, I could not bear to have the death of her brother upon my soul.

My supposition that the wolf pack had been stationed to watch for an imperial relief force was correct. The boy also related that Ascanius knew of the imperial troops' approach and planned to allow the relief force into the valley and then to ambush them on an open plain near the burned out region. Certes also told how Timiltuk's desert horsemen were to be the deciding factor in the upcoming battle. The use of these desert warriors brought me a chill; everyone on the frontier knew how fierce these mounted barbarians could be. The plan was simple; first Ascanius with his liquid fire weapon was to inflict casualties and chaos, then as the imperial troops turned to face the danger, Timiltuk's cavalry were to come upon their rear and destroy them.

We quickly broke camp, and as we did, I formed a new plan. Leaving one monk at the pass with a message warning of the upcoming attack, the rest of us wound our way off the mountain. The unconscious Certes was bundled up on a packhorse behind me. I needed him awake and hoped that the fresh air would revive him. He had at least one more service to provide before this day was through. There were many details to put in place before the battle; I would worry about him later. If the ancestors granted us good fortune, we would soon have our enemies. Where this would leave Snow Pine, I knew not. *I shall not doubt.*

Finding a high point from which to view the valley, we found the enemy arrayed as Certes had described. Ascanius and his troops were positioned on a high ridge from which they could launch the fire weapon onto the trail below. Across the small valley there rose a smaller wooded hillock where Timiltuk's horsemen lay. The men were lying flat, and would be invisible to anyone entering along the trail. Quietly they waited for the battle to begin. No fires burned, no talking was heard, they were as hunters awaiting the prey to draw near. Even their horses were quiet and held in readiness in the rear so that they could not be seen or heard and warn the passing troops of their presence. Putting away my view glass, I quickly met with my commanders. The contingent of Huashan Mountain monks were to stay with me, while the regular army troops were to quick march to the pass above the valley where Ascanius hid the Praxan families. They were not to attack but to hold the mountain pass until we could arrive. "Make them fear! Do my will!"

Into the valley the imperial troops marched with drums beating and flags flying, troops drawn from the best units of Old Hundred Surnames. Although warned of the ambush they kept to the main path appearing to be at ease and unaware they were entering the killing trap of the fire weapon. Through my view glass I watched as Ascanius's forces tensed waiting the signal. Even among the desert horsemen waiting across the valley for the opening of the battle, all eyes were glued on the approaching troops.

I watched as Ascanius waved his arm and the ropes were cut to free the mechanism of the launching machines. The weapon's arms sprang upright and the balls of fiery death were thrown toward the troops on the trail below. With the first arc of the fire weapon, the imperial troops moved in an almost counter-intuitive movement, for instead of turning toward their enemy above them, they turned and charged the positions where the unseen desert warriors lay hidden. At the same moment the monks I had kept with me struck the enemy sentries that held the horses. There came a most terrible sound as these gray ghosts went among the animals cutting their throats.

The men of the desert were suddenly faced with a screaming contingent of Chin'in's forces charging their front, while in their rear they could hear their only means of escape being slaughtered. The piteous sounds of the dying horses blended with the throaty shouts of the charging imperial forces "Make them Fear!" provided an appropriate chorus for the slaughter that was taking place. Although the desert warriors when mounted were an equal for any in the Chin'in army, when afoot they proved no match and were quickly chased down and dispatched.

The forces of Ascanius, at first stunned by the movements of the imperial troops, now gathered for a charge onto the vulnerable rear of the Chin'in forces below. It was now time for Certes to do his part. Returning to the boy, I slapped him awake, untied him, and placed him on a horse. "Give this to Ascanius, and tell him I know where the families are hidden and even now my troops are attacking the valley." His face drained of blood and grew white at my words.

"How," he choked? I did not answer but slapped his

horse and it bolted away. I needed this message to be delivered, now.

I watched with my view glass and saw Certes relay the message. It was as I hoped; the news that their families were in danger swept across them like a gathering storm. The wave of Praxan that had been preparing to fall upon the rear of the imperial forces suddenly crested and began falling apart as the word spread. As I watched, the old truth about the messenger who brings bad news was replayed before me as Ascanius suddenly reached for his shoulder sword and struck Certes from his horse. I was transfixed by the act as I watched Certes slump and fall. He was my enemy, and in battle, I would have killed him without thought, but he was also Snow Pine's brother.

The Praxan army faded away as shadows in the morning air, each warrior intent on reaching his loved ones before we could do them harm. It was never really a race, although to the Praxan, it must have appeared so.

Only small groups of desert warriors were still resisting, hoping against hope that soon their Praxan allies would relieve them. They were brave and fierce; even on foot they died well. When the battle was over, less than one hundred of the barbarians still lived. Timilturk was not among them, nor did we find him among the dead. Somehow the old fox had escaped. For the moment, he was as much a threat to the Praxan who had abandoned him as to us. I suspected he would retreat into the wastelands and lick his wounds. In the vastness of the desert, he was still the master. There he would nurse his hatred and wait. We would not see him for a while, but I knew one day he would return and Chin'in would pay for this humiliation. Our troops herded the survivors together, binding them into a line for travel. Although I admired their spirit, the part they played in creating the burned out areas brought bile to my mouth and I looked upon them with loathing.

"Take them to the nearest section of the wall and work them to death, see that none are paroled. Bury them in the wall; let their bodies become part of our defenses! Do my will."

Such was my anger that moment, with each victory on the field I found myself losing the one thing I held dear. Where is she? If she is in the valley, I may have just sealed her death.

I now joined my troops gathering in the field below. Among the imperial officers, I spotted General Liu Bang. Although not of Chin'in nationality, he was a formidable warrior and an old friend of my family. After the initial greetings, he motioned me aside and, while turned from the others, pressed something into the pocket of my robe. "This is for your eyes only, do not be careless." He then turned away laughing, as if we had just shared an intimate joke.

I dared not remove the message until I was away from the others. How weighty it seemed in my pocket as our troops prepared to move. I sent a message to Wang in the regional capital to move a contingent toward the valley. A pigeon had been released to inform Li Si and the emperor of our initial victory. If all went well, we would arrive just shortly after the Praxan engaged our forward troops at the pass. Stopping only long enough to gather the launching devices, and liquid fire balls, we moved onward. It was not until late in the afternoon that I felt comfortable in removing the message from my robe.

Chapter 23

Victory and Loss

Thus it is said that one who knows the enemy and himself will not be endangered in a hundred engagements. One who does not know the enemy but knows himself will sometimes be victorious, sometimes defeated. One who does not know the enemy or himself will invariably be defeated in every engagement.

Sun Tzu – Art of war

I first felt relief, as the wax chop that bound the rolled silk was unbroken. But upon opening it I found an erratic hasty message as if written under extreme stress or emotion. It was with dread that I deciphered it.

Older Brother –In my last message I told you of a new imperial policy where all "un-useful" books are to be burned. Yesterday, looking at the fire, it felt as if a piece of myself was being consumed. It is said that only books concerning agriculture, technology, military affairs, and medicine are to be spared.

In truth, the fire is the least of the bad news. Following the latest burnings several well-known Confucian scholars went to the emperor to discuss the wisdom of the policy; even the emperor's oldest son went with them to plead the case. We are undone! The emperor burst into a wild rage and has banished his son to the far West for supporting the scholars; he then ordered the whole delegation murdered. He commanded that a great hole be dug and that they be buried alive. I fear to report that Master Yi was among them. As dirt covered his face, his last word was "Shame."

Since then units of Old Hundred Names have rounded up thousands of scholars and have marched them to the Wall. It is as if Li Si bewitches the Emperor. I fear what comes next. Lord Chin seems obsessed with his own immortality. I cannot leave to join you now, as even loyal families such as yours feel insecure. If it becomes necessary, know that I will protect your family with my life. - Fan

Coldness gripped my heart. The situation must be terrible indeed; Fan had failed to use the title of younger brother or to mention the impending birth of his child. Everywhere my life was unraveling. Where was Snow Pine? What of my parents? What of this madness that has taken our emperor? There were no answers to any of my questions. Only the path of duty lay open ahead. I had to push my feelings and fears aside and finish this Praxan business even if in the doing, I lost Snow Pine forever.

The Praxan were now chasing the contingent of troops

214

which I had sent to block the passes. Our troops would not enter the valley where the Praxan families were hidden but instead would prepare to defend the high snowy pass against the Praxan army pursuing them, holding them in place until we could fall upon their rear.

With bad weather and good fortune, we should be able to contain them in a terrain from which they could not move forward, nor retreat. Liu Bang nodded his agreement with the plan. Even without battle, the weather would defeat them. Not even Ascanius, the old wolf himself, would escape. Those he loved were being threatened in the valley beyond the pass, but the deep snow would slow his progress, and he would be ours.

That next afternoon when our scouts returned to report, it was apparent that the plan had worked. The Praxan were arrayed just below the mountain pass, attempting to remove the forces that I had placed above them. Now with our troops blocking the way below and snowdrifts making other escape routes impossible, the once formidable Praxan forces were strung out along the trail, trapped.

General Liu Bang laughed as Old Hundred Surnames and the Huashan Mountain monk units moved into position, and the end move of the game became clear.

"Now we need only decide whether we will attack and root out these barbarians, or wait and let them be frozen in place and collect the bodies. The options are all ours, I say attack!"

Shaking my head, I countermanded the order. "We have already lost too many to this venture; we can let the wind and snow finish them. Hold in place! Send forward a delegation. They are to tell Ascanius that we will accept no conditions. He must surrender or freeze where he is. Do my will! Make them fear!"

It was a long night on the mountain. Several times in

the dark of night the Praxan tested our positions, attempting to find a way off the mountain, and each time they were pushed back. As the first morning light touched the high mountains, they massed and came again but the terrain kept them from creating a solid wide front and those who reached our forces died quickly. The Praxan had arrived in that most terrible battle position, as described in SunTzu's, **Art of War**, a place from where you cannot go forward nor retreat. Five more times during that day they came—always with the same results. It was as if they were choosing to die in battle rather than surrender. Their bodies became an additional blockage along the trail from whence they could not move.

Finally, in the late afternoon, they stopped coming, and all was quiet. We sent scouts forward to make contact, but all they found were dead bodies. It was obvious that in the end they had assisted each other in the dying. We found Ascanius' body with a small group of his officers. They had apparently died together. For me there was little joy in the victory. We now could turn our attention to those huddled in the hidden valley: the women, children, and the Praxan elderly. Is Snow Pine there? Will she survive our attack?

We waited for nightfall to enter the valley. I ordered the Huashan Mountain monks forward to gain control of the cave passage. They moved quickly and soon silenced all the Praxan watchers. We then filled the cave with soldiers and prepared to move at first light. Nothing stirred in the valley below. This was their last night to sleep as a free people.

During the early morning hours before light, the Huashan Mountain monks began their deadly work in the hidden valley. All sentries were silenced. When each of the families came from their tents, they were quickly taken. By early mid-morning, all of the Praxan families had been rounded up and were huddled together near the end of their valley. It had almost been too easy. The tents were now set ablaze as our troops went shelter-to-shelter being sure that no one remained.

For me the time was cruel torture. I had seen her, she was alive. Since my duties had not allowed me to approach her, she remained huddled with the families but she was alive. *She was alive! She was alive! She was alive!* All else was crowded from my mind. *She was alive!*

Later Snow Pine was to tell me that she also spent the morning in confusion. Her brother had brought her back to the valley as a prisoner, and for a period she had been kept under guard. However, as the time went by, her skills in medicine had been needed and soon she was allowed freedom to move among the families. Her father had vouched for her upon the life of his family; she would not run again.

When she saw the Chin'in troops enter the valley, she became afraid. She had seen me in the distance but I had not come for her. She did not know whether I saw her as a prisoner, an enemy, or as a rescued captive. Finally she resigned herself to wait for the answer. I would come, and then she would know. Her mind slowly repeated the words that had often given her solace. *Our paths are one, I shall not doubt.*

Yet on this day whatever plan I might have had for a reunion with Snow Pine was quickly shoved aside. Noise from the cave entrance drew my attention and I could see that a delegation from the capital had arrived. The leader moved toward me and without courtesy of greetings said, "General Sun Kai, you are relived from duty. Your Emperor has demanded that you attend him at the capital immediately! Go now, a squad of soldiers await you at the opening of the cave and will accompany you."

My heart sank; there would be no meeting with Snow Pine, I had waited too long. The manner of treatment that I received told me that the messenger believed I was not in favor and could be treated badly. There was no use in resistance, or explanation; my only path was to go. As I turned to leave, the Emperor's representative gave a command to my assembled staff that chilled the marrow of my bones.

"The Emperor has ordered that all Praxan taken alive will immediately be marched to the wall and there worked to death; all mention of them and their disloyalty is to be cut from our records. The Praxan from this day forward have ceased to exist. Make them fear, Do My Will!"

Within the recesses of my mind, I could hear myself screaming *NO!* I had just found Snow Pine again, and now she was lost, lost to the cruel wall that was winding its way across our land. I well knew what this meant; her life would first be one of misery and toil, until death itself became relief.

Chapter 24

Buy a crazy person lunch?

Over the next several days, Daniel and Lauren were inseparable. The two of them spent much of their time in the university library trying to find anything that might confirm or disprove the story. He knew that he ought to be putting the manuscript aside and concentrating on Eldredge's assignments, but he was drawn to the Sun Kai, Snow Pine story and to sharing it with Lauren.

One afternoon he had found her crying in the library reading room. Lauren laid the manuscript down; her eyes filled with tears. "How sad, does he find her?" she asked. "Please tell me he finds her."

Daniel looked at her shaking his head. "Well, now I know where you are in the story,"

He marveled at how he had come to love this woman

who could cry at the thought that Snow Pine and Sun could be separated.

"A promise is a promise," he reminded her. "You told me not to tell you about how this ends, even if you begged. Now you're begging, and you'll just have to wait and find out yourself."

Lauren wadded a piece of paper and threw it at him, "Thanks a lot, *now* you decide to keep your promises."

She pretended to be hurt by his rejection, but he knew that this was not so. She would have been more hurt had he broken his promise and told her. He sat down beside her, leaned forward and kissed her hair above her forehead.

Daniel sat back, scratching the back of his head.

"How do we prove this isn't a hoax? Maybe, we just want it to be true. I can see the headlines now." Daniel moved his hands, making a frame in the air. "World famous graduate students prove that the Chinese were here before Columbus! I mean, what is the likelihood of it being true, besides, I have Eldredge to deal with and he's asked me to catalogue more of the Cahokia material. I can't imagine he'd think our library research is the best use of our time."

She sat silently looking at him until he finished, then in a sugar sweet southern girl accent she opined, "I just can't imagine why you think a manuscript dealing with ancient Chinese, remnants of Troy, and the discovery of America is a hoax." She laughed at the audacity of their ideas, then said, "You up for buying a fellow crazy person lunch?"

They ate at the little ethnic restaurant where Lauren worked and had a discount, then spent the afternoon at the dorm doing the cataloging for Eldredge's project and preparing for class the next day. Neither of them talked about the skeleton in the cave, the coin, nor about the manuscript. They had spent so much time trying to find evidence supporting the manuscript that to have reached a blank wall where they couldn't tell if it were a hoax or true was more than either of them could face.

It was early evening before Lauren broached the subject. "Look, maybe the guy who translated the manuscript didn't present the case well. You know how the Chinese revere their history. Maybe...they wouldn't believe the story because it seems to present the first emperor of China as mercury-drinking mad man, and the Great Wall as a linear graveyard. Not to mention, that they'd have to say that the hero of the story was someone who refused to obey orders, was individualistic, and disloyal to the state. Not exactly good communist virtues." Lauren put her hands together as in prayer, mimicking a little bow, "How very un-Chinese!"

Daniel nodded, "Maybe, but that doesn't explain the American scholars refusal to buy into the manuscript."

"Yes, but maybe they're like Eldredge, love him dearly, but he can be a real curmudgeon at times. He knows what he knows, and anyone who dares to put faith in a story not thoroughly researched is going to get the old," she lowered her voice to mimic the professor, "A hint suffices the wise but a thousand lectures profit not the heedless," speech. But, I do wish we could talk to him about it though. The worst he could do is laugh at us."

Daniel winced at the idea. Having Eldredge see him as a joke was not something that he could handle at the moment.

"Lets not talk to him about our ideas until we have something substantial, I don't think I can go through another one of his how disappointed he is in me lectures."

Lauren, shrugged her shoulders in acceptance. Later after she had left, Daniel prepared for bed. He looked at the manuscript lying on the table. *What the hell, might as well finish it.*

Chapter 25

The Quest for Immortality

There is no calamity like not knowing what is enough.
Only he who knows what enough is, will always have
enough.

Lao Tzu

I do not remember much about the trip to the capital. The
scenery was a blur to me as my mind refused to focus on
anything other than upon the woman I left in the valley.
The monotonous sounds of the harnesses and hooves
marked time as we moved forward. The soldiers assigned
as my escorts allowed me the quiet of my thoughts. None
spoke; it was difficult to determine whether they saw
themselves as an escort of honor or guards taking a prisoner
to meet justice.

Upon reaching the outskirts of the capital, the escorts

took me to the home of my father in order to refresh myself before meeting with the emperor. When we arrived, it was Fan who opened the outer gate to allow our entrance. His greeting was one of both great friendship and concern for my well-being. Accommodations were quickly made for the troops, and he took my arm and walked me toward the house. "Older brother, it is so good to see you, even in these uncertain times."

I quickly asked him about my family; and he assured me that all was well with my mother and father. My sister Mai met us at the door. Although her face showed concern for me, I cannot remember her looking better. Some women are born to have children, Mai was such a one.

I made my way to the sitting room of my father. He rose slowly and came toward me. In my absence he had begun to look elderly, folded by the weight of years and events. He greeted me warmly. "It has been a long time my son. You are well?"

"Yes Father, I am well but tired. The emperor has called me to attend him."

At this, the smile upon his face froze and became a grimace. "Be careful my son, he is no longer the man you remember, and certainly not the person with whom you played as a boy. He now appears obsessed and can no longer tell his friends from enemies. Many of his old friends have made the mistake of thinking that past loyalties would protect them—but they were wrong."

He paused as if remembering before he continued. "Following the death of Master Yi, Lord Chin's troops attacked the Huashan Mountain temple. The monks who were at the temple when it was destroyed have disappeared. No one dares wear the gray robes in the capital."

This shocked me. It was impossible to believe that he distrusted the Huashan warrior cult that he himself had formed and which had served him so well. This news was sad indeed and did not give me reason to hope for my own future. I nodded in understanding, looking about to be sure no one was within hearing of our conversation. The tenseness I had felt in the capital on my last visit had managed to seep into my father's home. Even in the privacy of our dwellings, it was unwise to speak of the emperor.

"What can you tell me of his current mood? Does he still seek immortality?"

This time it was my father who looked about to be sure we were alone. "That is his one great obsession," he said. "It has become his only concern. He brings scholars from all over the empire to reveal the secrets of the immortals."

Even in my father's infirmities of age, he provided wise counsel. I trusted his judgment more than my own. We spent the next hour talking quietly of the family and about my upcoming meeting with the emperor. The more we talked, the less certain I was about my position, but the meeting could not be avoided. Slowly, as if dripped into a wine bag, a new plan formed in my mind, a plan to perhaps save myself and free Snow Pine.

That afternoon as I made my way to the palace, I again felt the tenseness within the city. The people stood in groups, but as we approached, all conversation stopped, all eyes looked away. There was a general feeling of unease, an unease born from uncertainty and fear. The squad of soldiers brought me first to the chamber of Li Si, the advisor to the emperor. He arose when I entered and stood rubbing his hands together in a dry washing manner. Although his words were gracious to the point of being unctuous, his eyes looked upon me as a vulture might look upon carrion. "The emperor has asked that you be brought to him immediately, upon your arrival," he said. I was then herded by the palace guards toward the inner chambers of our Lord. It was now apparent that I was not considered one in favor, and as we entered the chambers, the guards pushed me from my feet and I fell before Lord Chin.

As I looked up from the floor, my heart sank. Lord Chin was standing above me, but it was not the man I remembered. This was a caricature of my lord; the one above me had the face of a madman.

"You have come. Good. Now tell me why you have betrayed me. Tell me, was it for that woman?"

I shook my head, "No sire, this is not true. I have been, and remain, your loyal servant, even from the days of our youth."

He started giggling, a sound that chilled me as it did not spring from joy or amusement but madness. "Do not lie, you have betrayed my trust," he said. "You have delayed the destruction of these Praxan barbarians, and now you shall share their punishment."

With these words he sealed my fate. If I wished to survive, I must play my last gambit now. I steeled myself looking into his eyes, "My Lord misunderstands my actions, it was not the woman who interested me but rather her knowledge of the immortals." I looked to see if my words had impact before I continued. "The woman Snow Pine is a singer of her people's history and traditions, and within her songs are stories concerning the immortals which identify their homeland and the secrets of their power and longevity." I paused again. "It was for this, and no other purpose, that I have kept the barbarian woman."

The emperor's face now took on a new interest. "Immortals? She knows where they are?" It was as if we had not had the previous conversation. "Sun Kai, my faithful brother, let us talk of these matters. How is your noble father, well I hope?" He clapped his hands together, almost dancing with joy. "Bring us tea!" he commanded. I was then allowed to stand and was shown to a seat, all threats and coldness between us seemingly forgotten. From the side of my vision, I could see Li Si standing in a far corner against the curtains, listening, and frowning with teeth clenched.

"Tell me, tell me," the emperor demanded, even before the tea arrived. "What has she told you about the immortals and their powers?"

I told him of the ancient saga songs, and the legends of a race of immortals with dazzling powers. The songs described a high mountain upon which the gods lived. The stories made the gods seem almost human, gods with which a person as noble as the emperor might deal.

The tea arrived and filled the room with the smell of jasmine flowers and honey. I continued to tell him of the family of Praxan gods and how they might be approached.

"Snow Pine has often told me that the gods are fond of beautiful garments; perhaps we can tempt them with our silk. We could send a delegation."

"Does the woman know the way?" he interrupted as if time were short. "Will she take you there?" I told him that I thought she would cooperate but that when I left, the general who had relieved me had given orders for her and the others to be taken to the wall and worked to death.

"Who gave such an order?" he shrieked. He then turned to look at Li Si who seemed to be melting into the side curtains where he was hiding.

"Who gave such an order?" It was obvious that the emperor did not remember that it was he himself who had given the order. Chin again turned to me, "You must find her, I must know the answers. Go now! Do my will!"

I rose quickly and backed out of the chamber before he could change his mind. My meeting with the emperor did not relieve my mind or ease my stress. There is very little security in the momentary good will of a madman. I knew that I could not save all the Praxan, but perhaps I could save Snow Pine—if only I could arrive in time. The work on the wall was harsh and brutal. Perhaps she was already dead. I steeled my mind from such thoughts. She had to be alive. "Stay alive for me," I whispered to myself.

That night I left the capital on the fastest horse from my father's stable. In my pack was a pardon for Snow Pine, sealed with the emperor's own chop. Although I knew it was not good for the horse, I continued throughout the night and into the day without stopping for food or drink. It was as if my mind were closed; nothing entered except the need to move forward. Somewhere in front of me was Snow Pine.

I did not even think to care about what she would say to me. Would she hate me as an enemy, the destroyer of her family? I was consumed by the duty to find her, to protect her; whatever else happened was of a lesser concern. As I moved forward, I prayed to all my ancestors to protect this woman who had become more important than life itself.

Finally my horse crested the hill, and the wall came into view. I was taken back by the immensity of the thing. It coiled like a dragon over the land. On this day, however, I could not see it as a great architectural achievement of our empire, the defensive wall that separated the civilized from the barbarous. On this day as I looked at the workers scrambling like ants on the frame of a great beast, the wall did not look like achievement, but what it had become, a killing device for the Praxan people.

Chapter 26

The Escape

*Bend and you will be whole; curl and you will be straight.
Keep empty and you will be filled. Grow old and you will
be renewed.*

Lao Tzu

With mounting fear I rode toward the detail of men and women working along the mighty wall. The structure extended beyond my sight in both directions, and as far as I could see, thousands climbed upon its surface in never ending toil. The official responsible for the construction told me that if the Praxan I sought was still alive, she would most likely be found in this area. He had not been reassuring; saying many of the captives had already died and were buried where they fell in the wall. It was unlikely that a young woman would still be alive.

"Ancestors, please keep her alive," I pleaded as I approached the group. I had not moved ten yards down the wall when I saw her. *She is alive!* The thought came smashing into my brain and I was almost unmanned. My eyes filled with tears, which I wiped away with my sleeve. This would not do. She was standing there bent under a load of bricks, her face and hair covered with dust, and her clothing hanging in shreds. I recognized her immediately, as no amount of dirt or torn clothing could hide Snow Pine from me.

Pointing to her, I commanded "Bring that woman to me! Do my will!"

Snow Pine appeared dazed and confused, and swayed as she was brought to stand by my horse. She did not look up; it was as if she failed to recognize me. Again, my emotions betrayed me and my eyes filled. "Damned dust," I said, and again wiped away the tears.

"Place the woman in the wagon, and bring her to my camp. Be gentle fools! She has been summoned before the emperor himself."

I lifted Snow Pine over the side of the wagon, carried her into my tent, and laid her on cushions arranged as a bed. Not once did she look at me, and within moments she was asleep. Lying there, she seemed small and helpless, almost like a broken doll. She had been pushed beyond exhaustion and needed time for her body and mind to recover. While she slept, I removed her torn garments, and sponged her face, arms, and feet. Finally, I wrapped her in one of my robes. Sitting and watching her face in the half-light of the fire, I replayed in my mind all the events of our time together, recalling how close I had come to losing her forever. Regardless of what she thought of me when she awakened, I was filled with great gratitude that she had been spared and was still in my world. *Our paths are one, I shall not doubt.*

It was midmorning of the next day before I saw her

eyes flutter, and she slowly awakened. Quietly, I ordered a sweet jasmine and ginseng tea prepared, along with a sweetened gruel. When I returned to the bedside she was awake. Her face displayed no emotion, and her voice was but a whisper. "What of my family?" she asked.

I shook my head, "I'm so terribly sorry, I came too late."

"Too late?" Snow Pine repeated my words and slowly her face registered understanding. She seemed to sink deeper into the pillows as if all remaining energy had flowed from her. I sat beside her and held her in my arms; I could feel her tremble as great waves of sobs coursed through her body. It seemed like hours before she again became still. I held the cup to her lips and she drank the warm sweet liquid. But her stomach resisted the hot gruel, and no manner of coaching would tempt her to eat. We then sat quietly without talking. Having her alive was enough. She fell asleep in my arms.

When she awakened it was past midnight. I again ordered her tea and gruel. This time she was able to take both. It was strange having her with me once more. So much had happened since she left our home and yet nothing seemed worthy of discussion. She was mine and she was back. I was sure we both felt the same. Matters of greater import about our future had to be discussed, but even that could wait until the morning. Once she finished the meal, I lay down beside her and held her until she fell asleep again.

The next morning it was I who awoke to find her sitting next to me watching me in my sleep. "I knew you would come," she said, "knowing that kept me alive." It was now time for us to talk about what must be done if either of us were to survive.

I apologized that I could no longer allow her to rest but needed to ask her questions in regard to the Praxan's ancient homeland. Snow Pine shook her head as if questioning whether she had understood my request. I then explained to her my conversation with the emperor and his expectation that she could provide information regarding the homeland of the immortals which he had experienced in visions, perhaps even clues as to how to reach them. It was important that she remember what she could, because her knowledge was the reason I had been allowed to rescue her from the wall. She protested that the saga songs had been passed down among the singing families for generations, and that over time they had been embellished in the telling and retelling, and now no one knew or remembered if the stories were of real people, places, and deeds.

I assured her I understood, but we needed to find in the saga songs enough detail to convince Lord Chin that it was worth his while to keep us alive, and perhaps even send us in search of the immortals.

Since my meeting with Lord Chin, a strategy had formed in my mind that might save us. I was sure that Snow Pine would never be safe until we left the land of Chin'in. Escape was our only hope. We spent the next several hours reviewing her repertory of classical songs for any information regarding the gods and how we might find them. One that she remembered about the creation of the moon held great promise, as it told of the gods' great power, their human-like weaknesses, and of their immortality.

How Zeus Created the Moon

Great Zeus looked down from his mountain fortress
Saw her bathing in the warm blue sea
His heart went out to this beautiful woman
Surely her heart is meant for me.

Hera his wife, bade him no!
The woman is mortal, this cannot be
Mortals and Immortals must never be joined
Leave her in peace by the warm blue sea.

Disguised as sunlight he sought her there,
Showering her with golden beams of light
She turned and laughed in his soft warm presence
She lay seduced in his radiant might.

Tis a sad truth, the union changed her
Made her skin a golden hue
Her friends grew old and all left her
But the taste of age she never knew.

A new immortal was born that day
A woman alone, who could never belong
Hera above, seeing her sadness,
Made her first singer, of the people's song.

An immortal's life is one of sadness
All you know must someday die
But for an immortal this could not be
In loneliness she wept by her warm blue sea.

Zeus took pity upon his weeping creature
I loved you once, it is plain to see
He cast her skyward above his mountain
To float forever across the warm blue sea.

I wrote down several items that I thought might persuade the emperor. Most of the songs indicated that the gods lived on a high mountain, in a land far to the East, surrounded by a warm sea. The stories indicated that the immortals often took the form of humans and had many of the same desires in regard to carnal pleasures and material goods. Perhaps they were the kind of creatures that might be talked to, and with the right gifts, might be bribed.

The next day we set out for the capital. As our wagon moved forward along the dusty road, I feared how we would be received. Given his state of mind, it was unclear to me Lord Chin would listen or even remember that he had sent me in search of Snow Pine. His level of sickness was truly frightening. I decided to leave Snow Pine with my family and not take her to the emperor, given the possibility that he might have forgotten or changed his mind.

What I did not know was how all-consuming the allure of immortality had grown in our Lord. His own death had become like a dark well into which he looked and could not see. He had become frantic in his efforts to prolong his life, to find the elixir, to meet with the immortals of his visions. In desperation he had thousands of artisans at work building a model of his kingdom beneath a great hill outside of the capital in hope that, should he die, he might rule in an afterlife. I have been told that his tomb was a magical place where the constellations of the heavens were represented across the great ceiling in precious stones, and where great rivers and oceans flowed in a synchronized simulation of life.

It was with caution that I presented myself at Li Si's chamber and was surprised that I was quickly escorted to Lord Chin himself. It was apparent that our emperor had left orders to bring me to him at the earliest moment. Lord Chin did not arise when I entered and began my nine kowtows, which were now required of all who came before him. I had completed only five when he shouted, "Enough! What news have you brought me?"

I told him of my conversations with Snow Pine and

how the songs indeed spoke of immortals that lived on a mountain in a far land surrounded by a warm sea. I relayed to him several stories about how those immortals had dealt with humans and how, for gifts and services, they would often come to the assistance of one group or another. As I talked, he became excited and agitated. His eyes were bright with a wildness that was disconcerting. I felt as if my life and all those I held dear were in the hands of a mad child. He clapped his hands in glee.

"Do you remember the vision?" he stammered in his excitement. "The vision where I am sending you and Fan Shaofei toward a far mountain? This is the fulfillment! You see? You see? You must go to the immortals and bring back the secret of the elixir of life. I must have it! I will have it!"

Although this was exactly what I had hoped he would say, I felt it wise to speak of my concerns and not of my eagerness to go. "My Lord, the way is uncertain, we do not know how far or exactly where the land of the immortals lies. You know that I serve only you, but I am a warrior not a mariner."

The emperor would hear nothing of the possibility that I might fail. He roared in frustration, "It was my vision, you must go! Take what you need. You can draw treasures of silk, porcelain, and jade from my storehouse to offer as gifts. Go now! Do my will!"

I dared not talk further about uncertainties. "It will be as my Lord requires," I said. "I request that the woman Snow Pine accompany me. Her ancestors are from the land we seek. Perhaps they will guide our quest."

Lord Chin's eyes narrowed and for a moment I thought I had pressed too far, too quickly. It was my greatest fear that he would keep her hostage to guarantee my return. But, after a moment, he sagged and sat back on his pillows as if the excitement had drained him of all animation. He feebly waved me away. His eyes lost focus; bubbles came to his lips and he drooled. Twitching spasms seized his extremities.

"I must have it, I will have it," he mumbled weakly.

Li Si appeared from the back of the chamber, and the audience was over. He had a royal writ already prepared that directed Fan and myself to prepare for the journey. The writ was of such detailed instructions, I was certain that the emperor had planned this expedition for some time. I could tell from Li Si's demeanor that he was glad to be rid of me, but now that I hoped to flee this land where madness reigned, I pretended not to notice. The way was now clear to take Snow Pine from this place which held so much animus and danger for her. The future was perhaps uncharted, but we would escape.

On my return to my home, I found my family and Snow Pine anxiously waiting. I explained to them what the emperor had ordered. My mother and father were greatly saddened by the thought that I would leave them and perhaps never return, but the emperor's orders were not to be disregarded. I begged them to make the voyage with us but my father still refused to leave the comfort of their home.

The next several months were spent in exhausting preparation. It was necessary to construct boats of adequate size to be seaworthy for a long voyage in uncharted waters. Three great ships were prepared, large enough to contain the families of Fan Shaofei, Wang Yueming, and me, as well as treasures of silk, jade, and porcelain. Several small units of Old Hundred Names would be taken aboard to provide security. We worked in quiet desperation, in fear that, before we could escape, the emperor would change his mind.

Finally the day came. The ships were loaded with people and supplies, and we made ready to sail. The night before our sailing, we gathered at the shoreline to consult our ancestors and request their assistance for our undertaking. A monk came among us to cast the bones to see if our trip was auspicious.

Now, I grow tired of the telling, I grow tired of my imprisonment in the cave. This time of writing seems pointless now. We failed in our journey. I have lost Snow Pine. We did not find the immortals, and now only I remain, lost. For what purpose do I write this? Yesterday, I looked into the pool of water which captured my reflection. It is no longer Sun Kai who stares back but some strange, misshapen creature who is cursed to carry Sun's memories.

How I miss Snow Pine. She has come to my dreams for several nights. I cannot rest until I know; I must leave the cave which has become my prison before madness completely consumes me. My leg has become permanently bent and fixed in place, but I now move about better than a crab. Perhaps, I can find the remains of my beloved and bury her with appropriate honor.

That very night I left the cave and slowly and painfully began my search for the remains of my Snow Pine. Even in the darkness I could find my way to our old camp where we had spent such a happy time. It now seems like years ago but that cannot be. In the first light of morning I beheld the scene of our battle. All our homes were burned, and fences torn from the earth. It was as if our enemy had attempted to erase their memories of us. In the center place of our village, they had built a great fire and in the ashes I found the bones of my fellows. *Was this the fate of my beloved?* I picked up a fragment of skull, which had been crushed. The hollowed eyes with lipless mouth stared back at me, mute, with no answer.

The answer was not here among the dead. To know, I must talk to one of the living. Perhaps the vile and evil Shaman; he would know and I would enjoy the asking. That day I rested, hidden in the ruins of our village. My mind was almost lost in the giddiness of my thoughts. *Tonight I will visit the others; tonight they will tremble with fear.*

Chapter 27

Far to the West,
a Mighty River Flows

*Only the man of humanity can rightly love some people and
rightly despise some people.*
Confucius

I lay on a small hillock above the village and patiently
watched as they went about their daily chores. The
women talked and laughed as they cooked, washed, and
mended skins, with the children playing about their feet. If
I had not seen it myself, I would never have believed how
ferocious these people could be. In the mid afternoon, a
group of hunters came from the fields bearing two deer.
The women and children gathered about them, dancing and

singing in celebration. The deer were quickly hung and skinned, and each family took its share.

From his tent, Holtah, the cursed Shaman, came to bless the hunters and to get his portion, declaring, "This night there will be a feast of celebration to honor the hunters."

The Shaman's tent lay near the center of the encampment. I watched Holtah laugh and joke with the hunters, and my heart burned with fury as I remembered the part he played in the death of my love. Tonight, I would be the hunter and he would rue the day he had hurt Snow Pine. That he would die was a certainty but not before he told me what he knew of her grave.

The time in the cave had not been kind to me. We men of Chin'in never have great beards, and now mine was stringy and scraggy, my hair hung wild on my shoulders and my clothes were ragged, torn, and filthy. I little resemble he who had been sent to find the immortals. I moved from my hiding spot above the village toward a shallow creek I had seen earlier. I moved forward with the shuffling gait of a beast. As I lay drinking from the creek, I spotted a patch of feathers where some creature had taken a hawk. The patch of feathers triggered a memory from long ago when I was yet a boy.

"Hawkman," I said, "Hawkman." I pulled up the sleeve of my shirt to reveal the scars from that day so long ago when the hawkman brotherhood was formed. How young we were when we pledged to each other. "We are now true brothers by blood and brothers of the hawk. We shall be hawk warriors, who kill silently and without mercy." So much had happened since that day, so much which was unexpected. I picked up the feathers that lay about and tied them into my clothing and hair.

As darkness approached, I crawled closer to the village. I could see the Shaman at the central fire talking to a group of men as warriors danced in celebration of the days kill. Perhaps if I could sneak into the village, I could take him as he made his way back to his tent. Quietly like the beast I had become, I moved forward to find a place in the shadows.

It was near midnight; the fire had burned low before he left it to return to his tent. In the dark, I could hear him chanting and talking to himself as he made his way. My luck was holding, he had been drinking and he came alone. I allowed him to move past me before I limped from the shadows, and with a single blow from the club I had fashioned, he fell unconscious. I looked around to see if the noise had been heard, but no alarm was sounded, and no one ventured out.

He was very heavy and it took much time and most of my energy to drag him from the village back to my cave. I stopped often to rest and cover my tracks so that no one would follow and disturb the plans I had made for this Shaman who had taken Snow Pine from me.

When he awoke the next morning, obviously in great pain, he was startled to see me sitting, watching him. He was bound hand and foot and lay nude near a small fire at the center of the cave. It has been my experience that no man feels brave when bound naked. He did not recognize me from our past meetings, as I no longer was the man he remembered. Sitting there in rags and feathers, hair wild, and grossly filthy, I must have seemed an apparition from a nightmare. I did not speak or request anything from him, but took a burning faggot from the fire and placed it on the skin of his inner thigh. He screamed, his eyes wide with terror. I pulled the stick away and, grabbing him by the hair, brought his face near mine.

"You are about to die," I snarled, "but before you do, tell me of the foreign woman that you killed."

"Who?" he stammered.

"The foreign medicine woman," I yelled into his face. "Tell me!"

He looked at me in confusion and terror, still without recognition. "The foreign medicine woman?" he repeated.

I yanked his hair again, "Where is her body? Tell me quickly." I took a small burning stick from the fire and this time pressed it to one of his eyes. Boiling liquid from his eye socket spilled onto his cheek.

His scream filled the cave, and as his pain subsided, he sobbed, "We did not kill the medicine woman. She did not die, we sold her."

It took a second for his words to register in my mind. Snow Pine was not dead. "Do not lie," I warned. "Tell me of the woman."

The man was now blubbering insanely, hoping to tell me something that would get me to stop his torture. "She was sold to traders from the great river. They came after we killed the foreign devils of the village that were poisoning our children."

I started to deny the charge but stopped. What difference did it make what this fool believed? "Where are these trading people to be found?" I said. "Tell me quickly!"

He continued to sob, and brokenly told me that they sold Snow Pine to merchant traders who lived somewhere to the west, along the mother of all rivers. They came to his village twice a year, bringing red dyes and tools from the interior to trade for shells, which his people collected from the beaches. He had never seen their home, but had been told they lived in a place where two great rivers came together. They were called Trading People because they canoe up and down the great river with their wares.

When I felt he had told me what he knew, I slew him. I

241

did not think twice about his death; the man inside me who might have cared about life had died long ago. I then crushed his face with a rock and dragged him to the opening of the cave. I wanted him to be found. I then took my calligraphy brush and drew a picture of a qi-lin on the wall, our mythical dragon creature, putting feathers on its back and horns upon its head. In my condition, I could not outrun warriors who might pursue me. Perhaps, the violent death and desecration of their shaman's body, associated with the lair of a winged monster, would deter their coming. *Make them fear*, I thought.

Gathering what little I could carry, I moved west along the coast, seeking the mouth of the river. I came across several likely places but they did not seem large enough to be the one I sought. Whenever I saw humans, I avoided them. On two occasions, I slipped into human camps to steal food. If anyone saw me, they made no cry. I had become like a spirit, a creature of bad dreams. My only thought was to continue to move west until I had found the great river, and then move upstream to the village of the trading people. I had almost given up hope of finding the place when I noticed that the great water was no longer clear but was now brown with silt. Two days later I found the mouth of a mighty river, great beyond description.

This must be the one they call the mother of all rivers, I thought, turning inland. "Must find Snow Pine."

Chapter 28

A new beginning

When a great wound is healed, there will still remain a scar.
Can this be a desirable state of affairs?
Lao Tzu

For the next several months I stumbled and crawled my way northward, following the great river inward. Time passed, the seasons changed around me, but in my mind nothing registered except my mission: "Must find Snow Pine."

My humanness was fading and I was becoming what I seemed, a twisted grotesque beast whose mind was focused on a single goal, *Must find Snow Pine.* It could have been months, or it could have been years, but I finally came to the place where the two great rivers came together. It was as the Shaman described it. The village lay inland, on a small knoll, slightly above the river, against a great cliff. At its center was a mound; around its perimeter was a protective wooden wall. I could see many canoes pulled up along the bank, and before the city wall were stalls where people gathered to trade. These, I assumed, were indeed the people I sought.

I now needed a place to hide where I could watch the village. If Snow Pine were there, I would wait to see her. The cliffs above were pocked with shallow caves, which would provide the advantage of a hiding place from which to survey the village. The problem was that while the great height and steepness of the cliff would protect me from the villagers below, it also kept me from getting to the cave on the riverside. Cautiously I moved inland to the valley on the other side of the bluff, seeking signs of a cave that might have an opening that connected to the riverside cliff face. That afternoon I found a place where I could see the expanse of the valley, and sat to wait.

As the daylight faded, I saw what appeared to be black smoke rising from a dense patch of bushes. *Everywhere the world is the same,* I thought. I had seen similar places in my homeland, where caves could be found by watching for the evening flight of bats as they went to hunt. I was fortunate in my discovery, for when I reached it, I found the cave not only connected to the valley but also to the cliff facing the river. I had found a new home.

For the next several days, I lay hidden and watched the village. In the mornings, the gate would open and people would go about their daily lives of fishing, gardening, and trading. The village appeared to be a very active trading center, as each day numerous canoes would come and go, loaded with goods. My hopes of seeing her had almost fled when suddenly she came to the great gate. Snow Pine was radiant as her hair picked up the light of the morning sun. I was made dumb by the sight of her and as I watched, she turned, smiled, and waved to someone not yet in view. From behind her a small child appeared on wobbly legs. She scooped him up, laughing. My mind froze, *"No!"*

Yet there she was, tall, dressed in fine white skins, with hair trimmed in feathers, as beautiful as ever. My mind raced with possibilities. How could this be? I watched as she made her way to the riverside market area. She spent the day tending the child and arguing the price of what appeared to be herbs that were collected in her stall. By day's end, I knew that she was not a prisoner, but rather, had become one of these people. I could not take my eyes off her and lay watching until the light faded and she returned back to the village.

She obsessed me, and the next morning, even before the light broke the night sky, I was again at my perch overlooking the village awaiting her arrival. Each day she came, each day the same, playing with the baby and selling herbs. How I yearned to speak to her but each night as the light faded, she returned to the village, and the great gate of the city wall was closed. The space between the stalls and village lay open, with no place to hide and await her passage between the two. Once I might have climbed the wall in the night to find her, once—but that was long ago— I was not the man I had been.

My life became settled into a routine of watching Snow Pine during the day and sneaking out of the cave at night to find food. To provide warmth, I had fashioned feathers I found into a cloak that keeps out the rain and night air. On several occasions I was seen in the village while foraging for food. Who knows what the night herders must have thought when confronted by a bear-like creature with a shuffling gait and feathered cloak? Who knows what stories they must have told? I passed the season in this manner, watching by day and hunting by night, and had grown comfortable with my life. I no longer wondered about Snow Pine but rather found joy in her being alive and delighted in her life, which was played out before me each day. She was living, and safe; for me, that was enough.

Once during this comfortable routine, I became careless and was almost caught. The night was clear with a full moon and I left the cave to seek food. That day, the villagers had pulled a huge sturgeon from the river, a fish at least ten feet long, and had sliced off pieces to smoke and dry on racks arranged at the riverside. That night I was making my way toward the drying fish when dogs started barking and hunters rushed from the city gate. The first hunter came upon me from the side, but I turned quickly causing him to lose balance and as he fell, I crushed his head. The others who now saw me outlined in the light, stopped in fear. What must I have looked like, silhouetted in the moonlight? However, as their fear subsided, they began to pelt me with rocks, several of which struck home. Wounded, I slipped down toward the river and entered the water. The cold water soothed my wounds and the dogs could not find me.

It was near morning before I could circle the village and make my way back to the valley entrance to my cave. My body ached from the rocks that had struck me, and I was barely able to drag myself inside and lie there until the pain subsided. The next day, my pain was such that I could not drag myself to the cliff face to watch for Snow Pine. My view from the thicket, which hid the cave, allowed me to watch the valley. During the day, several bands of natives moved past, armed and hunting for the lair of the creature they had encountered the night before. However, bushes hid the entrance and they passed me by, moving on. For the moment I was secure. My mind devised a plan that would draw them away from the vulnerable valley entrance and focus them on the opening at the cliff face which was beyond their reach. Although my pain was great, that night I collected my paint and calligraphy brushes and drew a qi-lin on the cave wall similar to the one I left on the coast.

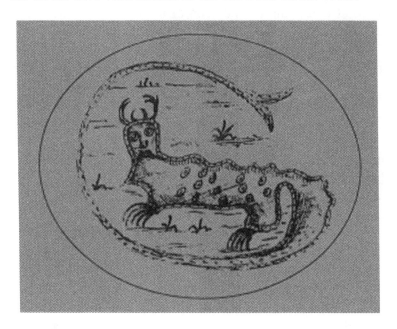

Daniel dropped the manuscript, *Oh my god!* The snapshot he'd taken wasn't exactly the same but close His mind screamed what he knew could not be. *Could the skeleton be Sun Kai?* Daniel picked up the manuscript, staring at it as if willing it to speak. Finally, unable to contain himself, he began to read.

Once I had the painting in mind, I took my brushes and paints onto the ledge. Although in great pain I worked throughout the night, and as the morning sun lit up the cliff above the village, the people looked up and beheld my handiwork. Looking down on them from the ledge above was a monster drawn from their worst dreams. The whole village gathered below to stare in awe at the great birdlike creature, twenty feet across, with scales of red and a blackened face. Great lips with teeth like knives seemed to snarl at them, and on the head of the beast were the horns of a deer.

Once a crowd had gathered below, I put on my cloak of feathers, adjusted a set of deer horns to my head and made my way out of the cave to crouch on the ledge in their sight. I stretched out my cloak of feathers and made swooping gestures like a great bird observing its prey. This was too much for them; the women and children screamed and fled back toward their tents. Only a few men were brave enough to fire arrows in my direction, and these fell short. On several occasions that day, the men gathered and attempted to fire arrows at me, but given the sheerness of the cliff, their arrows fell short and they could not climb close enough to see me well or do me harm.

My pain was still great, but hunger again forced me to leave my cave. That night no one ventured outside the village, and the gate was firmly closed. Not even dogs barked at my passing. I could see a great fire was burning near the center of the village, and a group of people were massed at the top of the mound, performing a ritual. Their actions represented no danger to me, so the purpose of their actions was of little interest. I quickly found the sturgeon meat, gathered several of the smoked pieces, and made my way back to the cave.

The next morning I was again at my cliff face, sitting, watching the village. To my amazement, the people of the village were almost gone. Obviously, the great fire and conference the evening before had been a time of decision. The leaders of the village did not wish to live under the eyes of my monster. In the morning light, only a few people remained, loading their canoes and preparing to leave. As I watched, Snow Pine came to the bottom of the cliff and stood looking up at the picture I had drawn. She stood staring for several minutes, calling out something I could not hear. Finally she waved, and turned away to return to her packing. By the time the sun was in mid place for the day, the people were gone.

That night, with great effort, I ventured downstream and found the new village. The people had placed their new home in a beautiful area of marsh and lakes, which unfortunately held no high positions from which I could hide and watch. The natives had already begun to build a new protective wall. Several groups of sentries made their way around the perimeter, and everywhere there was a sense of wariness. This was not going to be a village that I could enter without being seen. With a sad heart, I returned upstream to my cave along the cliff. My heart was low, I had failed again. My monster had been too fierce. I had not intended for them to move the village and flee. My own actions once again caused me to lose Snow Pine.

Over the next several weeks, life settled into a pattern. At times I was still in great pain but I hunted at night, and during the day, either sat at the cliff face watching the canoes along the river, or lay looking out from the valley entrance. The cliff face position was one that drew great interest from the people in canoes, moving below. They stared and pointed upward at the great creature, and often the men would shoot their arrows toward the painting but few came near. On several moonless nights, I went to their new village, but the gate was always closed to me. I was in despair of ever seeing Snow Pine again. Yet in my dreams, she would come, often to the place where I had last seen her, looking up, yelling something, and waving.

And then, as if by magic, she was there. I was lying looking out the valley entrance and saw her standing below with the child, looking toward the valley walls. She seemed to be looking into my heart. I froze, watching her from my hiding place in the thicket. She made her way along the valley floor gathering herbs. Snow Pine and the child spent the day there alone, and in the late afternoon made their way by me as they left the valley. I cursed myself that I had not the courage to go to her, but as the night came on, I convinced myself that it had only been my mind fashioning what could not be. She had not really come.

Yet the next morning she was there again, first looking at the valley walls, and then proceeding during the day along the path below. On this day, I left my hiding place; I must talk to her even if this was just a dream. As I stepped out in front of her, I could see she was startled. Standing before her was not the Sun Kai she remembered but the twisted creature I had become. I thought at first she would scream and run, but after a few seconds, she ran toward me. Only Snow Pine could have seen the man hidden within the creature before her. I was almost knocked down as she threw herself at me. It had been a long time since I had felt another human's touch. Even in my filthy state she crushed me to her, crying and calling my name. "I knew it was you! I knew it was you! Who else would have drawn a qi-lin?" She laughed, and held me close. She then drew back from me and picked up the child who had come forward to cling to his mother's leg. "Sun Kai, I would like you to meet your son, I call him Sun, after his father," she said. "And like his father, he will become a hawk warrior." She moved to show that she had fashioned a small hawk man necklace which hung from a dyed red leather thong about our son's neck.

The emotions of the moment and my continued pain

caused me to become faint and stumble. Snow Pine came quickly, and carrying the child in one arm and holding me up with the other, she helped me back to the cave. We spent the day talking, and watching our son play. She told me how she had been sold to a great trading tribe that had contacts from the coast where we had come ashore, to great inland oceans far to the northeast. Over time, she had been accepted into the tribe and her skills with herbs had made her a medicine woman among them. As she described the tribe, they seemed a noble people. When she had become obviously pregnant, the chief of the tribe had taken her for his sister-wife and she had moved in with the family. Our son had become a favorite of the chief and might, someday in the future, replace him in tribal leadership.

Snow Pine told me that I had become somewhat of a legend among the trading people and the neighboring tribes. They see me as a fierce creature who flies at night, coming to their camps to steal animals and small children. Mothers in villages along the river now use me to scare their children into appropriate behavior. *Be good or I will leave you for the Thunder Bird.* We laughed at the tales that have formed around my presence. Finally the talking sapped my strength and I slept. I awoke to find her sitting there, watching me, as she leaned forward, her tears wet my face and beard. Taking my face in her hands, and looking into my eyes, she said, "From this day forward, our paths are one. I shall not doubt. You and Little Sun are my family."

The next several months were a period of joy, even though my injuries did not heal and the pain began to increase. Snow Pine now tended me like a child, washing me and mending my clothes. Incense burned within my cave, giving a fresh smell of sage. She filled my life; I never tired of watching her move about, making this stark cave our home. She seemed not to notice my twisted body; we were together again.

Several days each week, Snow Pine came to the valley to search for herbs. We then spent the day together enjoying the antics of our small son. Snow Pine brought teas and herbs to relieve my pain, but even under her care the pain always came back, even greater. Snow Pine told me that she thought that the stones injured me inside in a way that she could not heal. She cried as she told me this, but even if my life were to end today, I am content. During her visits, she often reads the journal of our adventure and chides me in the order of the telling.

Today, when she comes I can no longer go to the valley to meet her. The pain in my side is now continuous, and I cannot walk. Medicines that Snow Pine brings relieve the pain, but leave me senseless. We were apart for so long, the thought of not knowing she is here is more than I can endure. After this day I shall refuse to take the herbs.

My beloved and I have talked of my death. I feel the end is near and today may be a good day to die. When I tell her this, she cries. Her tears wash my chest and I reach to touch her hair and give comfort.

"Be still beloved, few have lived as much as we, fewer still have loved as we." Now even the smallest of efforts tires me; I have strength for only one more request.

"Promise only that you will teach our son to wait, watch, and remember, for in time, our people will surely come." Snow Pine wipes the tears from her eyes, and promises she will teach our son the history of his father's people, and that I will be remembered and honored. Perhaps, one day, if our son follows his mother, he will become a great shaman and healer of this people.

Although Snow Pine does not wish to discuss it, we have planned for my death. Once I am gone, she will seal up the small alcove where I sleep, so my body will lay undisturbed. She is to seal my journal with bees wax and keep it safely hidden. Surely our people will come again.

As I lie here, my vision blurs, but calmness and clarity fill my mind. Snow Pine has placed our son in my arms and has come to lie by my side. I can feel his heart beating against my chest and the warmth of their bodies press upon mine.

"How can you not be among us?" she asks.

My mind continues to drift and I know that where I go they cannot come. Although there is sadness at our parting, I have come to believe that the only way one could remove sorrow from death is to remove love from life, and this would be a poor bargain indeed.

"I am satisfied," I whisper.

Chapter 29

Persuasive Evidence

Daniel finished reading the manuscript and sat staring at the two pictures, the photograph he'd taken in the cave, and the sketch from the manuscript . Not exactly the same, he thought, close, but not exactly the same. Could this be a crazy coincidence, or was the skeleton in the cave, Sun Kai? He called Lauren; he couldn't wait to show her the pictures.

When he arrived at the university library he found her in the first reading room. "You will not believe this," he told her taking a seat across the small table. "We may have just found the connection that will impress Eldredge."

Lauren was immediately caught up in the moment and began laughing. "It will have to be something big to impress him. Tell me what you've found."

Daniel reached into his pack, drawing out the manuscript and notepad. He opened the notebook and found the photo from the cave. "Remember, when I told you that I'd found what appeared to be a faded picture on the wall, just as you leave the cave? Well this is the picture I took of it."

Lauren looked at it, "It's pretty sketchy, are you sure you were actually seeing something or just a stain on the wall."

"Yah, I know," Daniel admitted, looking at the shadowy figure, "but look at this one," and he opened the manuscript to the sketch supposedly drawn by Sun Kai. "Come on, you gotta admit, they look very similar."

"I agree, they do look similar, not exactly alike, but that may be explained by changes in the drawing as a result of age." Lauren stared at the pictures. "So what are you saying, that Sun Kai is the skeleton?"

"I dunno," Daniel hesitated, afraid to make that great a leap, "but this is at least something that brings the manuscript, skeleton and coin together. If it is true, the coin is the hawkman symbol of the Huashan Mountain monks, and the manuscript may be a translation of his journal."

Lauren looked at the two pictures. "I hate to be the 'yes but' person, but if the skeleton in the cave is Sun Kai, and the manuscript was translated from Sun Kai's journal, how did it get to China? Why didn't you find it in the cave? And you have to admit, the pictures are not exactly the same."

Daniel felt crestfallen. "Then you don't think we should take this to Eldredge?"

"No, I think we should take it to him, but don't expect him to buy into your skeleton, coin, manuscript scenario. I expect he will be a very hard sell. But, we're at a brick wall, so lets talk to him and maybe he can think of something we've overlooked."

Daniel took a deep breath, considering the options. "OK, let's show him. But before we do, let's think this through, outline everything we know, everything we guess, and give it our best shot."

Daniel made a call to the department office to see if Eldredge could meet them later that day. He was available, and they were committed, so they spent the next several hours preparing outlines and evidence to bolster their case. It was with no small degree of trepidation they approached his office at four o'clock. Daniel was feeling a bit shaky in regard to the meeting. Remembering his lecture on the similarities between the Piasa and the Chin Dragon Banner, and Eldredge's reaction, he closed his eyes, almost afraid to knock.

Lauren leaned over and kissed him on the neck, then gave him her best *'we who are about to die'* smile. Seeing him frozen in place, she knocked on the door and hearing the *'come in'* they entered.

Eldredge sat behind his desk working on a stack of files. His face looked stern, but then broke into a smile.

"I was just thinking about you two, you've been doing an excellent job with the cataloging, come in, sit down. Why did you want to see me?"

Daniel cleared his throat. "Well, Lauren and I have been working on something, and wanted to ask your advice about it. When Eldredge's face showed noncommittal interest, Daniel went on. He related how he'd been climbing the bluff near the Piasa Bird area of Alton, and found the skeleton in a cave. He omitted the part about picnicking with Donna.

Lauren brought out the outline that they'd previously made, and related the Sun Kai story including the possibility that the Praxan were descendants from the destruction of Troy, and how they might have made their way to the northern borders of China. When Eldredge looked skeptical, Lauren quickly added, "I know it seems implausible, but there have been recent discoveries of Celtic mummies in Northern China. Come on, Irish in Asia? Having some of my Turkish ancestors show up in Northern China isn't any stranger than that."

Daniel broke in, telling Eldredge about the Chin'in dynasty and how much of the story in the manuscript could be made to fit into what was known about China's first emperor, even to details about the mercury poisoning.

"I know this must seem like a hoax, but if it is, then you need to ask yourself, who and why?"

Eldredge nodded, "You're right, this does seem like a hoax, and you're also right to question the who or what could be behind it and why. Do either of you know anything about the CAS?"

Both Lauren and Daniel looked startled. The Creative Archeology Society or CAS was the underground anti-progress group that sought to stop work at construction sites by seeding the areas with ancient artifacts or reproductions. Once an artifact was found, the government required that construction be halted until archeologists could determine whether a cultural treasure was being demolished. The CAS had become almost mythic in some of the wild hoaxes they'd pulled off. Anyone even vaguely aware of archeology was familiar with the tactics of the CAS. The idea that the CAS could be involved with his skeleton, coin, and manuscript, had never occurred to Daniel.

"Sure, we know who they are, but why would they do this? What would they have to gain? To the best of my knowledge, nothing is being developed in Alton. In fact, outside of a small tourist industry—bed and breakfast places, antiques, ghost tours, and stuff like that—the place is really dead."

"Who the hell knows why these Luddites do anything," Eldredge groused. "But this is just the sort of nonsense they would try." It was obvious from the forcefulness of his tone that he didn't hold the CAS or their activities in any esteem.

"Look, this is all speculation; you need a lot more than this to make a case."

Daniel pulled out the photograph. "This is a snapshot I took of the cave wall." He then opened the manuscript, "and this sketch was, according to the manuscript, drawn by Sun Kai. As you can see, they look very much alike."

Eldredge looked at the two pictures. He shrugged, "Yes they look similar, not exactly the same, but similar. You ever see Buddhist and Hindu statues with a Nazi Swastika symbol?" Both students just stared at him, not comprehending where he was going with the question. "First time I saw one, I wondered who had desecrated the statue. Yet in fact, it's an ancient symbol, first used in India and China as a religious symbol, and much later, misused by the National Socialists in Germany. Recently, what appeared to be a pre-Colombian Star of David was found on a cave wall in Kentucky. Do you suppose the Jews discovered America, or just that it is a very aesthetic looking symbol, found and used by differing people in different places in the world."

Daniel started to protest, "But a simple symbol like a Swastika or Star of David is very different from a complex picture such as this."

Eldredge frowned, "Yes, but the idea is the same, and remember, the pictures are not exactly the same, and you have the problem of how the Sun Kai manuscript made its way back to China." He glanced at this watch,

"Look guys, I'm a bit busy right now," he said pointing

to the stacks of files on the desk. "Tell you what, give me what you have, I'll look at it and get back to you. However, I must tell you that I tend to think this is some kind of bizarre hoax."

Daniel and Lauren thanked their professor, and gave him a copy of the transcript, as well as the drawings they had made of the cave and the Piasa Bird. They both had the feeling that he was only vaguely interested, and perhaps a bit put off by his students being involved in an ad hoc project of which he was unaware, but it was still their best shot. His demeanor told them they should not expect too much from his review. He followed them to the door of his office, and before closing it, he gave them a parting piece of advice.

"Look, don't get too caught up in chasing fairy tales. Our field can't stand a lot more of these hoaxes from groups like the CAS, if we're to maintain credibility."

Driving back to the dorm, Lauren leaned against him. "I don't care what he thinks, I put my faith in Sun Kai and Snow Pine," she kissed him on the neck, "and you."

They spent the rest of the evening together in his dorm room, each preparing for the next mornings classes. As he held her in his arms to kiss her goodnight she leaned back so that she could look into his eyes. "From this day forward, our paths are one. I shall never doubt." She began to cry and held him tight.

"Ditto," he said.

She struggled from his arms, banging her forehead on this chest." You!"

Chapter 30

To await another day

Standing at the podium, Dr. Frederick Eldridge looked over his 8:00 am class. The students, although in their seats, were not quite ready, still getting out their papers, still finishing last minute conversations begun in the hall. The hour was too early for a graduate seminar, but he felt little sympathy for the students. He himself had spent most of the previous evening at the dig site, trying to reason out the latest findings from the Cahokia Mound. He had also finished skimming the materials from Daniel and Lauren.

Gaud, he thought, *how naïve, all caught up in a document given to them by a mysterious Chinese scholar who didn't leave an address where he might be found. Spare me. With all the work yet to be done on the Cahokia artifacts, why are they wasting their time on nonsense? Daniel and Lauren are good students, but the're really off the mark with the manuscript.*

Eldredge looked up from his musings. "Class if you will! Let's get oriented. First drafts from your projects are due next Tuesday." This last brought about a few groans, but the class was now together and ready to begin. "This morning we will be looking at the early peopling of the American continents. We will look at what we know to be true about the people here, what some think is true but probably isn't, and then some anomalies that don't seem to fit into the picture at all."

Dr. Eldridge looked over the classroom and saw that the class had all begun to take notes, with the exception of Daniel, who appeared to be drawing something. It looked as if Lauren was distracting him, and they were both leaning together looking at his picture.

"Mr. French, please review for us the land bridge explanation of the early settlement of North and South America."

It took only a second for Daniel to compose his thoughts. "Ah, well, we know that about 12,000 years ago during an ice age, the water levels in the Bering Sea fell until a land bridge was formed between Siberia and the North American continent. Scholars assume that small groups of hunter-gatherers came across this bridge over a period of several hundreds of years. They migrated southward, following really big game like ground sloths the size of hippopotamuses, and Volkswagen-sized armadillos." The class laughed at the big game reference. Daniel smiled and continued.

"This migration view is known as Clovis First, named after a commonly shaped spear point found near Clovis, New Mexico. Until recent discoveries which date back

40,000 years, it was generally accepted that these groups were the forerunners of all the Amerinds or First Nation people of both North and South America. Some studies have looked at this migration in linguistic terms and found evidence in the usage of common terms for '*the people*' in places as far apart as Alaska, the North West Territories and Navajo country in New Mexico."

Eldredge nodded, "Outside of your big game references, that's essentially correct. The ground sloths were indigenous and weren't chased from the north and the armadillos moved south to north. So, back to the question. Is there any evidence that other people outside of these hunter gathering groups came to the new world? Please leave out the Vikings, as we all know of their settlements. I'm thinking of earlier people. Mr. Franks?"

Brandon Franks cleared his throat. "I was reading a paper the other day about some recent discoveries that have led scientists to think that people have been on the Northern and Southern continents well before 12,000 years ago, maybe even as far back as 20,000 to 40,000 BCE. If that's the case, they may have come from places other than Siberia, maybe by water. Recently there were some papers describing a kelp river that might have allowed people from the Pacific Rim to have made the crossing."

Eldredge broke in, "I read the same article based on artifacts from California, Pennsylvania, and Peru, or remains like footprints, cooking fires, and strange cave markings. Are there any other findings that would make us think that people other than those across the land bridge came here?"

Now several hands went up. Eldredge pointed to Lauren. She looked about with some uncertainty, "There is the blood type problem. We know the predominate blood type in the Asian group that we think came across the land bridge is B, while the predominate blood type of the Amerinds is almost exclusively A or O. While that does not tell us the 'who' of the matter, it does suggest other migrations."

Eldredge nodded again, "That's true but who do you think are the 'who'?"

Several students laughed and raised their hands.

Bob, one of the younger students, spoke first. "If we're to believe the books by Van Danikan, perhaps the new world was visited and populated by ancient astronauts."

More laughter, Eldredge frowned and shook his head. "Let's not go there, Danikan finds a large arrow scratched on a mountain side which pointed to an open plain and thinks this proves that ancient astronauts are using these as airport landing signs. Any of you see any large arrows pointing to Lambert International Airport lately? Surely his astronauts were as accomplished as the poor souls from St. Louis. Any other ideas?"

Again, Daniel replied. "Well there are the writings of St. Brendan the Navigator; his journal seems to indicate that he found the new world."

"Yes, there is always St. Brendan the Navigator," Eldredge replied. "But, he did not talk about bringing a group of Celts with him, and his vows of celibacy should preclude him being the answer to the blood type problem. Besides, in his journal, he speaks of talking to a whale, an assertion that somewhat tarnishes his credibility."

"Well there's some indication that Buddhist monks toured the California coast," one of the other students added.

"Yes," Eldredge said, "the monks in California, again, even if we concede that their tour might have happened, it would not explain the blood type problem, but it might explain why some of the early Amerind pottery of the area looks like some of the early pottery from China. Of course there is also the story of the Jewish hermit, Maba, who supposedly lived in an Oklahoma cave, or the Welsh nobleman, Prince Madoc, who founded a colony in what is now Georgia."

"Maybe all of this is the work of the Creative Archeology Society," another student suggested. At this comment, all the students laughed, although some uneasily, as they saw color flood the professor's face. They had all heard the stories of his hostility toward the group and were suddenly uncomfortable. The relationship between full professors and graduate students is always an uneasy relationship, and it was not wise to bell the cat. The laughter ceased as quickly as it had begun.

Several years before, Eldredge had been burned by the *Society,* and he was not a man who saw much amusement in his own embarrassment. Writing an article and putting your academic reputation on the line for a fraud was not something that he wished to revisit. It had cost him dearly in academic prestige, grants, and appointments. The CAS was unfunny indeed. The very idea that these Neo-Luddites were going about sprinkling artifacts in building sites and on roadway construction sites irritated him to the nth degree. He knew many of these anti-progress nihilists were university students who stole the artifacts from their archeology departments. Among the rather anarchistic archeology graduate students, the CAS escapades were the stuff of legend and admiration. For Eldredge, the CAS was just the latest group of reactionaries, and no laughing matter.

"Let's move on," he said abruptly. "Any other ideas beyond these crazies?"

Again, Lauren raised her hand. "All across the archeological findings in North America we find anomalies that don't seem to fit. Whether it's a Star of David found in Kentucky," she smiled at him, "or the legend of Prince Madoc who reportedly was teaching natives the Welsh language, or Buddhists in California; none of these really answer the blood type problem."

"You're right, Lauren," Eldrege said. "All of these form subtexts, like the Vikings, interesting but with no substantial impact on the history of the continent's migrations."

Now another hand went up; it was a quiet student near the back who rarely participated. "Professor Eldredge, what about the Latter-Day-Saint's views of ancient America? If their doctrines are true, wouldn't that be bigger than a subtext?"

Eldredge hesitated before responding, as he might actually be talking to a Mormon and didn't particularly wish to offend. "You're right, the Mormon ideas, as outlined in their religious texts, about groups of people coming across from the holy lands and establishing themselves in South America, if true, would be bigger than a subtext. In fact, if true, their story would not only explain the blood type problem but also provide an explanation for similarities between old and new world temple building.

The student again interjected, "I've read many reports from their archeology scholars at Brigham Young University which seem to provide scientific backup for their theories."

Again, Eldredge frowned and cut into the discussion. "The problem with the Mormons is in your statement about 'their archeologists.' The error they are making is that they start with '*the truth*' and then set about proving it. That's not science, its religion. They over-subscribe to those artifacts that seem to support their case and under-subscribe to equally obvious materials that detract."

With this, the student looked down and that ended the conversation. Clearly, Eldredge was not going to subscribe or give much credence to the Mormon doctrines.

Eldredge looked out over the class and asked a concluding rhetorical question.

"Do we have any non-controversial early findings of people from other places coming to the New World? The answer is no! But, then again, we do have the blood type problem. We have early Amerind stories about visits from beings with white skin and abundant facial hair, which some take as *'proof,'* but nothing conclusive." He paused to allow the statement to be put into the students' notes. "We seem to be going in circles now. Let's take about a thirty minute break and come back and hear some student reports on last week's findings from the Cahokia sites."

Eldredge shuffled his notes putting them back into a file folder. "Mr. French and Miss Caurcas! During the break, could you join me in my office?"

Daniel looked at Lauren who gave him a tight but reassuring smile. Eldredge had obviously read the materials and had questions. When they entered his office, he sat them down and offered coffee. "Well it's a damn interesting story," he said, "but again, not likely to be true. I'm afraid I concur with the departments that criticized your mysterious vanishing Chinese student; it seems like an elaborate hoax. Think about it. Not only do you have Chinese in America, you have Trojans in China! Besides, it reads like a love story and romantic love is a modern phenomenon. Couples two thousand years ago didn't think in those terms. Don't waste your time."

Both students started to talk at the same time, "But."

He waved his hand to end any further discussion of the matter. "Look I know you kids are caught up in this thing, but your best bet is to forget it. It is just too unlikely to spend your time on. Really, you can't have your names, or for that matter, the department, associated with nonsense like this. It's not good for your future."

Lauren looked at Daniel and they both remained quiet. Eldredge was not going to support more investigation of the matter.

"Besides," Eldredge continued, "our department's focus is on the Mississippian mound culture at Cahokia, not some 'Chinese discover America' theory. That's a National Inquirer headline, not archeology." He paused, his look giving no opportunity for rebuttal.

"Look! Both of you have been very important to me and my effort to catalog materials from the Cahokia field site, and I don't need you distracted." He paused before going on, letting the threat/invitation of working with him sink in.

"If you don't mind I'll keep the manuscript, and as time permits, perhaps we can talk of this again."

Both students nodded; the materials were safe with him and they could always get at them later, so long as they were in the department. "OK, let's get back to class."

Eldredge remained seated as the students left, and put the transcript, pictures, and notes on the shelf behind him among his many stacks of papers. He hoped he'd been able to dissuade them from their wild goose chase. They were too good to begin their careers chasing nonsense.

Chinese discover America, he thought. *God, sounds more like a tabloid headline, than an article in Science.* He rubbed his eyes and leaned back in his chair thinking of all the work he had yet to do on the new material they had collected from the Cahokia site. Even after all his years of work on the project, not much was known of the Mississippian Mound Culture which had flourished in the bottomlands at the confluence of the Missouri and

Mississippi Rivers. Little was left at the site today except some large dirt hills and an educational exhibit building, yet in their day, these people had created a trading society which reached from the gulf coast to the Great Lakes, and from Oklahoma to the Atlantic coast. The archeological remains showed that the village had contained about 20,000 people at the turn of the first millennium of the Common Era, which would have made it larger than Paris at the time. If he could just get it together in the next several months, he could submit a paper and abstract for the conference in the fall. Lauren and Daniel were doing excellent work on the project; they were great teaching assistants, perhaps he would add them as second authors. *They would like that, and it would be well deserved,* he thought.

He then opened the desk drawer and took out one of the sandstone pieces he had uncovered at the mound site. The rock was a rounded piece and on one side was a drawing of a man in a feathered cloak and on the reverse the texture of a snake. *Wonder what the hell, this was about,* he thought. His mind went through the possibilities, of Indian gods such as Quetzacoatl, the feathered serpent of the Aztec, and Toltec traditions. *Too far north for them,* he mused shaking his head in negation of that mental path.

He sat tossing the piece from hand-to-hand, weighing the possibilities of his thoughts. Look at the nose on that guy. Probably it will turn out to be something like the Southwestern Thunderbird, a common symbol associated with shamans who were said to have the glance of lightning and voice of thunder. Again, Eldredge shook his head weighing the possibilities of his thoughts. Too far North for that, can't remember seeing any of those closer than Colorado. He then put the piece back in the drawer and gathered his papers; it was time to get back to class. Walking back, Eldredge's mind went over his conversation with Daniel and Lauren. Well, thank god they decided to be reasonable.

Epilogue

That afternoon Lauren and Daniel sat relaxing in the dorm, talking about the class and Eldredge's decision. The idea of working with an established professor was a real coup, and even better, they would be working together. It was said that Eldredge was generous with his publications, often listing his assistants as co-researchers. Having some publications to show when they went out into the real world—whatever that was—would not hurt their postgraduate vitas.

"He's probably right," Daniel said, "the material about the Piasa and manuscript may be too good to be true, the similarities of the pictures a coincidence. We should focus on the Mound Culture."

Besides, they both had class assignments to fulfill, papers to create, grades to make, and a post graduation future to plan together. The mystery of the skeleton, and the Sun Kai-Snow Pine love story would have to wait for another day. Daniel was a little irritated at the thought of giving up the manuscript project materials to someone else, but as he sat looking at Lauren, all in all, his life was not working out badly.

Lauren smiled, "I still put my money on Snow Pine and Sun Kai, and even if we know what happened to him, what about her? Maybe working for Eldredge at the Cahokia site will give us some clues about what happened to Snow Pine and little Sun."

Daniel laughed, "I love you, cuz you a crazy woman, you never give up!" He fished in his pockets for the coin he had picked up that first day in the cave. He didn't know why he hadn't shared this finding with Eldredge, but somehow it seemed right. Daniel looked at the Chinese character for 10,000 on the reverse side of the coin. *That's how long I am going to love this woman* he thought. He dug out a red string from another pocket and threaded it through the opening, fashioning it into a necklace. He reached over to her and placed it around her neck. "Michael tells me the Chinese believe the red string brings good luck and joy," he said.

She smiled, leaned toward him kissing his neck, and snuggled into his arms. "See, it's working already."

That night after Lauren left; Daniel sat in front of his computer fingering the thousand dollar check he'd received from his Uncle Fred as a graduation present. *Just about enough,* he thought. *Eldredge said he didn't want my name or the department associated with this nonsense, well so be it!*

He laid the check down, clicked on the Word icon, cracked his knuckles, sighed, and began:

Flight of the Piasa

He stared at the title, leaned back in his chair, lacing his fingers behind his neck. *What the hell, Mark Twain wouldn't have had anything to say if it weren't for Samuel*

Langhorne Clemens. What's in a name? Leaning forward again, he typed.

A novel written by Raymond Scott Edge

The Teller's Tale

*Be of unwavering good faith, love learning,
if attacked, be ready to die for the good way.*
Confucius

My name is Sun Kai; I am of the Chin'in people. In my life I have been many things....

**The story of Snow Pine continues in the sequel
"She Who Remembers" available in 2008.**

The strain of placing the limestone slabs into the wall pulled at her muscles and Snow Pine straightened, rubbed her back, relaxing in the half darkness, surveying her work with satisfaction. Cooled by the perspiration of her efforts, she watched as the boy played, moving back and forth between the light and darkness marking the cave entrance. Turning once again to the task she picked up another broken slab of limestone, heavy and cold to the touch. With each placement the opening into the shallow alcove became smaller. *Soon my love, you will be safe,* she thought, and placed the next stone in the wall she was building to protect the body of Sun Kai from discovery by anyone or anything that might seek shelter in the cave. "My love, what shall I do without you?" she said aloud, knowing that only stillness would answer. At first she had thought to block the outer entrance to the cave as a way of protecting the body, but the idea that this would mean that she herself could never again visit this place, pushed that from her mind.

The opening had now shrunk to the size of a single stone, which she picked from the pile and then hesitated in the placement. *Two worlds, two lives,* she thought, one which began long ago in an ancient land and belonged to the man who now lay hidden behind the stone barrier she had erected. How far they had come, how many leagues from home, and now his body lay in this cave beyond any map. She smiled as bittersweet thoughts of him filled her mind, his smell, the sound of his voice, his dreams, the way his body felt. Even as she entered this second life beyond the lighted entrance she knew that her love for Sun Kai would never change. *Not while I breathe* she thought. His last words again came to mind, a final request that she "watch, wait, and remember." He was right, one day, his people would come, and she must be ready so that his body could be taken and buried in his homeland. *He deserves that*, she thought, *to be buried with his ancestors, not here, lost and alone.* Steeling her resolve for the task she placed the last stone.